Healing Sarah

Other Books By Lorin Grace

American Homespun Series
Waking Lucy

Remembering Anna

Reforming Elizabeth

Healing Sarah

Artists & Billionaires
Mending Fences

Mending Christmas

Mending Walls

Mending Images

Mending Words

Mending Hearts

Healing Sarah

AMERICAN HOMESPUN 3

LORIN GRACE

CURRANT
CREEK PRESS

Cover photos: Deposit Photos by: nature78, angelnnov, and hydromet
Cover & interior photos: The Metropolitan Museum of Art Public Domain Photos

Cover Design © 2018 and formatting by LJP Creative
Edits by Eschler Editing

Published by Currant Creek Press
North Logan, Utah
Healing Sarah © 2018 by Lorin Grace

First printing: March 2018

ISBN: 978-0-9984110-5-7

For Grandma Eileen—
I love you forever.

Acknowledgments

THERE ARE NOT ENOUGH WAYS to thank those who helped me bring about this book. Huge thanks to Tammy and family for letting me crash at her home while I conducted research in the Boston Area. A special thanks to Kristen Hollenbeck who gave me a personal tour of the Brandford College memorabilia room. (I want to tell more stories about the college!) Also to the patient librarians in the special collections at Haverhill and Amsbury libraries.

I have been blessed with several author friends to guide me. Thank you Emily, Sally, and Cindy, whose ideas, critiques and daily advice keep me going.

Thanks also to Michele at Eschler Editing for the edits (any mistakes left in this book are not her fault). Nor are my excellent proof readers to be blamed. Especially Nanette who scours each book for errors. Thank you!

My family, for sharing their home with the fictional characters who often got fed better than they did. And my husband who encouraged me every crazy step of the way, and who is my example for every love story I dream up. The real one is better.

And to my Father in Heaven for putting these wonderful people, and any I may have forgotten to mention, in my life. I am grateful for every experience and blessing I have been granted to form my life.

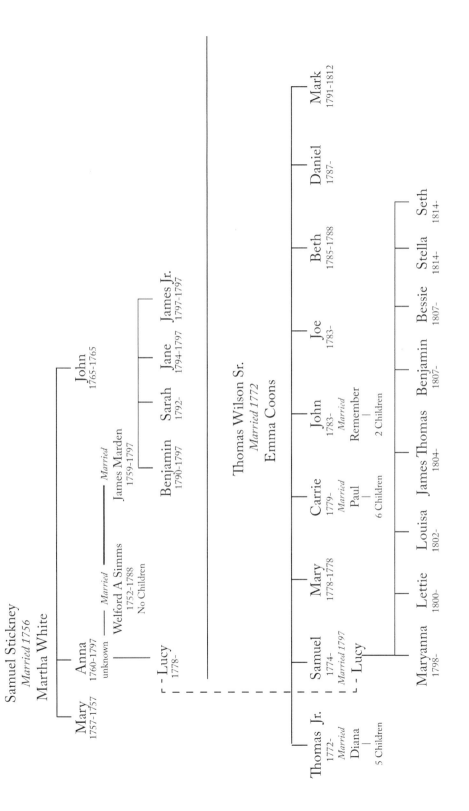

Samuel Stickney
Married 1756
Martha White

Mary
1757-1757

Anna
1760-1797
Married
James Marden
1759-1797

Married
unknown

Married
Welford A Simms
1752-1788
No Children

John
1765-1765

Lucy
1778-

Benjamin
1790-1797

Sarah
1792-

Jane
1794-1797

James Jr.
1797-1797

Thomas Jr.
1772-
Married
Diana
5 Children

Samuel
1774-
Married 1797
Lucy

Thomas Wilson Sr.
Married 1772
Emma Coons

Mary
1778-1778

Carrie
1779-
Married
Paul
6 Children

John
1783-
Married
Remember
2 Children

Joe
1783-

Beth
1785-1788

Daniel
1787-

Mark
1791-1812

Maryanna
1798-

Lettie
1800-

Louisa
1802-

James Thomas
1804-

Benjamin
1807-

Bessie
1807-

Stella
1814-

Seth
1814-

One
Massachusetts, May 1816

A FAKE COUGH CAME FROM the corner of the classroom. Sarah set the cloth down, leaving half the verse from James on the board, and consulted the watch she wore about her neck. Ten more minutes would be painful for both of them. And, unlike her other students, she would be seeing Benjamin often over the summer as well as in the years to come.

She tapped Benjamin Wilson on the shoulder and held out her hand. The eight-year-old took off the cone-shaped cap he wore, and his blond hair stuck up in all directions. "I had hoped we could complete the last day without you ending up in the corner. Tell your parents I'll be by to talk to them on Sunday."

"But, Aunt Sarah—"

She frowned to remind him of his place.

He lowered his head but kept his eyes on her. "I mean, *Miss Marden*, it's the last day of school."

She set the hat on the shelf. "Good, then it shall give you plenty of time to think before fall term. Mr. Stanworth is not going to be as lenient."

Benjamin shifted from foot to foot. "Must you tell?"

"Not if you tell your parents first." By now he should know that the tale of his classroom woes would reach Lucy's and Samuel's ears long before he reached home. His twin rarely wasted time recounting the injustices received at the hand of her brother.

Head hung low, the boy started to shuffle out the door but turned and rushed back to Sara, flinging his arms around her waist. "Please don't tell, Aunt Sarah. Pa promised to take me down to Boston."

"All the more reason to be honest, then."

"But what if he gives me a lashing?"

"Benjamin Samuel Wilson, you know as well as I do that your father has never given any of his children a lashing in his life. More likely you'll be asked to clean the chicken coup." Sarah patted his head. "Hurry on now. It looks like a storm is coming. Your brother and sisters are probably most of the way home by now."

Benjamin gave her a final squeeze before running out the door. Sarah let out a sigh. At least none of her sister's children would be in her classroom this fall. Benjamin and Bessie would be the last for the next few years.

Even without her niece and nephew, the year had been more difficult than the previous three combined. The last two weeks of April had been enough to almost convince her to give up teaching altogether. The other teachers had the same problem in their classrooms. They all blamed the rash of poor behavior on the unseasonably cool weather following a mild winter that had area farmers fretting over the possibility of a second year of drought.

The tap of Miriam Dawes's patents sounded in the hallway dividing the four-room school. The petite blonde poked her head in the doorway. "Well, I am done. I don't think I shall miss it." The smile on her face reflected that of the male students who were escaping school anticipating a summer without books.

Sarah took a moment to admire the golden hues of her colleague's dress. Perhaps someday she should give up her browns and grays for more colorful clothing. "Why would you miss this? George is a handsome man, and by all reports, Ohio will be a wonderful place to start your life and family."

Half the color drained from Miriam's face. "Oh, Sarah, I am so scared. In a week I'll be Mrs. Wells, and in less than three months I'll be living in a place I've never seen."

Sarah walked to the doorway and embraced the young woman. "Ohio does seem far away, but with New York's proposed canals connecting to the Great Lakes, travel will be ever so much faster in just a few years. You can come visit your family and bring all your children. Just stop by the school to see me."

Miriam took a steadying breath and stepped back. "Thank you, but I am sure you will have a family of your own by then. I really must go—so much to do before the wedding, and mother gave me instructions to pick up more thread. I thought the sewing was finished. I can't believe there is anything left to sew." The patter of the first raindrops on the window drew Miriam's attention. "I hope it doesn't rain on Tuesday. Can you still help mother clean up afterward? Parmelia informed me she couldn't help just before she left. Today of all days! I warned the board not to hire her."

Sarah avoided discussing the under-teacher who would take Miriam's place next year. "You know I will. You'd better hurry before the storm gets worse."

"This has to be the coldest spring of my life. I'll end up wearing my pelisse during the ceremony, and no one will see the dress we made. It is so pretty! I can't wait to show you." Miriam pulled the long coat tighter and hurried out of the building.

Sarah stood in the center of the vacant classroom. Here and there a scrap of paper or bit of chalk pencil cluttered the floor. Most likely the same lay hidden in the shelves of the now-empty desks. Cleaning now would save her the trip back in the morning. She should have required her students to scrub down the room before they left, like Miss Dawes. But this group of students would be likely to start the sort of mischief that ended with her maps being soaked and one of the smaller girls facedown in a puddle. The minimal sweeping and dusting her students had completed was halfhearted at best and still required her to set Benjamin in the corner for putting a spider in Bessie's hair.

Retrieving a bucket and armful of dustrags, Sarah set about cleaning her room. She tied an apron around her waist and tucked her skirts up several inches to keep from getting any mop water on the hem.

The top of the chalkboard was out of reach. If only she had her sister's height! Making use of one of the student benches, she climbed up to remove the alphabet she had so neatly chalked along the top last fall. Sarah had just cleaned the *J* off when she heard heavy footfalls in the hallway.

Sarah stretched to reach for the *K*.

A deep male voice called from the doorway. "Excuse me, miss?"

The bench tipped, and before Sarah hit the floor, she caught a glimpse of a broad-shouldered stranger. Had she not been concentrating on angling her body to miss the bucket, several words in addition to *handsome* would have crossed her mind.

She failed to dodge the bucket and found herself sitting in a puddle of water—and staring up into the softest brown eyes that crinkled at the edges as if their owner were stifling a laugh. His lips refused to smile, although she sensed they wanted to.

The stranger extended a hand. "My apologies. I did not intend to startle you, Miss—"

"Miss Marden! What are you doing?" Preceptor Colburn rushed into the room.

Biting back a groan, Sarah took the offered hand and stood carefully, keeping her wet back to the wall.

Mr. Colburn advanced, his face red, his eyes focused on—

Her ankles!

Sarah yanked her tangled skirts out of the apron ties.

"Miss Marden, there are strict rules about entertaining gentlemen inside the classroom."

The stranger interjected. "It is my fault, sir. I simply meant to inquire about the whereabouts of my sister, and I am afraid I startled Miss Marden as she diligently cleaned her room."

Mr. Colburn looked at the half-cleaned boards and puddle. "Did you not hear? The boys in Mr. Stanworth's upper class will be coming in next week to scrub down the entire building as punishment for putting gunpowder in the stove." He shook his head and turned to the stranger. "Made quite a clatter and upset the entire school for several minutes. Claimed they wanted to make firecrackers."

Sarah squelched the desire to roll her eyes. Minutes? More like hours. The boys in her class had discovered that the sound of a primer dropping on the floor elicited a scream or two from the girls. At least the older boys had been given an appropriate punishment. Too bad she hadn't known about the cleaning crew earlier. It would have saved her dress.

Mr. Colburn's attention rested on the young man. "Now, who were you looking for?"

"My sister, Miss Miriam Dawes."

"Timmy?" Sarah covered her mouth, hoping neither man had heard her whisper. But from their stares, she could tell they had.

The younger man recovered first and held out his hand to the principal. "Dr. Timison Dawes. Nice to meet you, sir."

The short, pudgy man pumped Tim's arm up and down. "Dr. Dawes, I believe your sister has left for the day. Or, rather, left for good, with her getting married. The board shouldn't hire women. They are always leaving." The man looked again at the puddle Sarah stood in. "Well, Miss Marden, clean the floor, and I'll see you in two weeks. At least I never have to worry about replacing you."

Sarah felt the color drain from her face. It stung to admit she had no better prospects than to work at the school for years to come. Hearing someone say it out loud ripped open the wound.

Water dripped from her dress, forming a pool at her feet. The dress clung where it shouldn't. Waiting for the men to leave before she went in search of a mop was the wisest course of action.

Both men stood silently. Mr. Colburn must be waiting for her to respond. "I'll get it cleaned immediately, sir. And please remember, I am not teaching summer term. With so few enrolled, you asked Miss Page to teach the lower grades."

"I wish you had taken the post." The preceptor grumbled as he left the room.

Timmy—he was much too old to be called Timmy—remained. "Tell me where the mop is kept."

"No need. I'll get it. Miriam told me she needed to pick up some thread. She is most likely still at Swanson's. If you hurry, you can catch her."

The grin he gave her threatened to buckle her knees and land her back on the damp floor. "Knowing my sister, I don't need to hurry as she will be chatting with someone. Now, where is the mop?"

"There is a closet at the end of the hall." She hoped he would be gone long enough that she could fix the dress where it clung to her posterior.

Sarah stared at his retreating form. It had been almost a decade since she had seen him, and those shoulders hadn't been broad back then. Sarah reined in her thoughts. This was Timmy, who had smelled of barn cats and earned more than one black eye from the Wilson brothers for trying to steal a kiss from her behind the school, the church, and on one occasion the outhouse. He definitely didn't smell of barn cats anymore.

This would not do. In a week he would go back to where ever he lived and she would return to … nothing.

Two

TIM FOUND THE CLOSET EASILY enough. The symmetrical layout of the four-room school left few options. Though the school was four times the size of the school he'd attended with Sarah, memories of standing in corners and writing lines for teasing the girls flooded his mind.

His heart had stopped when he'd seen Sarah cleaning her board. She hadn't grown an inch taller in the years since he had seen her last. He wondered how many of her students could see over the top of her head. He had never achieved the height of the Wilson boys, so her size suited him.

Sarah. A spinster? The last time his mother had mentioned Sarah in a letter, her banns to one of the Wilson boys had been posted … Mark? The preceptor had addressed her as "Miss," though, so she wasn't one of the many war widows, although she wore gray. Choice or mourning? Why hadn't Miriam or his mother ever told him? They had written him letters about every unattached woman on the North Shore but had left Sarah out.

He returned to Sarah's classroom with the mop, pausing at the door. Sarah stood behind her desk, attempting to ring the water from her dress. Tim doubted she was aware of how nicely the dress outlined her silhouette. He knocked the mop handle against the doorway and pretended to be more focused on the implement than on her.

Sarah jumped and turned to face him, color infusing her cheeks. "Thank you for getting the mop." She held out her hand.

Instead of giving it to her, Tim crossed the room and started to clean up the puddle.

"You don't need to clean my mess. You should go find Miriam." Sarah scooted closer, keeping her back to the wall. Had it not been so many years, he would be tempted to laugh.

Water splashed in the bucket as he wrung out the mop. "Why don't you gather your things, and I'll give you a ride home. As I remember, it is a ways out to the farm. Did you bring a cloak or something?"

Sarah walked backward to the far corner and retrieved her pelisse. "I don't live with my sister anymore. I live with Mrs. Emma Wilson. Her house is less than a mile from here, and I can walk."

"But would it be wise? It's raining, and you are already soaked through."

Sarah fastened the brass buttons of her pelisse. "What of your sister?"

"We'll stop and see if she is at the store. They aren't expecting me until tomorrow, so Miriam won't be looking for me." Mother would send someone around to bring her home, in any case.

Home. Tim thought of the large house with the view of the Merrimack River. It had never felt like home after his father died and his mother remarried. Perhaps it would now that she was widowed.

Sarah pulled a ledger out of her desk and added it to a pile of books. "Miriam hasn't seen you for years. You really should go home."

Tim paused to survey his cleaning. Not bad for an army doctor. "If you are afraid I will try something to earn me a black eye, I've learned my lesson." The last time he had tried to steal a kiss was fifteen and a half years ago. Sarah had new birthday ribbons. It was her eighth birthday. In five separate visits, Samuel, Joe, John, Daniel, and Mark Wilson had all let him know in very certain terms that Sarah was not for him. Driving the point home, Mark's right fist had connected more than once with Tim's nose and eye to make sure Tim understood.

Sarah brought a hand to her mouth, and her cheeks pinked. "Oh, I hadn't thought—no, I didn't think you would…"

With effort, he kept his face neutral. That blush had caused him to do foolish things before. "I'll empty this bucket, and we can go."

Tim berated himself. He'd promised Samuel Wilson he would leave Sarah alone forever. Besides, he had no intention of remaining after Miriam's wedding. If he stayed, he'd be stuck in town forever.

Sarah took a deep breath and gathered her books. She hadn't lied. She wasn't thinking of the kisses he used to try to steal. For one crazy moment, she wondered what letting him kiss her would be like. Pure folly. Mark had left her as good as widowed. Timmy would have no interest in the local spinster when there were so many young ladies in town due to the shortage of men since the war.

Everything else she could leave in the classroom over the summer. The half-erased row of letters annoyed her. At just nine inches over her five feet, Timmy, er, Dr. Dawes, wasn't as tall as Samuel Wilson, but he should be able to reach them.

"Dr. Dawes—"

"Tim."

Birds would fly north for the winter before she called him Tim. "Would you mind erasing *M* to *Z* for me?"

As she suspected, he reached the letters with ease. "Anything else?"

Sarah shook her head. "No, I have everything I need."

"Allow me." Tim tucked the books under one arm, and Sarah had no choice but to follow him out of the school.

Although a light rain fell as they left, the dark clouds threatened a deluge at any moment. Timmy, Dr. Dawes, Tim—nothing sounded right in her head—tucked her books in a box under the seat before helping her up into his buggy.

He handed her a large oilcloth. "The open buggy allows for speed but is not always the most convenient in inclement weather." He untied the horse and guided it back a few steps before joining Sarah. "I am afraid you will need to direct me."

"Oh, Em—Mrs. Wilson's place is just north of the church on the opposite side of the street. After her husband died, she wanted to be closer to the center of town for her midwifery, and with her twins, John and Joe, working the farm, she thought it would be better to have a place of her own. That was before Joe left."

Tim drove to Swanson's store first. "I won't be but a minute." He dashed in and came right back out. His sister had left a quarter hour earlier. As they turned up High Street, the rain began to fall in earnest. "How long have you lived with Mrs. Wilson?"

"I moved in with her my last year at Bradford Academy. Lucy had her twins, Benjamin and Bessie, that summer, and even with Samuel's additions, the house became crowded. Besides, moving in with Mrs. Wilson allowed me to go all three terms, not just fall and spring."

"Have you been teaching ever since?" Tim slowed the buggy at an intersection.

"No, I worked with Mrs. Wilson for a couple of years and filled in as a teacher for a term or two both here and at the academy. Then, with the war, a position opened at the school. With men in short supply, the board couldn't be so picky about who they hired, and I got the job. They have a hard time keeping the female teachers for two terms, so the fact I finished my third year qualifies me for veteran status." Sarah hoped she'd answered him adequately as she didn't want him asking the questions most of her acquaintances glossed over.

"That's right. My sister only taught two terms. George wanted to marry a month ago, but they promised her a four-dollar bonus if she stayed."

Sarah cringed. No one had ever offered her a bonus, and no one ever would.

Three

THE PROMISED DELUGE ARRIVED, OBSCURING the houses on either side of the street. Tim stopped the carriage in front of the house Sarah indicated. Despite his questioning, she hadn't been very inquisitive herself. Which had been fine with him. People were bound to ask why he had stayed away so long. He was sure that would be the question of the hour when he returned home, followed by "Why don't you set up practice here?"

He hurried around the buggy to help Sarah down. "Run up to the porch. I'll get your things." He wrapped the oilcloth around her books before sprinting to the porch himself.

Sarah opened the door and motioned for him to follow. Soon they both stood dripping in the entryway.

Mrs. Wilson called from the kitchen. "There you are, Anna. So nice you didn't make her walk in the rain, James."

James? And why had she called Sarah Anna? A tug on his sleeve interrupted his confusion. Sarah mouthed "Please" before motioning him to follow her into the kitchen.

In a voice louder than a sergeant, Sarah addressed Mrs. Wilson. "What are you making? It smells wonderful." Sarah unbuttoned her long jacket but did not remove it.

Emma set a third bowl on the table. "You will join us, won't you?

It is far too rainy to drive all the way home right now. You can put your horse in our barn."

Tim looked at Sarah, and she pointed to a small structure behind the house. "There should be room in there," Sarah whispered.

Tim took one step and paused. "Who are James and Anna?"

"My parents."

Sarah's parents? He had no memory of Sarah's parents, as she had been raised by her sister. That meant Anna and James must have been dead for twenty years or more. Tim shook off the thought as Sarah nudged him toward the door. "I'll be back in a moment."

He wasted no time getting the horse under the roof of the two-stall shed. A goat and pig eyed him as if trying to decide whether they should protest his invasion of their space. He didn't bother returning to the front door, opting for the kitchen entrance instead.

Mrs. Wilson looked up at him. "Who are you? Why didn't you knock? Is it your wife's time?" She hurried to the corner and grabbed a leather bag not unlike the one he used to store his medical implements.

Frantic footfalls echoed on the floor above and down the stairs. Sarah rushed into the room wearing a faded gray dress, her unbound brunette hair streaming down her back and past her waist. "Emma, this is Dr. Timison Dawes, Miriam's brother. Do you remember him? He used to go to school with us."

Mrs. Wilson turned to study him. Tim had the uncomfortable feeling he should be cowering. "Aren't you the boy my Mark thrashed for kissing Sarah?"

"Yes, ma'am." If Mark could read his thoughts now, he would have another black eye. But to touch Sarah's hair might be worth the risk.

Mrs. Wilson turned to Sarah. "He hasn't broken his word, has he? Told the twins he would never touch you again."

Sarah led Mrs. Wilson to the table. "No, Emma, Dr. Dawes has been a perfect gentleman."

"Doctor?" Mrs. Wilson pulled out of Sarah's grasp and came to stand nearly toe to toe with Tim. "Doctor? Are you the one who said I was unfit to deliver babies? I'll have you know I delivered you and your siblings!"

Sarah wrapped an arm around Mrs. Wilson's waist. "Dr. Dawes just arrived today. He is only here for Miriam's wedding." Sarah turned them both to the table. "I am starved. Why don't we eat?"

After settling the older woman at the table, Sarah stepped out of the room, then returned with her hair bound in some sort of net. Shame. He had rarely seen hair like melted chocolate sweetened with honey. Her hair had gotten him into trouble more than once. How long had it taken her to get the ink out of the ends of her braids all those years ago?

Sarah took her place at the table, looked to Mrs. Wilson, and began to pray. When the prayer concluded, both women relaxed.

"Did you see Mrs. Larkin today?" Sarah shouted, asking about their neighbor across the street and Emma's good friend.

"No, that boy of hers has smallpox and they are under quarantine."

Tim hadn't seen any notices since coming to town. Sarah's brow furrowed, and she gave him a quick shake of the head. "Today was the last day of school. I heard Noah Larkin placed first in arithmetic."

"That is good. I thought the child would die of smallpox a few years back. He is such a good boy. He promised to come kill my old rooster. I think it is time that old bird was made into a good meal."

"Are Lucy and Samuel planning on staying after church?"

"I hope so. I like the new minister."

Sarah nodded and looked out the window, then at him, her words no more than a whisper. "It looks like the rain is stopping. Are you finished?"

He wasn't, but he placed his bowl in Sarah's outstretched hand.

"I'll be right back, Emma. I am going to show Dr. Dawes out," she shouted.

Tim followed Sarah to the hallway.

"Thank you for playing along. I never know exactly where she is in her memories. When you came in, she mistook me for my mother. If you had left suddenly, it would have been harder to coax her back to the present."

"And smallpox?" Tim took his hat from the stand where he had set it.

"We had an outbreak a year or so before the war." Sarah sighed. "Emma's confusion becomes far worse when associated with memories of family, so I try to keep conversation to the neighbors and things like that."

"So she has been like this for a while?"

Sarah nodded. "A year or so, but it has been worse this spring. I am sorry to delay your return home."

Tim gave her a slight bow. "My pleasure."

Sarah's answering smile made the odd detour worth every minute.

Shutting the door behind Tim, Sarah let out a sigh. He had been kind to stay, but after such an odd experience, she doubted he would come again. Which was for the best. Seeing him made her want to forget every vow she'd ever made. Marriage was not an option. She took another deep breath before heading back into the kitchen.

"Anna, I am so glad you came back."

It took longer than normal to settle Emma this time. Sarah often wondered if she should let Emma stay back in her memories or help her face the reality that often the people Emma was addressing were no more than ghosts.

Some events were painful for both of them to relive. Tonight, before coming completely to herself, Emma recalled the messenger who'd brought the news of Mark's death. After sobbing through two handkerchiefs, Emma had retired for the evening, leaving Sarah to pull her own emotions together. Each time this happened, his death felt too near, as did all the memories. How could she ever move forward when she kept reliving the past with Emma? It had been three years since the messenger had knocked at their door. Emma had lost a son, but Sarah had lost more.

Until tonight, she hadn't realized that the little details of her time with Mark were fading. Had he smelled faintly of soap like Tim? No, there had always been a bit of fresh-cut hay, even in the winter months, identifying Mark. When they were young and played blindman's bluff, she'd found him by following his scent. Odd that going in the barn no longer brought memories of Mark. But on night's like this, Emma's pain brought back memories of her pain too.

For a moment in the carriage sitting next to Tim, she thought she might follow Lucy's advice and find someone else to love. But love bred pain. Another reason she was better off a spinster. After all, she had had her love. There were many girls who had yet to find the opportunity for love. As Mrs. Garrett often loudly pronounced as she left church each Sabbath, men were in short supply.

Sarah locked the doors and removed the key, hiding it under the silver sugar bowl. Emma had wandered out a couple times during the night over the past few months. Both incidents had occurred after Emma experienced one of her particularly draining spells. Sarah rather not risk that tonight would be one of those nights.

Sunday she would talk with Samuel. The Wilsons needed to know their mother was getting worse. Sarah dreaded the conversation, as John would insist he was right to request Emma come live in her old home, and Sarah along with her, as his wife.

But visits to the house Emma had raised her children in often resulted in episodes like tonight's. Sarah wondered if Emma had been out to the old house while she was at school.

Sarah took extra care in banking the fire and extinguishing the lamps. The thought of not being able to find the key in case of an emergency lurked at the back of her mind. The Wilson brothers would never forgive her for keeping that secret if a fire killed their mother.

The evening meal concluded, the family retired to the parlor. Miriam and mother were bent over a table, consulting a list.

Ichabod noticed Tim first and laid aside the book he was reading. "Tim?"

A predictable cacophony of hugs, questions, and offers of food followed. Tim accepted the leftover roast chicken and answered his family's queries between bites, avoiding the stickier questions when possible. He simply had no intention of staying as long as Mother wanted him to. Fortunately, no one asked when he had arrived.

A knock on the door announced the arrival of George Wells. Tim didn't know the groom well, but he would be ever in his debt for changing the subject to the upcoming wedding. Tim took the opportunity to slip away to his old room.

A hastily set fire burned low in the Franklin. Usually the stoves lay dormant this time of year.

The wind scraped the branches against his window. It would be easy to climb out and escape the questions Mother would reiterate until he answered them to her satisfaction. There had been a time when Tim had put the tree to very good use to avoid grammar tests and lessons on the family's shipping business.

His stepfather had threatened more than once to fell the tree. But it shaded Mother's withdrawing room, and her needs prevailed. Instead, his stepfather had nailed the window shut in July. At the time, Tim had thought him the vilest man on earth.

But Tim had been face-to-face with evil more than once in the last few years, and not always from the troops on the other side of the line. He'd seen the scars left by fathers who had done far more than nail a window shut or deny supper. Every sin Reverend Woods had ever warned against and some he never imagined had been lain before Tim in the camps and fields of war.

By the time Tim realized his stepfather should be revered rather than hated, it was too late to forge a friendship, as his mother was widowed again. His half brother, Ichabod, only seventeen, had taken over the Marsh shipping business. His stepfather had been generous with Tim, leaving him a partnership in the will if he ever wished to quit doctoring. Ichabod had all but begged him to join him on the docks.

He had to admit that escaping the medical field was tempting after experiencing the carnage of war. But on his list of things worse than a field hospital was the dockyard. He had no desire to enter the shipping trade. Not after seeing it kill his father all those years ago. The new steamboat had been a colossal failure. Designs had improved over the years, thanks to men such as Robert Fulton, but Tim rather stay firmly on land.

He ran his hand down the window, tracing his reflection. He couldn't see any further into his future than he could through the glass.

Four

"Oww!" Sarah wrung her hand and stuck her finger in her mouth, the pain easing as her finger cooled. She tried again to get the pudding pan out of the brick stove. The center of the dessert jiggled, and the edges had turned a brown bordering on black. No point in cutting it. Sarah tipped the pan over the slop bucket. "Well, Peggy Piggy, you'll eat well tonight."

For once the bread had turned out, not that she dared slice it to make sure. For years she had heard her sister and Emma praise the fireplace her grandfather had built nearly eighty years ago, but her food turned out only marginally better there. It seemed as if the pigs were the only ones who appreciated her efforts. Her thirteen-year-old niece cooked circles around her, though fifteen-year-old Lettie cooked only marginally better. But at least most of Lettie's food remained edible. Lucy and Emma had spent countless hours trying to teach Sarah the basic domestic skill. At least as a school teacher she could buy bread if she couldn't make it and she didn't ruin porridge or boiled eggs too often.

Sarah took the slop bucket out before Emma could return to see the evidence. Stomping to Peggy's pen, she fumed. Two days ago she'd burned the bread, and so she'd used the crumbs and half a pound of the few carrots they had left in the cellar to make the pudding. She shouldn't have left out the orange-flower water. Too bad the *Universal Cook* couldn't tell her how to find an orange flower. Returning to the kitchen, Sarah resisted the urge to toss the cookbook in the fireplace. Instead, she set it on the shelf.

The book was one of the few things Mark had given her. He teased her as much as the other Wilson brothers did about her cooking, but he also showed faith in her. She caressed the spine and was transported back to the Sunday after she'd graduated from Bradford Academy.

Mark had waited until they could be alone—not a small feat. Emma had managed to use the occasion to get most of her children and grandchildren together, as usual claiming Sarah as her own. As the sun set, Samuel insisted he get the little ones home early. And Mark had volunteered to see her home before Daniel could offer. That night cemented her preference for the youngest Wilson brother.

She had known since the day of Lucy's second wedding to Samuel that she would marry one of his brothers and one day be a Wilson too.

Mark slowed the carriage as they crested the hill near the farm where she had been born. He pulled the book wrapped in brown paper out of its hiding place.

"I wanted to tell you how proud I am of you. I know we all tease you since we can use your gingerbread as cobblestones, but I know you're capable of most anything you set your mind to. Maybe you'll learn better from a book." Mark shoved the parcel into her hand.

Nervousness radiated from him as she untied the strings. Her heart dropped. She'd hoped for the next volume of the Romance of the Pyrenees series. She longed to read it but had been unable to borrow it from either of her fellow students who owned a copy. She thumbed through the book while trying to phrase a gracious response. Sarah reread the line "To Dress a Turtle" and giggled.

Mark shifted in his seat.

Sarah looked up. "Mark, this is perfect. There are so many recipes. There is even one for turtle. Can you imagine what might happen if I tried it?" Her giggle gave way to a full laugh.

Mark joined her.

Sarah leaned over to give him a kiss on the cheek.

Mark turned his head.

Her first kiss as a woman had been pleasant. She touched her lips with her fingers. The memory hovered near the surface, but the sweet warmth of that night six years ago had faded away.

She would keep the cookbook. Even if it didn't help culinary skills, it held memories of her first and only love.

Tim tossed the letter from a fellow doctor on the table, troubled that Dartmouth wouldn't be hiring for months. Not that he'd seriously considered anything farther north. Massachusetts was cold enough. If he confessed to his mother that he had no idea what his future held after the wedding, she would insist he stay. Every letter since the war had ended had been filled with pleas to come home. In the last five years, houses he didn't recognize had sprung up in the fields where cows had once grazed. A new church and school attested to the growth in the area, and Dr. Morton had repeatedly insisted there was more than enough work for another physician in town.

A scratch at the door interrupted his musing. He opened it to Miriam's tears.

"Cook says the stableboy drank the brandy, and there is none left for my cakes. Mrs. Reynolds needs my help slicing a pound of almonds, and the currants we saved are filled with mold!" She fell into his arms, sobbing.

Tim awkwardly patted her back. "If I go purchase more brandy and currants, will that help?"

Her answer was comprised of a snorting sound and a nod, and she released her hold. "Ichabod has gone down to the warehouse. He says they received a shipment of fine French brandy."

"So you need me to go buy some currants, then?"

"Yes, and some ribbon. Blue, but not too dark—about the color of George's eyes would be perfect." She kissed him on the cheek and ran down the hall.

The color of George's eyes? Tim had failed to take note of that aspect of his brother-in-law to be. He hurried down the back stairway and conferred with his mother as to the amount of currants required.

Mother couldn't tell him the color of George's eyes either. And neither one of them braved asking Miriam.

The house smelled of the failed carrot pudding, and Sarah couldn't concentrate on the silk painting for Miriam's wedding. Tucking a few coins in her reticule, she headed for Swanson's. If they had some currants, she could make—nothing. But if they had licorice, she could eat it and be just as content.

The air was fresh and felt so much warmer than the past week. Maybe spring was here for the rest of May. So far this year the almanac had proved to be most inaccurate. Emma joked that Mother Nature was changing into an old woman. Considering the temperature fluctuations, Sarah seconded the opinion.

Half the citizenry filled Swanson's this afternoon. Not being in any hurry, Sarah wandered among the piece goods. A pale-pink muslin caught her eye. Would it be enough of a color to keep Lucy from bothering her about her choice of dress?

"I think you should consider the green."

Sarah whirled around, almost knocking a paper packet out of Tim's hands. "Ti—Dr. Dawes, you startled me. Did you need some fabric?"

"No, Miriam sent me to find some ribbon matching George's eyes. Perhaps you could help me?"

Sarah stifled a giggle. "So what color are you looking for? Blue, brown, or gray?"

"You don't know, then?"

"I don't make it a study to remember men's eye color." Never mind. She didn't need to look to confirm the particularly soft amber brown of Tim's eyes.

Tim wiggled his brows. "Not even mine?"

Fearing to be caught in a lie, Sarah turned and moved to the end of the counter, to the ribbons. "He has white in his eyes, correct?"

Tim laughed. "He also has black, but Miriam asked for blue, though not too dark."

"You are in luck. There are only three shades to choose from." Sarah held up the lightest. "I don't think I've seen eyes this color."

"That leaves two." He weighed the ribbons in his hands.

"How much ribbon do you need?"

"Six yards."

"You could purchase both colors and hope you run into George to compare before you see Miriam."

"Excellent suggestion. That way she can't be upset with me for having the wrong color. But what will I do with the extra?"

Sarah placed the spool of light-blue ribbon back in its place. "I don't know. What do men usually do with ribbon?" *He is leaving in a few days. Surely a little banter can't hurt us…*

"When we were in school, some of the boys would buy it for their favorite girl for her hair."

"Well, six yards should be enough to give a length to half of the eligible maidens in town. But be careful if they all show up to church with the same ribbon. Some of them could end up being fined for fighting on the Sabbath."

Tim held the ribbons up to Sarah's hair. "I could just give it all to you, then."

Sarah willed the heat she felt not to show on her face. "Sadly, I am too old to wear ribbons in my hair. I would end up dividing it among my nieces."

"How many nieces do you have?"

"Excluding Maryanna, who wed in March, there are four, plus John's daughter." Sarah looked around for something else to purchase as they meandered toward the line at the main counter. A placard announced a sale on raisins. Raisin pie seemed easy enough.

"That would be enough for a yard each, and you could keep a yard for yourself. My sister keeps all of George's correspondence tied in a ribbon. I could write you some letters."

Sarah tripped, nearly falling into a woman and her basket of purchases, but Tim caught her by the elbow just in time, and a new sort of unsteadiness filled her. It remained when he released his grip.

Tim waited as Sarah purchased a pound of raisins and a couple pieces of licorice. Looking at her gray dress, he wished he had gotten her to choose the green fabric. Was she mourning for someone?

She tucked the candy into her little bag and seemed surprised to find him still standing near her. "You waited?"

Tim offered his arm. "Shouldn't I escort you home? Is it not the proper thing to do?"

"No—Yes. I mean you didn't need to. I live only a couple blocks away, and I don't require an escort."

"Require?"

"I mean I don't need one. I am perfectly capable."

Tim worked to stop a frown from forming. "Is it any escort you don't need, or just mine?"

Sarah closed her eyes and took a breath. "That is not...I mean—" She waved her hand in front of her face. "I am used to being alone, and I don't want you to be late with your purchases. Miriam is liable to be frantic. Good day, Dr. Dawes."

He watched her scurry down the street. One thing hadn't changed, and that was that Sarah Marden could run away as fast as any boy in the school could chase her.

Good thing he would only be here a week.

five

With the ceremony over, the room grew uncomfortably warm. Tim inched around the edge of the parlor to one of the windows, intent on opening it before one of his sister's friends fainted from the warmth. Or worse, pretended to swoon to gain his attention. Mother maintained the wedding would be just a small thing—family and a few friends, but from the looks of it, his sister had invited every female student who had ever graced Bradford Academy's doors. Tim praised his stepfather's wisdom of sending him to the all-boys' Atkinson Academy in New Hampshire before he'd gone to Harvard for his studies. There were far too many flirtatious misses at Bradford for his taste.

One of the ladies flicked her fan, nearly hitting his shoulder.

"Pardon me, miss."

"Oh, Dr. Dawes, I shouldn't be so careless."

Or calculating. "I see you are suffering from the warmth of the room. If you will allow me to pass, I'll open a few more windows to rectify the situation."

The woman's smile faded. "Oh, but of course." She stepped to the side, closer to another woman. As he passed them, he heard the second whisper loudly, "Parmelia, I can't believe you accosted the doctor."

"Oh, I shouldn't have."

I agree, miss. You shouldn't. If only that were the worst of it.

Three feet shy of his goal, an elderly widow stopped him.

"Well, if it isn't Timmy Dawes! You finally decided to come home and heal your mother's heart." The woman waved a black, lace-edged sleeve in the general direction of the room. "You should be able to find a bride among this group. My eldest granddaughter is the one in blue. She has recently formed an attachment with a man from East Stoughton, where she was raised, but her sister is quite unattached. It would be nice to have her settled so near. They are such a comfort to me since the magistrate's death."

Finally—a clue to her identity. "I am sorry for your loss, Mrs. Garrett. If you don't mind, I need to open this window."

Mrs. Garrett grasped his arm. "You are needed here, boy. We lost far too many men—more than in the Revolution. It is your duty."

Tim nodded. There were no words. He tugged at the sash, but the window wouldn't budge. He tried again.

"If you remove the locking dowel, you will be more successful, Doctor." Sarah's voice carried a hint of laughter in it.

He followed her instructions, and the window rose with ease. "I had forgotten about my brother's little invention with the dowels. Ichabod came up with it after his father vetoed installing hidden shutters to keep out the Indians."

"He isn't the first boy to become enamored with the windows in the academy—a few of the buildings there were built over a century and a quarter ago and have shutters to protect against Indian attacks." Sarah stepped back, allowing Tim access to the next window.

When Tim turned to make another comment, she was gone. He found her with Emma and what had to be one of Emma's sons. Judging by Sarah's gestures and the son's reddened face, their conversation bordered on an argument. Tim wove through the crowded room, and as he neared them, he caught snatches of their hushed conversation.

"I promised Miriam I would help clean up."

"Ma needs to go home."

"Then take her."

"But I shouldn't—"

"For the thousandth time, I am not your sister or sister-in-law. You don't need to be my guardian." Sarah moved her hands to her hips.

Tim decided to interfere before the fight grew more intense. "Mrs. Wilson, Miss Marden, John, I hope you are enjoying the gathering."

Sarah blushed and looked at the floor.

Emma laid a hand on his arm. "Perhaps you could solve a dilemma for us. John insists I return home, but Sarah has promised to help your dear mother."

"Nothing simpler. I also promised my mother I would help clean once my sister leaves. I can escort Sarah home afterward."

John glowered. Sarah looked from Tim to John and then to Emma.

"See, son, I told you there was another option." Emma took her son's arm.

"But, Ma, you'll be alone."

"As I am most days when Sarah is teaching."

John gave Sarah a long look before turning his attention to Tim. "Very well, but know that *nothing* has changed."

Tim recognized the threat immediately. The Wilson boys were still protective of Sarah. Evidently she understood too, as she took a step forward and raised her chin. "John—"

Tim interrupted, giving a slight bow to Mrs. Wilson. "Thank you for coming. John, nice to see you again. Don't forget to take home some cake." He gave a slight nod to Sarah. "I'll find you later."

When he heard the sound of his name over the heads of the guests, Tim followed his mother's voice to help with whatever she needed now. Too late he realized that several young women surrounded her.

"Dear, these are some of Miriam's friends—Mrs. Garrett's grand-daughters, Miss Mina Frost, and her sister, Miss Ester." The girls gave the slightest of curtsies, which amounted to lowering their eyes and dipping less than half an inch. "And this is Miss Parmelia Page. She took your sister's position at the school and co-taught this past term." Miss Page fluttered the fan she had hit him with earlier and attempted a curtsy that would have toppled her had her friend not taken a firm grip on her elbow. "And this is Miss Clara Brooks. She is a teacher at Bradford." Miss Brooks bobbed her head slightly.

Reciprocating with a slight and awkward bow, Tim looked each lady in the eye. "Ladies, it is a pleasure. I hope you enjoyed the day."

The youngest Frost girl spoke up. Tim had already forgotten her name. "Didn't Miriam look divine? That color of blue so suits her. And her smile—just like an angel in one of the paintings we saw at Mr. Peal's museum when we visited our uncle in Philadelphia."

The other ladies nodded and made comments of agreement.

"If you will excuse me, it looks as though I need to open a few more windows." Tim retreated to the glare of his mother and the nodding heads of the others. He scanned the room. The women outnumbered the men almost two to one. Did George have no friends he could invite?

Slipping into the smaller withdrawing room, Tim opened a window there. Miriam had gotten her nice weather. It was almost unseasonably warm. Too bad the lawn was in such dismal repair, or some of the guests could enjoy the spring day.

The minister stood alone in the corner of the room. Perhaps a conversation with the man would keep the young women at bay.

Sarah slipped unnoticed into the hall. Why did she always have to fight with John? And to be caught doing it at her friend's wedding! And for John to threaten Tim! She wasn't eight anymore and didn't need someone watching out for her every second. And if she ever wanted to kiss Tim Dawes behind the church or anyplace else, she didn't need John's permission! Not that she would…

Maybe the weather would continue to be fair and John wouldn't have so much to grumble about. She swore farming brought out the worst in men. Sarah waved her fan a few more times and mustered a smile. Soon the guests would leave.

The sound of rushing footfalls caused her to move farther down the hall. Ichabod ran toward her, waving his arm. "Miss Marden, Miriam needs you. Upstairs. Her dress."

Sarah started for the front stairway, but Ichabod shook his head. "No, this way."

The servants' stairs. Sarah had never used any before, but so few of her acquaintances had houses with more than one set of stairs. She followed Ichabod up the narrow staircase to Miriam's room, where he tapped on the door. "Miri? I brought Miss Marden."

The door flew open and a hand reached out, dragging Sarah into the room. "I am so glad you were still here. Look at me! I am positively shaking. I am afraid George will think I am… that I… What am I to do?"

Sarah looked around the room, hoping for some idea of what was going on. An empty glass sat next to a pitcher. "Sit down and sip some water. What happened?"

Filling the glass only halfway, Sarah led Miriam to the bed. Miriam's hand shook so violently the water still threatened to spill. "We were downstairs receiving Mrs. Palmer's felicitations. When she finished, George leaned over and"—a blush rose in Miriam's cheeks—"he whispered in my ear that if we were going to get to Cambridge by nightfall, we needed to leave and I should go change my dress. By the time I got up here, I couldn't pull the bell. Not that I want Mrs. Reynolds helping me, even if she was my nurse. Mother can't see me like this. I knew Icky was hiding out from the Frost girl in his room, so I asked him to find you."

"Do you need me to help you change your dress?"

"No—I mean yes. I need you to help me stop shaking as if I've seen a ghost."

Sarah coaxed Miriam up and started to unfasten the tiny buttons running down the back of her dress. "Are you afraid of something?"

The answering whisper came so faintly the sound faded before Sarah understood what Miriam had said.

"Can you say that again?"

"George."

"Why? Has he ever hurt you?"

"Never!"

"Then why are you afraid of him?"

"Tonight, Mother said—Oh, why am I asking you? You've never been married."

"But I was engaged."

"That is not the same."

Sarah finished the last button. "Over the top or step out of it?"

"Can you get it over without messing my hair?"

"Of course. I may not have been married, but I did help Mrs. Wilson for a couple of years as a midwife." Sarah gathered up the back of the dress and slipped it over Miriam's head.

"Are other women this scared?"

"I suppose most are a bit nervous."

"But do they shake?"

"I don't think so. But Maryanna ran to the privy every ten minutes for the entire hour before her wedding. I thought Lucy would tie her down so we could finish her hair."

"I'm scared. Mother said …"

Sarah shook out the dress and laid it on the bed. "Tell me this. Do you enjoy kissing George?"

Miriam blushed from the neckline of her corset all the way up to her perfect hair. For a moment, she stopped shaking and whispered, "I do."

"It seems to me if you enjoyed kissing him yesterday, you still will today, and tomorrow, and next week." Sarah picked up the traveling dress and prepared to slip it over Miriam's head.

Miriam stuck her arms in the sleeves. "But what about tonight?"

"I don't remember much of my parents, but I am old enough to remember when Lucy got married. She is expecting for her eleventh time, and she still gets all doe-eyed and sweet as maple-syrup candy with Samuel, and then they go off and kiss. I think if being a wife was scary, my sister would be the first to run away. Hold still while I do your buttons."

"Eleven? Are you sure?"

"Lucy bore three of them when they were too small to live. But that is not a thought to follow."

Miriam held out her hand. "Look, I am not shaking."

"And you don't need to." Sarah drew Miriam into a hug. "I shall save my pennies and write to you, my friend."

"You'll need more than pennies. The new postage is twenty-five cents for four hundred miles, and we are going nearly six hundred."

Sarah opened her reticule and pulled out a dollar coin and pressed it into Miriam's hand. "This is to make sure you write me at least once. You can use the rest to write your mother and brothers."

She clutched the coin to her chest. "I shall write you twice, then, as Icky can share with Mother. If Tim stays here, I won't need his quarter either, so you best get him to stay."

"I have no influence there, I am afraid."

Miriam tilted her head. "At least keep him away from Parmelia if he does stay. She wants him worse than she wanted my job."

"No such thoughts on your wedding day. Shall we go down?"

Miriam shook her head. "I am meeting George at the servants' entrance. I don't think I could live through the long goodbyes. I'll be—I mean, we'll be—back in a week to get our things for the move west. You will come and see me off?"

"Of course."

"Hug my mother for me." Miriam slipped out of her room and down the servants' stairs.

Sarah went to watch out the window as her friend met her husband. They stopped to kiss before getting into the carriage. Sarah blinked back a tear and left the bedroom.

Why is a guest up here? And sneaking into the servants' stairs? "Have you seen Miriam?"

The woman stopped and turned to face him. *Sarah.* "Dr. Dawes, I didn't see you. Your sister left just now for Boston with George, or is it Cambridge?"

"What are you doing up here?"

"Miriam asked me to assist her in changing dresses. I assure you I have not been pilfering the linens."

Tim reached the doorway where she stood. "I never thought you would. But why are you using this stairway?"

"These are the stairs Ichabod brought me up and the same your sister left by. As I assume my coming down the grand staircase would be noticed and raise questions, I figured I'd better leave as I came." Sarah turned down the stairs again and then stopped. "Did your mother send you looking for Miriam?"

"Yes."

"Then I suggest you go announce that the couple has slipped away without saying their goodbyes."

Tim started to follow her.

Sarah stopped again and pointed to the other end of the hall. "I believe the announcement is best made from the grand staircase."

Tim watched her retreating form and felt as if he had been dismissed. It seemed Sarah Wilson was the only unmarried female in town who didn't want to be around him.

Too bad she was also the only one whose conversation did not border on the inane.

Six

GRABBING THE BROOM FROM THE corner, Sarah swept a few non-existent crumbs into an imaginary pile and debated whether she should walk home after all. The sun was hastening its decent, and she hadn't seen Tim for the past half hour. The day's unusual warmth remained, and her spencer would be adequate for the walk.

Only a couple slices of cake wrapped in brown paper and tied in the lighter of the blue ribbons Tim had purchased remained on the sideboard. Emma had already taken one home for them. But the thought of the dried-currant-and-nut confection made Sarah's mouth water. Her stomach rumbled. Like the rest of the wedding guests, she had not eaten after the ceremony, politely saving the packets of cake and sweets to enjoy at their homes.

She wiped the sideboard again and contemplated slipping a packet into her reticule for the walk home. She picked the smaller of the packets up and studied it. Would it be missed? Cleaning up, she had seen almost an eighth of the enormous cake still sitting in the larder. Moving the packets to the side, she scooped a single crumb into her palm. A voice behind her caused her to jump.

"I won't tell. You are probably starving." Tim reached around her and picked up one of the packets.

Sarah whirled around, a hand over her heart. "Dr. Dawes! You should have made your presence known!"

"And miss your debate over pilfering a slice of the wedding cake?"

"I wouldn't."

"I know." Tim handed her the larger piece. "Take it. We have more than enough to last us the week. Even Ichabod will be sick of it."

Sarah cradled the cake in her hand, having left her reticule with her wrap.

"Come, let's see if there is something more we can eat before I take you home. Cook and Mrs. Reynolds have abandoned the kitchen. They deserve a week's holiday." Tim led the way back into the empty kitchen. He opened cupboard doors and looked in a couple of jars. "Cheese and a few molasses cookies?" He offered her a handful of the cookies.

Sarah balanced the cookies atop her cake. Tim unwrapped the cheese and cut two wedges. He handed her one. "Well? You had better eat. I'd rather you not faint on our way home. I've managed to dodge two girls attempting just that in my presence today."

"I would never—" Sarah felt the heat rising. Did he assume she would play the empty-headed school girl trying to catch his eye?

"Of course you wouldn't. But you haven't eaten all day, and, like all women, your corset is most likely tied too tight. And you have been working hard. If you were to faint, it would not be some ploy to gain my attention. You would be embarrassed, and, no doubt, Mark or one of the other Wilsons would come thrash me."

Sarah swallowed the lump in her throat. "Mark is dead."

The smile on Tim's face disappeared. "My apologies. I had not heard. I thought it was Daniel who had passed."

"We've not had word from Daniel for more than a year. He was a seaman. Emma assumes the worst, but his brothers continue to hope he was lost at sea and will yet be heard from." To avoid further conversation, Sarah took a large bite of one of the cookies.

Tim looked around the room. Sarah wished she had not brought up Mark's death, but she had assumed he'd known. Everyone knew. She took another bite. Discussing Mark on her friend's wedding day seemed inappropriate.

"Do you have a wrap?"

The words barely penetrated the thoughts swirling in her head. Sarah pointed to the back of a chair. "I moved my spencer in here when I dusted the small parlor where the women left their wraps. The handkerchief on the table is not mine. I suspect its owner will show up to claim it soon. Her name should start with a *P*."

"*P*? How do you know?"

"It is embroidered on the corner."

"How many women were here today who would monogram *P* on their handkerchief?"

"I can only think of two—Mrs. Palmer, the new reverend's wife, and Parmelia Page, the teacher who will be taking your sister's place." Sarah didn't tell him she found it carefully tucked in the corner of the horsehair chair.

Tim examined the cloth. "Perhaps we should deliver it on our way home. I doubt it belongs to the reverend's wife. She cried during the ceremony, and this one looks unused." Tim put the cloth in his pocket and picked up the wrap. "Shall we go?"

He held the short jacket as if he expected to help her with it like one would a child. For the briefest of seconds, his fingers brushed her arm, and a tingle raced through her. It couldn't be. Their conversation about Mark must still be affecting her. She composed herself before turning to face him. "Thank you, Doctor."

"Why is it you insist on calling me doctor?"

"It is your title, is it not? Why would I call you otherwise?"

"Everyone else around here calls me either Tim or Timmy." He opened the back door to usher her out. "One woman called me Timison today."

Sarah suppressed a smile. "You didn't call her out for the slight, did you?"

Tim took the packet of cake from her and offered a hand to help her up into his buggy. "I haven't called anyone out over my name for years."

Sarah settled herself in, laying the packet of cake in her lap. "Oh, my reticule!" She started to stand, but Tim held up his hand.

"Where is it?"

"I left it hanging on the chair in the kitchen."

Tim crossed the yard in bold strides. *He certainly looks fine in his fancy suit.* What a thought!

Tim returned with her bag and a small package. "Your reticule and your ribbon."

"Thank you. But do let me pay you for the ribbon. I am giving it to my nieces, after all."

"But I am giving it to you."

Sarah tried to ignore the warmth in his voice. He'd played the flirt well even as a child, and it captivated her. Not that she admitted it then—nor would she now.

With the slightest movement of the reins, he coaxed the horse into a walk.

Sarah searched for a safe topic. "I still cannot believe anyone would dare call you by your given name."

"Timison? I don't mind it as much now, but I prefer Tim."

"I suspect she was one of Mrs. Garrett's granddaughters, as she is a stickler for proper names. But I assume she would have instructed them to call you Doctor."

"Where does Miss Page live?"

"In the boardinghouse Widow Webb runs, around the corner from Emma's."

They turned a corner, and Tim slid an inch closer. Accidental probably, but it made her feel unsettled in a way she hadn't felt for a long time. Perhaps it was a result of the wedding and remembering

Mark, or maybe he just had that effect on all single women. No wonder they were all trying to stake their claim on him. But she wasn't one of them—not even with those soft-brown eyes and the faint scar on his cheek, which added to the slightly roguish air he'd carried even as a seven-year-old. The wheel hit a hole. Sarah bounced into Tim's arm but quickly slid back.

"Sorry."

"No problem. I should watch better."

After a moment of riding in silence, he offered, "My sister loves the embroidered painted-silk picture thing you made her."

"You mean the remembrance? I wanted to give her something she could take with her. I assume she can frame it in Ohio. It is rolled up and should hardly take up any room in her trunk."

"Where did you learn to paint silk? You captured Miriam and George's likeness expertly." Tim shifted in his seat, and this time she was positive he had moved closer.

"The preceptress at Bradford, Miss Hassltine, taught us how to paint the watercolors on silk and then enhance them with embroidery. Occasionally someone commissions one for a wedding or funeral. It is enough to keep me busy in the evenings. Since Emma—I mean Mrs. Wilson—no longer needs my help in her midwifery. And it brings in some extra money."

"Did she need your help often?"

"She took me as often as she could. She was training me to take her place, but husbands don't like trusting their wives to a 'woman who has no experience herself.'" Sarah didn't add that Emma had been forbidden to use her skills unaided.

"Did you like midwifery?"

How could she not? Each new baby was such a joy. Of course, those who did not survive or whose mothers who did not brought the deepest of sorrows. "Most of the time."

Tim looked at her with an intensity that made her turn her head to hide her blush. "One of the doctors who taught us believed women would make excellent physicians. What do you think?"

"I think that if we were allowed in medical school, it would be a benefit to all. Doctors would stop the practice of bloodletting forever."

"You do not believe it helps?"

"How can it? When a person loses too much blood, whether from an accident or childbirth, they become weak or die. It does not make sense that removing blood from an ill person does anything other than make them weaker still. If anything, they need more, not less."

"You are not the first person to express such an opinion, and in most cases I am inclined to side with you. Despite our modern age, there is still so much we do not know."

"I hope we learn how to keep so many women and children from dying during childbirth." Sarah toyed with the strings of her reticule while her emotions calmed. Even though she knew her mother had been ill prior to delivering James Jr., it was still the premature birth that had killed them both. And eight years ago, Lucy had nearly died after giving birth to the twins.

"That would be a very good thing." The carriage rattled across a bridge, making conversation impossible for a moment.

When they reached the other side, Sarah asked, "Do you enjoy being a doctor?"

"In general, I believe so, but not in times of war. I went straight from Harvard to the war. There were days when I longed to deal with a child with the grippe or a woman whose child was born without one of the diseases plaguing her profession. Then it was a mercy to see the child die. But I still hated it almost as much as performing amputations."

Sarah gasped and sat back.

Tim looked as chastened as she had ever seen a man look. "My apologies. I should not have spoken thus. Sometimes the atrocities of war fill my mind so."

"I am not unfamiliar with that of which you speak. It seems when midwives gather, we do much the same thing."

"Still, I should not have spoken of such things."

Sarah laid her hand on his arm, and for a moment she forgot what she intended to say. "Do you think you will enjoy being a doctor now?"

"I think I will if I can find a place to settle down. Mother wants me to look for something here on the North Shore."

"Could you just set up shop, so to speak?"

"I wouldn't want to take patients from other doctors. It is hard enough to earn a living or support a family for many doctors. It is best to be partners if there are multiple doctors. In Boston, Dr. Warren is building a general hospital, the third one ever in this country. I hope for an invitation to work with him, although the building is far from complete."

"Samuel studied under a Dr. Warren. Is it the same?"

"I don't think so. Dr. John Collins Warren is about the age of Samuel, so he must have studied with the father, who died last year. I had forgotten Samuel studied medicine. He didn't finish, did he?"

"No. It isn't much of a secret now, but Samuel faints at the sight of blood. Even the smell is enough." Sarah suppressed a giggle.

"That would make being a doctor or surgeon very difficult. He is one of the best woodworkers around. I am sure he would have been excellent in surgery."

"He has a talent for bone setting."

"Useful to know."

They rode in silence for a minute. A chill wind blew through the trees, and Sarah shivered. With how unseasonably warm it had been today, the unexpected drop in temperature caught her off guard.

Tim reached under the seat and pulled out a blanket. "Would you like this?"

Sarah nodded, afraid if she spoke her teeth might chatter. He pulled to the side of the road and unfolded the blanket. Their hands touched as she took it from him, and they both froze. Sarah tugged the blanket away, the warmth flooding her having nothing to do with the wool cloth.

Tim lifted the reins, and they resumed their journey.

Seven

I<small>F HE HAD BEEN TEN</small>, the temptation to kiss her would have won out. In the dimming light, her blush had nearly caused reason to fade.

It had been a long time since he had allowed himself to feel anything for a woman. Of course, most of those he'd been around the past few years were either the devoted wives of soldiers or women of questionable morals. Either way, it served him best to ignore the fairer sex. Until he knew his plans, he wasn't going to look for a wife, especially not in a woman the Wilson men still protected.

Tim recognized the boardinghouse from his last trip to Sarah's.

"Her name is Miss Page?" Tim slowed his horse and stopped near a hitching post.

"Yes, Parmelia Page." Sarah moved to get down.

Tim raised his hand to stop her. "I'll only be a moment. You'll stay warmer if you don't get out."

At the door he lifted the brass knocker only once. Movement on the other side kept him from tapping a second time. A stooped woman dressed in black from her cap to her boots opened the door.

"Male visitors are allowed on Tuesdays, Fridays, Saturday evenings, and Sundays after two o'clock. Today, if you have forgotten, is Wednesday." She started to close the door.

Stopping the door with his hand, Tim spoke through the crack. "My apologies. I am not here to visit but, rather, to return a lost item." He held out the handkerchief. "I believe this may belong to Miss Page. It was found as we cleaned up after my sister's wedding."

The door opened again, and the old woman extended her hand.

"Oh!" A high-pitched squeal sounded from the dim hall behind the woman. "My favorite handkerchief! I worried that I'd lost it on my walk back this afternoon."

Tim recognized the speaker as one of the women who'd swooned to attract his attention. He doubted she'd lost her handkerchief at all.

"Well, Parmelia, thank him so he can leave." Judging by the direction of the woman's wrinkles, her frown was a semipermanent facial feature.

"Just five minutes, Mrs. Webb. He rode over here just to return it."

Tim stepped down a step. "Actually, I—"

Mrs. Webb cut him off. "Two minutes. Here at the door." She retreated into the hallway. Tim wondered if she made use of her dark dress to lurk in the nearest shadows.

"Oh, Dr. Dawes, how kind of you to track me down." Parmelia stood closer than necessary, her eyelashes fanning an odd little rhythm.

Tim handed her the cotton cloth. "I'm pleased to locate the owner on my first attempt."

"Oh, you guessed it was mine?" The eyelash fanning increased in speed.

"No, Miss Marden guessed the handkerchief's origin."

"Sarah?" Miss Page's voice squeaked a high, grating note, and the lashes stopped for several beats. "She recognized it?"

"Only guessed." Tim turned to leave. Two minutes was much too long for this transaction.

A hand on his arm stopped him. "Oh, I do need to thank you properly. Perhaps if you come by Saturday evening. I am cooking, and I could save you a piece of my mince pie. Everyone says it is the best they've ever eaten."

Dislodging her hand, he took another step down the stairs. "There is no need to thank me further. My mother is very jealous of my time when I am home. Good evening, Miss Page." He turned and descended to the street.

He heard Miss Page following him. "Oh, who is—Why, Sarah, I didn't realize. Whatever are you doing out so late? Shouldn't you be caring for Widow Wilson? Everyone says she—"

Tim cut her off before she could finish saying something hurtful. "Miss Marden was good enough to help my mother after Miriam and George departed. We are en route to her home now. If you will pardon us."

"Oh, you must be unaware of Miss Marden's duties, or you would never have delayed her." There was a hard edge to Miss Page's voice as she spoke.

"Thank you for your concern. I am sure Miss Marden appreciates your diligence on Mrs. Wilson's behalf."

Mrs. Wells appeared at the door. "Miss Page! Get back in here at once. Shame on you, Dr. Dawes, for luring one of my girls out of the house after dark!"

Miss Page ducked her head and ran up the stairs. The door slammed.

Back in the carriage, the air was filled with tension. Tim opened his mouth, but Sarah spoke first.

"I should have warned you about Mrs. Webb. She is very protective of her girls. At least she did not have her broom."

"Her broom? You sound as if you've met with the broom before."

"Mark has. However, I got sweeping duty for a week." Sarah laughed, a musical sound he wanted to hear again.

"You lived there?"

"My second year at Bradford. Before Emma had her house. Samuel decided it was too far for me to travel each day. It also allowed him to move my nieces into my room while he completed the addition."

"Your room?"

Sarah smiled. "Yes, Samuel and Lucy always allowed me the privilege, just as Papa had allowed it to Lucy, as I am so much older than their children."

Tim guided the horse around a mud hole at the corner. "Was it difficult being raised by your sister?"

"Lucy is almost fifteen years older, so she had always mothered me a bit. I won't lie—there were times I appreciated when Emma stepped in as a grandmother figure, especially as I got older. I think it was hardest on Samuel when I needed to be reprimanded."

"You needed to be reprimanded?"

The musical laugh again. "Don't all children?"

"Of course, but I am having a hard time imagining you doing anything untoward."

"Ask me no questions, and I'll tell you no fibs."

"That's from a play, isn't it?"

"Yes, *She Stoops to Conquer*. The twins memorized the entire script, and they would do the parts in different voices. Joe always wanted me to play Kate."

The parlor curtain fluttered, and Tim pointed with his chin. "Someone is waiting for you." He stepped out of the carriage and offered Sarah his hand.

As soon as her feet touched the ground, Sarah slipped her hand out of Tim's and looked at the window. Parmelia was correct. She should have been home hours ago.

The front door flew open. Sarah recognized the look in Emma's eyes and braced herself for the confusion sure to come in the next few minutes.

"Mark, is that you? Have you been keeping Sarah out unchaperoned again? How many times have I told you? Now that you are engaged, you must be more circumspect."

Sarah hurried to the porch in hopes of turning Emma back to the present. Tim followed behind.

"Sarah, do I need to speak with Lucy? Hasn't she explained to you what could happen?" Emma peered over Sarah's shoulder at Tim. "You are leaving for this new war in just a few days. Do you want to leave Sarah with a child and no marriage? How would she pay the fine? They won't let her teach if she is found to be morally deficient!" Emma's voice rose to a pitch that carried easily in the clear night air.

Heat flooded Sarah's cheeks. Whatever would Tim think of such a conversation? The 'Emma sometimes lives in the past' excuse didn't cover wild imaginings. This conversation never existed in the past, as far as she knew. She reached for Emma's hand and guided her back into the house. Tim still followed.

"Emma, this is Dr. Dawes. Do you remember him?"

"You mean little Timmy Dawes who always tried to kiss you? What are you doing with him? What will Mark say?" Emma turned to Tim, whose face grew as red as Sarah assumed hers had. "You should leave now." Emma waved him away like she did the chickens.

Sarah closed her eyes for a moment, hoping it would all just go away. When she opened them, Tim opened the door, then gave her a little nod before passing through it and shutting it behind him.

Oh, dear Emma! Sarah gathered the woman in her arms and took her to the warmth of the kitchen, wondering how long this lapse in memory would last.

"Come, Emma, let me brush your hair."

Tim looked back at the house as he guided the carriage around the corner. Sarah's mortification had been palpable. He had heard of the maladies of old age affecting the memory. Having witnessed Mrs. Wilson lost in some version of the past twice now, he pondered the implications. No wonder John had been so insistent Sarah return home earlier.

There could be little truth in this memory. Sarah was a teacher, so he dismissed any words impugning her character as the thoughts of a mother worrying over a son. Hadn't his stepfather given him the same lecture every time he returned from Harvard for a break?

He wondered if there were any cures for the elderly. He had all his copies of the *New England Journal of Medicine and Surgery, and the Collateral Branches of Science* in his trunk, but he couldn't recall the malady of dementia being covered. There were articles on the moral approach to the treating of the insane. The ancient Greeks had written about the phenomenon of madness in the elderly, and Dr. Morton may have a book on the subject in his library. Mrs. Wilson was the first instance of the affliction he'd witnessed as a doctor. There had been the old man who'd run out in the snow in his nightshirt when Tim was six or seven, but he didn't remember the man's name.

Could he learn anything from talking to Mrs. Wilson or Sarah? Not that he would mind furthering his acquaintance with Sarah. No, he wouldn't mind one bit.

Eight

"No teacher who is shown to be morally deficient may teach."

You know this is talking about you.

Stay away from Dr. Dawes, or Preceptor Colburn will know why too.

SARAH TURNED THE PAPER OVER. Blank. The poorly formed lettering reminded her of her nephew Benjamin's. Yet no child could have written the note as all the words were spelled correctly. Sarah took it into the kitchen.

"Anna, dear, so nice of you to visit today. I thought you would be tending your garden. Ours is ever so lovely."

Sarah looked at the stunted plants in the garden. *Lovely?* Wherever Emma's mind resided this morning, she would not be a good person to ask for advice.

Who could have written the note?

Sarah waited until Emma turned her back. Then she dropped the paper into the fire.

⇥ ✖ ⇤

Tim meandered through the shop on High Street as he waited for his mother to decide on her purchases. He never understood how picking out a spool of thread could take longer than a few seconds. Wandering past the books, he read the titles. A book of lectures caught his eye, and he thumbed through it before setting it back on the shelf.

"Oh! You should buy that. It is quite the thing. They have been running an advertisement for it in the *Intelligencer*."

For a second, Tim considered pretending he had not heard the voice he'd come to know as Miss Page's. But he turned to her lest his mother cite him for his rudeness. "Miss Page, thank you for the recommendation, but I am not in need of a book at the moment."

"Oh—" This time the exclamation sounded disappointed.

Did she start every sentence with *Oh*? Tim would rather not listen to enough conversations to test his theory. "Excuse me. It looks as if my mother has finished."

"Oh, but … oh, I wanted to make sure you knew of the lecture being given at the Church tonight. Reverend Palmer is hosting a man of science who is going to discuss the sunspots and the red-and-yellow snow and the end of the world. It will be most fascinating."

"Snow?"

"Oh, haven't you read in the paper? It fell in Italy just before Christmas. Surely it is a sign, don't you think?" Miss Page's eyelashes started beating the annoying rhythm of the other night.

Tim recalled having seen several articles a week past on the phenomena but assumed a logical explanation existed. Not wishing to encourage the woman, Tim stepped around her. "Thank you for telling me. Now, if you will excuse me, my mother awaits." He hurried across the room faster than necessary.

His mother gave him the slightest of frowns but kept her thoughts to herself until he escorted her outside. "You did not need to cut your conversation short on my account."

"Do not worry yourself. I did not."

"Timison, you must start talking to women if you ever intend to marry. According to Miriam, Miss Page is an excellent conversationalist. You could do far worse." His mother adjusted her shoulders, a sign the lecture had just begun.

Tim cut her off. "I don't recall it being so cold here this time of year. Is my memory that poor from being away these past four years?"

"There is nothing wrong with your memory. Nor mine. If you think to distract me from—"

Tim took the wooden bridge slightly faster than necessary, the clanking of the wheels drowning out his mother's voice.

"Timison George Dawes! Your father warned me not to spare the rod when you were younger. How did you ever grow up to be so difficult?" A hint of humor colored her voice.

"Blame it on all the maple sugar candy I took when no one was watching."

"Oh, I knew it was you. But with Miriam moving so far, I do hope you will settle nearby. I am so jealous of my friends and their grandbabies!"

"If I start or join a practice here, there is no guarantee of grandchildren anytime soon. Without a wife, such a thing is practically impossible. And despite the many women introduced to me since I returned, I have yet to meet one I am inclined to court." Tim hoped his mother did not catch the lie. Considering he couldn't remember a time when he hadn't known Sarah, *meet* wasn't exactly the right word.

"You mean to tell me not one of your sister's friends or schoolmates has caught your eye? Why, there were nearly a dozen at the wedding."

"I am aware of the variety of women you managed to invite to the event. I do not require variety as much as I do quality. That, I am afraid, is in short supply."

"Timison! How dare you speak of our North Shore girls that way."

Tim patted his mother's knee and drove on without a reply.

"Samuel? Whatever are you doing here?" Sarah closed the door and gave her brother-in-law a hug. She so desperately needed the strength it offered today. He held her until she stepped out of the embrace.

"I had a delivery to make and thought I would stop by to see Ma and my favorite little pumpkin."

"What would your children say if they heard you call me that?"

Samuel rested his hands on Sarah's shoulders. "We discussed this many times, and my answer is still the same. I love you as if you were my own. How could I not? You're the one who taught me what fatherhood meant before I figured out how to be a husband. And as you well know, I've never called any of the other children pumpkin."

"Oh, that's right. You nicknamed us all after different foods. Although I think Lettie is not fond of carrot. What shall this next one be—beets?"

He tipped his head back and laughed. "I could never name a child after a food I hated. There are still two or three choices left in my garden. Where is Ma?"

Sarah pointed to the kitchen. "She wanted to make bread today. As usual, she is making far too much. You will take some home, won't you?"

"Tell me. Is she getting worse? John is of the opinion she is declining."

Sarah felt tears forming. "I'm sorry, but he is correct. Have you seen him today? Is that the real reason for your visit?"

"Perhaps we should take a walk after I speak with Ma." Samuel entered the kitchen. From the greeting he received, Emma seemed to be firmly rooted in the present.

In the corner of the parlor, Sarah returned to her painting. She hadn't failed to miss Samuel's evasion of her question. Had John gone to give Samuel an earful directly after the wedding yesterday, or had he taken the opportunity as it had arisen?

"Walk with me down to Swanson's. If I return home without some peppermints, you know I will have a rebellion on my hands."

Sarah tied her hat on and followed him out the door.

"John did come to visit me last night. He is of the opinion I should be able to rein you in. But I pointed out to him that when we moved Ma to the little house so he could take over the old one, we never intended for you to be a nursemaid. We assumed in time you would—" Samuel cleared his throat.

"—marry Mark." Sarah filled in for him.

"Actually, I thought you were leaning toward Daniel at the time. But I did expect you would be married by now and that one of my other daughters would be living with Ma as she attended Bradford."

"It was perfectly wonderful to have Maryanna and Lettie here during their schooling, and you know Louisa will be welcome this fall."

"And Ma will be alone during the day while you teach, which brings us back to John's concerns. He thinks Ma should not be left alone."

"And it is my duty to be her constant companion."

"Something like that."

Sarah stopped. "He wants to propose again, doesn't he? Only this time not only will I inherit his children, I will need to look after Emma as well. I can't do that. You know I harbor no regard for him in that way. Besides, Emma is always so confused after going back to the house. Half the time I need to explain to her that Thomas is dead. That is always so draining. I can't do it. Last night she mistook Dr. Dawes for Mark, and it took more than an hour to calm her as she relived getting the message of his death."

Samuel escorted Sarah across the street to the green, where he found them a bench under a tree. "That could not be easy for you either."

Sarah dabbed at her eyes with her handkerchief. "It was particularly difficult to have Dr. Dawes witness Emma's"—she waved her hand, not sure what to call it—"a second time."

"Twice? I had no idea you had been in Tim's company so often."

"Only twice, but both times of little consequence."

"Remind me to ask about him after we discuss Ma. How bad are things?"

Nope, not going to remind you. "Some nights she has tried to go see old patients. So now each night, I lock the door and hide the key so she can't leave. With the horse gone, she walks, and I am afraid I might not hear her leave."

"Do we need to get someone to help you? Perhaps one of my girls or my nieces. Both Thomas Jr.'s and Carrie's daughters are of an age to help. Lettie is already helping at John's, but Louisa may be able to come."

"Lucy should deliver this child in July." Sarah didn't need to wait for a confirmation. "Louisa will be needed at home until fall. As for your nieces ... Emma's lapses can be quite confusing. I am not sure a girl of fifteen or sixteen is equal to the task. If we could find a woman nearer Emma's age, it may be of more help. But I can't think of anyone who needs a job as a companion."

"I will put the question to Lucy. So you know, John did not ask me outright again for my permission where you are concerned, but he still sees marriage to you as a solution to several problems."

"I wish he wouldn't put me on his list of problems to solve. It isn't like I am Mark's widow."

"Hmmm. Then you might consider wearing brighter colors. Just the other day I had someone inquire about my widowed daughter. I assume the difference in surnames adds to the confusion."

"Then it is fortunate I am not truly widowed, or I would have the same last name and it would be even more confusing." Sarah tried to laugh, but the sound came out flat.

"I know how much you loved him, but think of your mother. She found love again."

"You forget that Mama didn't receive much caring in her first marriage, according to Lucy and mother's journal."

"I wasn't very fond of Mr. Simms. And even less so after reading the journal. But James Marden was one of the finest men I knew. I don't know if I lived up to him as your substitute father. He did love your mother very much."

Sarah gave Samuel a side hug. "If Mama had lived long after Papa died, I don't know if she would have married again. If she'd had a choice, I think she would have married Papa from the start." Sarah thought about her parents. Her vague memories, more feelings than anything else, had been supplemented by Lucy's stories and her mother's journal. But one thing she clearly remembered was Papa hugging Mama and laughing. "I want what Mama and Papa had, what your parents had. And I've watched you and Lucy." Sarah paused and made a face. Samuel laughed. "I want someone who will look at me the way you look at Lucy. Even after all these years, you still look at her the way you did when I wasn't old enough to understand."

Samuel nodded. "Hence, John's proposals are not accepted. I'll try to make sure he doesn't offer another one. But we do need to work on something for Ma. I'll see if Lucy is up to a Sunday dinner, along with Carrie, Thomas Jr., and John. I don't dare not invite Ma, but we need to discuss things without her."

"I can probably talk her into walking down to the creek with the children and me."

"Good idea—only, we will get the older girls or perhaps Mary-anna and Phillip to go. I want your opinions on this. Now, shall we continue to our destination?" Samuel stood and offered his arm. Sarah took it, and they proceeded to High Street.

Sarah considered discussing the note she'd burned with Samuel. But there was really no point as Dr. Dawes would be leaving soon and she would have little opportunity to see him while watching over Emma anyway.

Parmelia and Miss Brooks exited the milliner's just as Samuel and Sarah were passing. Parmelia whispered to her companion before addressing Sarah. "Oh, Miss Marden, we were just discussing yesterday's wedding. You were there—didn't you think Miriam's dress was too—"

"Gorgeous for words? Why, George couldn't take his eyes off his bride." Sarah cut Parmelia off before she could utter an unkind word.

"She looked fine enough, I suppose, but that brother of hers—I can find no fault with his attire at all." Parmelia's statement brought a giggle from Miss Brooks. "I was just speaking to Timothy. He regrets he cannot attend a lecture with me this evening."

"Timothy?" Samuel raised a brow.

Miss Brooks wound the strings of her reticule around her fingers. "I believe Miss Page is referring to Dr. Dawes. We really must be going."

Samuel waited until they were out of earshot. "I am going to assume Miss Page's feigned use of your old friend's name was for your benefit?"

Sarah shrugged.

"Why didn't you correct her?"

"If Dr. Dawes has given her permission to address him by a Christian name other than his own, I could hardly presume to interfere." Sarah entered the door Samuel held for her.

"So, you are competition for Miss Page."

"You know Tim and I are only old friends. Besides, he is to leave shortly. Oh, look, a new shipment of licorice." Sarah hoped Samuel didn't realize she had been looking around the store in hopes of finding something, or someone, else entirely.

Nine

THE TEN-YEAR-OLD MESSENGER REFUSED TO leave until Tim had
donned his coat and collected his bag of doctor's instruments. Only
when Tim mounted his horse did the boy run off into the gathering darkness. Tim crossed the bridge and realized he wasn't sure of
the exact location of Dr. Morton's home. He rode past the doctor's
surgery but found it empty. A lamplighter supplied the address.

The two-story white house sat back from the road far enough to
provide for a small garden of sorts. The lamplight revealed a neatly
trimmed hedge and lawn—exactly what Tim expected from the
doctor. Everything where it belonged.

A maid answered the door and escorted Tim to an upstairs
bedroom. Raised voices filled the hallway.

"You need your rest," said a man.

"Not until Dawes arrives." The pain-filled voice spoke slowly.

A woman's voice entered the conversation. "Alexander, I am sure
Dr. Norris can explain the situation to Dr. Dawes."

"Monkey pox! I want—"

The maid rapped on the door. When she announced Tim,
a collective sigh echoed throughout the house.

"About time." Dr. Norris crossed his arms and leaned against
the bedpost.

"My apologies. After your messenger left, I realized I couldn't recall the location of your home."

"I hope you learn the locations of a great many homes quickly, then, if you are to take over my patients for me." Tim was hopeful the gray pallor of Dr. Morton's face had more to do with his current ailment than with his age.

"Your patients?"

Dr. Norris stepped forward. "My partner is of the opinion that while he is convalescing, you should see to his entire practice."

"Norris, you are too busy to take my patients, and if you have your way, Dawes here will only get the ones you don't want to deal with and you will be overburdened." Dr. Morton's voice strengthened as he argued.

His wife patted his arm. "As you can see, my husband and Dr. Norris are at a bit of an impasse. But the fact remains that between the two of them, they see far too many patients. With his broken leg, it will be weeks before Alexander can make any calls, and those he can see in his office will be limited. My husband has been talking for days of again approaching you to join them. His accident has merely hastened the proposal. Now, if you would be good enough to accept, I can give him a dose of laudanum and he can rest."

Dr. Norris crossed his arms again. He looked as sour as he had fifteen years ago when he'd treated Tim's measles. Tim addressed Dr. Morton. "I would be more than happy to help you out as I have yet to decide what I am doing next. I had hoped to go to Dartmouth to work with a doctor there, but with the problems they are having, I don't dare until the governor decides the school's fate."

"Then may the wheels of government work slowly. My wife will show you my books and records. I do ask you to come consult with me daily. Now, Doctors, if you will please leave. Mrs. Morton is quite insistent that I rest."

"Gentlemen, if you will wait for me in the parlor, I will be down in a moment." Tim wondered if Dr. Morton's wife wouldn't have made the better doctor had she been allowed to attend medical school. He'd heard rumors that as a midwife, her skills were eclipsed only by Mrs. Wilson, and none surpassed her in bone-setting.

Dr. Norris stopped at the bottom of the stairs, blocking Tim's descent. "You should know I am not in favor of Dr. Morton's proposal. You have been an army sawbones these past years, but you know nothing of the illnesses we suffer here, and of women, et cetera. I keep telling him we must give you a trial to see if you are competent."

Tim thought a moment before answering. Angering Dr. Norris would serve no good end. "I can understand your reluctance. I do have letters, but I am sure they will do little to change your opinion of me. Illness is as much a danger to soldiers as cannonball or musket fire. And as for women, between the wives and other camp followers, I have more than a little experience in both childbirth and women's complaints."

"I bet you do." Dr. Norris crossed the room and claimed the chair that by size and fabric would be the one usually reserved for the master of the house.

Refuting the implication that he'd seen the fallen women who'd trailed after the soldiers in anything other than a professional capacity would only stir things up more, and so he remained silent on the matter. "How did Dr. Morton break his leg?"

"He fell through the rickety porch out at old Dobbs's place. I keep telling him he shouldn't make as many house calls, especially to the older patients. Half of them aren't sick anyway—just afraid of dying and hoping a good doctor can cheat the Grim Reaper."

Tim chose to stand near the fireplace rather than sit. "Were there many splinters?"

"Don't know. Mrs. Morton had it all cleaned and set before I arrived. Don't know why she bothered to ask me to come."

"I asked you to come because my husband wished it."

Dr. Norris did not bother to stand when Mrs. Morton entered the room.

Mrs. Morton rubbed the bridge of her nose, concealing a sigh. "Norris, remove yourself from Alexander's chair. In fact, you may leave if you wish. I don't think I have anything to discuss with you. I only asked you to stay in case my husband had something further to relay. He does not."

Dr. Norris moved to the settee. "I wish to remain." The heat of the doctor's glare nearly started Tim's coat ablaze.

Mrs. Morton turned her full attention to Tim. "These are a spare set of keys to the surgery and office. The small one is to his file box, and the midsized one fits the drug cabinet. This book contains his appointments. I usually help out a couple days a week, but I think I will be needed here." She waved her hand to indicate the floor above. "Come by tomorrow afternoon and let us know if you have any questions. Since it is Friday, he only had a couple of appointments in the morning. Saturday is usually full of minor emergencies—boys falling from trees and such."

Tim took the keys and smiled. He had been one of those boys.

"And if you will please put this sign in the window of the office." She turned back to Dr. Norris. "Now, if you will both excuse me. I prefer to be with Alexander. I believe our maid has your coats and hats."

Tim followed Dr. Norris out of the house and was relieved when the doctor had no more words for him. For a second, he wondered if he should have refused. He turned over the pasteboard to read: *Dr. Morton's patients are now in the care of Dr. Tim Dawes. In an emergency, please inquire at 10 River Street.*

The sign had been neatly written and embellished. Tim looked back at the doctor's house and noticed a similar placard next to the door. Dr. Morton must have been certain he would help. Mother would be happy to learn he would be staying until at least Independence Day.

Ten

THE BREEZE DANCED THROUGH THE clothing as Sarah hung it on the line. This Friday morning, it seemed like spring was finally here to stay. About time too. Maybe John would stop his grumbling about the farm and crops, even if they did need more rain. Last year's poor crop had only deepened the dark mood hanging about him since his wife passed. The entire family had endured almost a year and a half of his nay-saying. If Sarah thought for a minute her marrying John would improve his person, she would be tempted to do it. But there were too many reasons to avoid such a marriage, not the least of which was that he still pined for his deceased wife, Remember.

Sarah shook out a sheet as well as any thoughts of John. She couldn't force herself to enjoy his company.

Emma descended the steps. "It is such a lovely day. Are you weeding the garden today?"

"There isn't much to weed yet. We only planted it a week ago Saturday. But the flowers in the front are looking poorly." Sarah pulled the last linen from her basket. "Maybe we should work on them together."

"You mean you'll work while I talk. Bending over is so much harder to do each year."

Sarah breathed a sigh. Emma was herself today. They walked around the house to the ailing flower bed.

"Is your calendar correct, dear?"

Or maybe not. "I believe so."

"I hoped it wasn't. It says I'll be sixty-six next week."

"Would you like to ask the boys and Carrie over?" Sarah knelt on a piece of oilcloth. The late frost two weeks ago had damaged many of the flowers she'd planted from seed last fall.

"No, I'd rather not have them fuss over me. Besides, we are due at Samuel's on Sunday, and Lucy will most likely bake me some little thing to commemorate."

"I could bake you a cake or pie."

Emma laughed. "And have it meet the same fate the last of our carrots did earlier this week? I love you, little miss, but please, please don't cook for me."

"How did you know I tried to bake?"

"Piggy Peggy isn't as dumb as we think she is. Even she wouldn't touch it." Emma bent over and pulled out a withered stock. "Not much of a flower, is it?"

Sarah turned to see Emma's flower and spotted Amity Barns coming up the walk. It struck Sarah that Amity resembled the withered flower, only in her case, damage from a horse's hoof and not a frost had prevented her from blooming.

"Mm-mmi-iss, Wil-ilson, need help." Amity rested her hand at her waist, revealing the shape her dirty brown dress camouflaged.

Emma looked at Sarah and mouthed one word. "Please?"

Midwifery. Emma had been forbidden to practice her trade. But it couldn't hurt just to see what Amity needed. Sarah set down her trowel and stood. "Would you like to come in for something to drink?"

"Y-yes, Missss Mard-din."

Sarah followed Emma and Amity into the house, trying to remember the girl's age. She was somewhere between Louisa and Lettie, maybe fourteen. But not really—the accident had left her blind in one eye and with slurred speech. The intelligence she'd showed her first three years of school had been reduced to that of a young child. Sarah should go get Mrs. Morton, but she would tell her husband. Then Dr. Norris might find out, and then Reverend Palmer and the magistrate. The fine would equal more than a month's pay for Mr. Barns, and that would hurt Amity. Although there must be mercy in the law for a girl who had been reduced to an imbecile. Sarah bit her lip. Just this one visit. If Emma remained in the present today, she would be able to at least guess when the girl could expect her lying-in. Then she would talk to someone.

"Would you like tea? Or cider?"

"No, I-I fat-t cow."

Sarah ushered the girl into a chair. "A cup of chamomile tea won't make you grow fat, sweetheart."

Emma sat next to Amity. "Did someone tell you that you are fat?"

Amity nodded.

"Who?"

"Da-da say grr-ow lık-ke a fat-t cow. I s-say I hurt. He say no eat."

Sarah sat on the bench. "Have you had any food today?"

Amity shook her head. Emma got up and filled a bowl with the peas porridge left over from breakfast. Sarah sliced some of the ham left from yesterday's supper. Amity shoveled the food into her mouth as if she hadn't eaten for days. Sarah longed to brush the girl's hair and wash her face, but if she was correct in her assumption, cleaning Amity up could mean someone looking too closely at her.

When she finished, Emma patted her hand. "What do you need my help with?"

Amity again rested her hand on her rounding belly. "Wr-r-ong. Bad. Sick-k."

"Will you come lie on my bed and let me see?" Emma stood and started guiding the girl out of the room. Sarah ran ahead to lay one of the oil cloths over the bed.

"Amity, Miss Marden helps me. Can she stay in here with us?" Again, Emma didn't wait for an answer. "Lie down right here."

Amity bent to take off her boots. Sarah knelt to help her. The girl had not been careful where she walked, nor had she scraped them off for a while, and her stockings were unwashed. How many times had the woman's charity circle made Amity one of their projects? Dropping off clothing from time to time didn't come close to fulfilling Amity's needs.

"Amity if you will lie back, I am going to feel your stomach." Emma demonstrated by patting her own midriff.

Amity did as asked. Emma conducted her examination through the girl's clothing. Emma's brow furrowed and she looked up. "Sarah?"

"Did it hurt when Mrs. Wilson touched you?"

Amity shook her head.

"May I do the same thing she did?" asked Sarah.

Amity nodded.

Sarah conducted the examination as Emma had taught her. The baby was bigger than she expected. But through the dress and petticoat, they could only guess. She looked up to see that Amity's eyes were closed.

Emma patted the girl's hand. "Are you tired, dear? Why don't you sleep for a bit?"

Sarah followed Emma out of the room. "How has she hidden this so long?"

"I don't know. I think because she didn't realize what was happening. I think the baby could be here as early as mid-July. But I know I am not myself most days, and Dr. Morton asked me not to do any more midwifery. I think either he or Mrs. Morton should look at her. Amity has had some sort of attacks or seizures since the incident with the horse."

"But what of the fornication laws?"

"I doubt Amity understands how this happened. Reverend Palmer won't press charges, I am sure. As far as the judge, the general outcry from the charity circle will keep him from levying a fine. However, her father…I don't know what he will do. He has refused offers for any help with Amity over the past two years."

"Perhaps it is better to let her think she is fat for now." Sarah cleared the cup and bowl Amity had used. "When she leaves, we'll go talk to the Mortons."

Tim knocked on the door of Dr. Morton's home. By day, the house looked less imposing. The maid opened the door and showed him to the parlor, where he found Mrs. Wilson and Sarah visiting with Mrs. Morton.

"Dr. Dawes, I am glad you are here. Let me see if my husband is ready for company, and we can go discuss this problem. It may well be that Dr. Dawes will need to be involved as well." Mrs. Morton swept out of the room.

They barely had time to exchange pleasantries before the maid returned and led them up the stairs. Curiosity ate at Tim. What problem could they all need to discuss? Maybe Mrs. Wilson knew she needed help.

Mrs. Morton directed them to several chairs placed around the room. "Mrs. Wilson, please tell my husband what you told me."

"Amity Barns came to our home this morning asking for help. I don't think she had eaten in days, so we fed her. But her problem wasn't so easily solved. I believe she will deliver a child in late July or early August. She has no idea, so I only felt her through her dress."

Dr. Morton shook his head. His wife looked grave. "Did you attempt to question her at all?"

Sarah spoke. "No, we let her take a nap and prepared some mint tea packets for her to take home. From what she said, I think she is not eating because her father told her she was fat. I thought it best to let her believe he was right."

"I wish I could go down to the docks and talk to Barns myself. He tries, but he is too proud to take help. We already know he won't talk to any church women. And Norris won't show the girl the compassion she needs." He turned to his wife. "Have you spoken with Amity in the last couple of years?"

"No, she doesn't talk when I am around."

Dr. Morton frowned. "Mrs. Wilson, for now I am going to give you permission to see one patient, but only if Miss Marden is there. Over the next two weeks, invite Amity over as often as you can, around noon. Dearest," he patted his wife's hand, "you will drop by. Hopefully we can get Amity used to you. Dr. Dawes, you will also just happen to stop at the house and pray the girl likes you. With her seizures, the delivery may require your assistance. If she can keep the secret for a few more days, perhaps I can get Barns to come here for a discussion."

Tim looked at each person in the room. "May I ask just who it is we are discussing? I am rather confused at the notion of letting a woman think she is fat when she is expecting."

"Not a woman. A child. Amity Barns turned fourteen last month. She has been under my care since a horse kicked her in the head at the age of twelve. The injury resulted in blindness in her left eye, a stutter, and a perpetual state of confusion. To this add seizures, which she has experienced with increasing intensity and frequency over the past several months. She lives with her father in one of those rundown apartments near the docks. Even if she survives her lying-in, the baby will need to be placed. Honestly, I don't know with the seizures if she or the baby will survive." Dr. Morton leaned back against the headboard. "I know she will let me treat her, and with any luck, I will be up and around by then, but the chance of something out of the ordinary happening earlier is too great."

"I can stop by whenever necessary," said Tim.

Dr. Morton looked at his wife. "Dear, why don't you get our guests some refreshment. I am sure Mrs. Wilson will be happy to help."

Sarah started to follow the women from the room, but Dr. Morton called her back. "Miss Marden, how is Mrs. Wilson?"

"She is having her lapses more often. Are you sure about this? What if she thinks Amity is someone else?"

"Amity trusts her enough to seek her out. I think she must understand something, or she would not have gone to see a midwife. If I put someone she doesn't like in the room with her, she screams to the point of passing out. Dr. Norris won't go near her if she is conscious. Hopefully she will be comfortable enough around my wife and with Dr. Dawes. Are you confident in delivering this baby if you need to?"

Sarah paled. "I haven't delivered one in over two years, and never alone."

"But you were taught by the best. Don't tell my wife, although I suspect she knows. Perhaps you can accompany Mrs. Morton to some of her calls."

Sarah pondered for a moment. "Only if I don't have to leave Emma and the husbands don't object."

"Oh yes, those troublesome creatures." The doctor's eyes drooped, and he yawned. "I suspect my wife snuck another dose of laudanum in my tea. Dawes, we will talk later."

Tim held open the door for Sarah. Seeing her nearly every day would not be difficult.

Mrs. Morton and Mrs. Wilson sat in the parlor swapping tales of difficult birthings. Sarah joined them on the couch. Had Tim not delivered his own share of babies, he may have run from the room. The tales became a debate of birthing chair versus other positions. Mrs. Wilson contended births required a number of positions and a birthing chair was not always available or practical. Somehow this moved on to the topic of doctors hurrying too much and the use of forceps. This earned Tim three sets of glares.

Tim stood. "I believe my presence is no longer desired."

Mrs. Wilson waved her hand dismissively. "Horse feathers. You may learn something—if nothing else, to listen to the mother. She knows what her body is telling her. Even little Amity will do things she has never seen or been taught because they are natural."

"We are not saying that sometimes extreme measures aren't needed, just that men want to rush things. With more and more doctors being involved in deliveries—" Mrs. Morton shrugged.

The maid entered with a tray.

Mrs. Morton gestured to Tim's vacated chair. "Do stay, Doctor. We need to improve our plan for Amity."

The shortbread had more to do with Tim's decision to stay than did the cajoling of the women.

Eleven

Forty dollars is a lot of money.
Stay away from Dr. Dawes.

The handwriting matched that of the last letter. Too bad she'd burned it.

When Sarah heard Emma stirring in her bedroom, she knew she had better get breakfast soon. She ran up to her room and hid the letter in the first volume of *Pride and Prejudice*.

Sarah cradled two-year-old Seth, his head nestled on her shoulder. His soft, rhythmic snoring enticed her to join him in his slumber. However, the reverend punctuated his oratory quite often by pounding a fist or raising his voice, and she had no desire to join the list of red-faced parishioners who found themselves awakened by one or the other. Next to her, Benjamin fidgeted. Samuel reached over Bessie's head and tapped her twin brother's shoulder. Benjamin sat still for a minute, then began swinging his legs.

Warm contentment filled Sarah. Twenty-four years she had sat in this pew with her family—first in her mother's and father's arms, and then next to Lucy and Samuel, eventually holding each of their little ones in turn. She looked over to the other Wilson pew, where Emma sat with John and his children. Today Emma's oldest son, Thomas Jr., joined them with one of his sons. Sarah couldn't remember the teen boy's name. Emma's only living daughter, Carrie, sat next to her. Neither of Emma's children had brought their spouses.

A sharp kick to Sarah's calf brought her attention back to her nephew. Benjamin hung his head. Sarah glanced at Samuel, who had missed the event since four-year-old Stella had climbed onto his lap. Bessie stealthily moved to the vacated place next to her mother.

What would it be like to escape this pew with its never-ending game of musical chairs? Sarah pretended to adjust little Seth so that she might look back to the pew where Maryanna sat with her new husband. Her oldest niece was faced in the direction of the preaching. As she turned back, she noticed Tim sitting next to his mother. One corner of Tim's mouth raised in a half smile, and he winked.

The audacity to wink in church! Who on earth would he be winking at? Sarah turned her attention back to the front of the room. Several widows sat in the pew in front of the Wilsons. Perhaps Tim hadn't been winking at anyone and it had been a trick of the light.

Seth replaced his snores with his thumb and shifted to look around.

When Reverend Palmer ended his sermon with a loud amen, little Seth's face puckered up. Sarah hurried to distract him before he could cry. Fortunately the hymn was one of her favorites, and she rocked her nephew as she sang Isaac Watts's words:

I sing the mighty power of God
*   that made the mountains rise,*
That spread the flowing seas abroad,
*   and built the lofty skies.*

I sing the wisdom that ordained
    the sun to rule the day;
The moon shines full at God's command,
    and all the stars obey.

Halfway through the song, Seth made a dive for his father. Samuel momentarily balanced both his youngest children on his lap before Sarah coaxed Stella into her arms. They accomplished the switch in time for Sarah to sing the last stanza:

While all that borrows life from Thee
    is ever in Thy care;
And everywhere that we can be,
    Thou, God art present there.

Halfway through the prayer, Stella loudly made an urgent need known. Several parishioners near Sarah almost succeeded in containing their laughter until after the amens were said.

Sarah rushed out of the church and around the building. While she waited for her niece to complete her visit to the necessary, she vowed that someday she would sit at church without a child in her arms for an entire meeting.

The younger Frost sister, Miss Brooks, and Miss Page were gathered at the end of Tim's pew, effectively blocking his escape to the aisle. They tossed polite words at his mother and cast longing looks at him. Why couldn't he be as quick as Ichabod? The three women continued to chat as people squeezed around them, trying to leave the church, the Widow Garrett and her other granddaughter among them. A black lace fan flashed in the widow's hand as she tapped it on Miss Frost's shoulder. "Come, Ester, you are making it difficult for others to exit."

The girl bowed her head and hurried from the building. Miss Brooks took Miss Page by the arm and dragged her after them.

Tim's mother took his elbow to escort her out. "I thought they would never leave. Next week I am running out with Ichabod! Ester Frost is too young for you, anyway. I don't think she has graduated from the academy yet. Promise me you won't court anyone so young."

"Of course, Mother."

They were among the last to reach the door, where Reverend Palmer wished each of the congregants well as they left. He shook Tim's hand with a firm grip. "Dr. Dawes, I am glad you will be with us for at least several more weeks. I see some of our young ladies are endeavoring to persuade you to stay longer, but I fear their exuberance may be having the opposite effect."

Tim nodded politely.

"Will you be seeing Dr. Morton this afternoon?"

"Yes, I am going there directly after I see to Mother."

The reverend pulled a sealed missive from his coat pocket. "Would you deliver this to him? It is a copy of the letter I sent to our good judge requesting no charges be brought against the girl. I can only pray the Lord's justice is poured out on the man who did this to her. I am not aware of anyone looking to adopt, but I will keep my ears open. I believe there is an orphanage in Salem taking babies."

As Tim tucked the letter in his coat and followed his mother down the steps, Sarah came around the side of the church with the niece she had been holding in her hasty exit. Tim bowed slightly. "Miss Marden, had I known you were behind the church all this time, I would have endeavored to meet you." As he hoped, Sarah's face pinked.

Her eyes darted around the still-crowded churchyard. "I assure you I was not waiting for you. Good Sabbath, Dr. Dawes." She continued to the tree where the rest of the Wilsons congregated, pausing to speak with Miss Brooks and Miss Page. Both women turned to smile at him as the little girl pulled Sarah away.

Tim looked for his mother, hoping to find her before he was trapped again, and found Ichabod helping her into the carriage.

His brother loosened the reins. "I can see her home if you want to go to the doctor's now."

"Would you mind dropping me by?" Tim didn't wait for an answer as he climbed up on the back seat.

"So, you have them chasing you now? You can keep all the old ones. Just leave Miss Ester Frost alone."

Twelve

IT HAD TAKEN SEVERAL MINUTES to get all the children to leave the house with Emma, Maryanna, and her husband, Philip. The gathering around Lucy's table took on a solemn air, Thomas Jr., Carrie, John, Samuel and Lucy took their seats with grim expressions. Sarah thought of those missing—Joe, where ever he was, then Daniel, and, of course, Mark.

Thomas Jr. started the family meeting. "Samuel, I think you should lead the discussion as I don't know nearly enough of the situation. Your letters are few and far between."

Samuel leaned forward. "Ma seems to spend more and more of her time somewhat addled. When I stopped by a couple of weeks ago, she thought I was Pa and tried to kiss me." Samuel's face reddened. "If my boys had been there, the situation could have become much more embarrassing, as Ma and Pa always behaved in front of the grandchildren. The hardest part is when she realized I wasn't Pa, it seemed as if she'd just learned he died. Sarah says this happens often. Sarah, please share with everyone what you told me."

"I don't know that there is much to say. At least once a day she seems to think I am someone else, or a much younger me. The fact I am no taller than most twelve-year-olds doesn't help. Although she is just as likely to mistake me for Lucy. When she is talking, she will forget words. You can see the frustration on her face, almost like one of the little ones when they are learning to talk. Even though I had Samuel remove the horse from our stable last month and put it in the livery, she has still tried to leave to go help women in the night. The only time she seems to be in the present is when being a midwife, which she isn't supposed to do anymore. It doesn't help matters that Mrs. Larkin hasn't been in the family way for ten years. Emma is insistent she must help. As neighbors, the Larkins are very helpful, as Mrs. Larkin's grandmother went through something like this before she died. The biggest problem is, I can't take care of Emma on my own anymore. She has problems cooking, and she will just get up and try to leave for no reason."

Carrie spoke up. "I could send Constance over for the rest of the summer."

"How old is she?"

"Twelve."

Sarah bit her lip. "I think whoever comes to help should be older. At least old enough to understand the madness Emma experiences."

John nearly jumped out of his seat. "Madness? Ma is not mad. Why, just last Wednesday she helped with the children and there were no problems."

Sarah raised her brows. "None?"

"No." John crossed his arms.

"But she did call your daughter Carrie all day and had her bawling again. Then, when she came home, she spent the evening talking to me as if I were Mama. Fortunately, I agreed Samuel should marry Lucy and it ended."

Samuel kissed the back of his wife's hand, and she gave him one of those smiles Sarah envied.

Carrie spoke next. "What is the harm of Ma living in the past? She isn't hurting anything."

Sarah looked to Samuel for an answer. How could she tell them their beloved Ma would scream and scratch and kick and yell when she didn't get her way?

"Ma grew upset with me when she thought I was Pa and slapped me across the face when I wouldn't kiss her."

A collective gasp echoed around the table. None of Samuel's siblings would call him a liar, but disbelief radiated from them.

Samuel looked at Sarah. "Does she get that way often?"

More often than I care to admit. "She broke a cup when she threw it at the wall." *And missed my head.* "And sometimes she has tried to hit me." She tugged her sleeve down, making sure to hide the scratches from that morning. Emma had refused to go to church until Sarah convinced her Reverend Woods had passed years ago and that no sermon on the importance of properly officiated marriages would be preached. The former minister considered Emma and Thomas's marriage to be a mockery of both church and state and had gone as far as to mention it at Thomas Sr.'s funeral. Emma had never forgiven the old minister.

John leaned into Sarah's side. "I proposed my solution more than once. If Sarah would just agree, she and Ma could come live with me."

Lucy spoke before Sarah could. "John, that would hardly solve things. Sarah would not only have Emma to worry about, but your children. If I thought my sister had feelings for you, I would encourage marriage, but it is evident she's never harbored anything beyond a sisterly affection for you. Forcing her into a marriage only convenient for you is not a solution. Even at your house Sarah would need more help."

Samuel nodded and started to rise. "John, I refused you Sarah's hand. She has refused you. No more talk of this."

Thomas Jr. put his hand on Samuel's arm, forcing him back into his seat. "As I see it, we need to find an adult woman to move in with Sarah and Ma. My wife's sister Dorcas Smith is a spinster, and since their father's death last year, has been passed from house to house. Currently she is down in Billerica. I could inquire if she were willing to come. I believe she marked her fortieth birthday this past fall. Surely she would be old enough to understand Emma's needs, and she is a fair cook."

"Sarah could use that." John's muttered words went mostly unnoticed.

Sarah studied him for a moment. Why would he want to marry her if he disliked her so much? Of course, he disdained everyone and everything since losing his wife. If only Joe would come back for more than a two-day visit. But Joe might make the problem worse.

"How long would it take her to get here?" asked Samuel.

"Inside of two weeks. I could go get her as early as next Saturday if she agrees." Thomas Jr. turned to Sarah. "Is there anything else we need to know?"

"I lock the house and remove the key each night to stop her wanderings. I am just as worried she will accidentally start a fire and I won't be able to get the key in the door quickly enough." She had feared fire ever since the barn had burned down when she was six.

"We could send Louisa over during the day if that would help." Lucy rubbed her rounded stomach. "At least until this one joins us."

Sarah smiled at her sister. "Thank you, but it is mostly evenings that are difficult. Dr. Morton has asked Emma and me to work with Amity Barns for a few weeks, and I don't know if Louisa should be there."

Samuel cleared his throat. "So, along with extra help, I suggest we all try to stop and see Mother a bit more often. Thomas Jr., I know it is harder for you, but Carrie, John, and I can all get in more often. If we can stay for a while, Sarah can take a walk or run an errand without worrying."

John scowled.

Sarah nearly swallowed her last request, but something needed to be said. "One more thing. Can we please not take Emma to

John's? It really seems to upset her. Coming out here isn't as bad, but being in the old house makes her go back to a different time."

"Ridiculous," said John.

"John, I know you think Dr. Dawes and I are wrong, but she has had an episode every single time she has been there since school was out."

"Little Timmy? You are taking advice from him?"

Lucy laid a hand on John's arm. "Tim Dawes grew up to be a very competent doctor."

John shook Lucy's hand off. "But what is she doing even spending time with him? We told him to stay away years ago."

"Sarah is no longer a little girl, and Dr. Dawes is not trying to sneak kisses behind the church." Lucy turned. "Is he?"

Sarah hoped her face remained neutral. "Not behind the school or outhouse, either."

John sat back.

Thomas Jr. stood. "I'll send a letter to Miss Smith first thing. If there is nothing else, I had better be leaving. I left my wife at home with a nasty toothache and would like to be home before sunset."

The siblings hugged each other and Lucy. John went in search of his children without acknowledging Sarah. Thomas Jr. and Carrie chatted for a moment before taking their leave. Lucy slipped out the back door, most likely the baby she carried having made an escape rather urgent.

Samuel laid his hand on Sarah's shoulder. "Ma is worse than you are saying, isn't she? No, don't answer. You are too old for me to punish for lying. Is there anything else I can do?"

"If Benjamin could come chop some more wood this week, it would be nice. We are going through it faster than we should at this time of year."

"Aren't we all. I saw in the newspaper the Canadians had another snowstorm. It is like spring forgot to come this year. I don't agree with the reverend that it is the end of the world, but I did plant a bigger garden this year. Not that more plants are doing better, but I hope there will be at least a few that grow."

"I hope so. Emma weeded our garden last week and killed all the bean plants before I realized what she was doing. I replanted yesterday."

Lucy came back in. "Your mother has the kids playing some game out in the side meadow. When she is in her right mind, it is hard to believe there's a problem at all."

"I'll go hitch up the team to take you two back to town."

As soon as the door shut, Lucy lowered herself into one of the rockers. "This one kicks something awful. Must be a boy. How much do you see of Dr. Tim Dawes?" Her big sister studied her. "Ah, you blush."

"It doesn't matter much, does it? He plans on leaving as soon as Dr. Morton is up and about. I only see him because of Amity. And there are so many women who want his attention." The words of this morning's letter ran through Sarah's mind. Lucy would not know her shame.

"You are sure about that?"

"Yes, I've accepted that I had my chance with Mark, and every girl should get one opportunity to love. There just are not enough men out there for a woman to be in love twice."

Lucy rocked back and forth for a moment. "Has John brought up marriage often?"

"Only twice since Miriam Dawes's wedding. I think it reminded him of his wedding to Remember. He must see we wouldn't suit. Neither of his children wants me as a mother after being their cousin and teacher, although they are old enough to understand I am not truly their cousin." Sarah sat in the other chair.

"My poor girl. It has been an awkward life for you, hasn't it, balancing a sister who isn't your mother, a man who isn't your father, brothers who are not your brothers, and then Emma, who has been a cross between a grandmother and a friend."

"It may be difficult to explain, more so if I had married Mark, but at least I know you all love me. Well, all but John. He seems more annoyed with me than anything."

"I think John loves you too, but more as a sister. He doesn't want to get hurt again by losing a wife, and his children need a mother. Since you were engaged to Mark, he thinks he should take care of you. I never realized until Joe left how seriously John considers it his duty to see that everyone is cared for. I always thought he was just part of the twins who played jokes and laughed at everything. John is just trying to fix a problem as he sees it." Lucy stifled a yawn.

"I am not fond of someone thinking I am a problem to be fixed. It is almost as bad as the students who grow taller than me and think they know more because they can see the top of my head."

Lucy laughed. "They are nitwits."

"Careful—your own children number in that group. I remember the day Maryanna realized she was taller than me and started telling me to do her chores just like she would Lettie and Louisa."

"Not sure how I got a domineering girl like her for a daughter."

Sarah raised an eyebrow. "Really?"

"Are you saying I am the same?"

"If the cap fits…"

Sarah and her sister laughed until tears formed.

Thirteen

AMITY SPENT MOST OF THE dinner staring at her plate. Tim and Mrs. Morton ignored her as much as possible, both having realized she was likely to bolt if they spoke to her. The only person who'd earned a smile from the shy girl was the maid. When the meal concluded, Mrs. Morton whispered to the maid, who in turn whispered to Amity. To Tim's amazement, the girl followed the maid from the room. Amity's father moved to stand.

"Don't worry, Mr. Barns, she has only gone to the kitchen to get some gingerbread. Our maid will watch out for her. My husband would like to speak with both of you in his room for a moment." Mrs. Morton led them up to the bedroom.

Several cushions had been added to prop Dr. Morton's back and broken leg.

"Come in. Mr. Barns, I trust you know Dr. Dawes is seeing to all my patients over the next several weeks?"

Mr. Barns looked around the room and appeared as ready to leave as had his daughter at the table.

"Do take a seat. I have a concern about Amity I need to discuss with both of you."

Tim sat, and Mr. Barns followed his example.

"On Friday Amity went and visited Widow Wilson. Do you know her?"

"She be the one who helped me wife deliver Amity."

Dr. Morton nodded. "Only Widow Wilson doesn't do much midwifery anymore. However, she did pass her skills on to Miss Marden."

Mr. Barns opened his mouth as if to comment, but the doctor quickly went on. "Mrs. Wilson and Miss Marden are of the opinion that Amity is with child."

"No, she ain't. My girl just is getting fat like her ma."

"I'm sorry, Mr. Barns, but after seeing Amity today, my wife agrees."

"You lie!" Mr. Barns jumped up. Tim joined the man, not sure if he was of a violent persuasion.

Dr. Morton spoke calmly. "Widow Wilson conducted an examination of sorts with Amity fully clothed. She is of the opinion that Amity will deliver the baby in about six to eight weeks."

Mr. Barns collapsed back in the chair. "She is wrong! My little girl ain't sinful. She wouldn't do that."

Lifting a paper, Dr. Morton said, "This is a letter from Reverend Palmer. He sent the same one to the magistrate, along with one from me. It is my professional medical opinion—and the reverend agrees, Amity did not act wantonly—that a man took advantage of her."

"Who? I'll kill him!" Mr. Barns leaped out of the chair, causing it to crash to the floor.

"I wish I knew. I would hunt him down and see he is jailed."

"Jail ain't good enough for the man who hurt my baby girl." Tears poured down Mr. Barn's face.

Tim helped him back into the chair. "I quite agree, Mr. Barns."

"Sadly, Amity is hardly likely to tell us who fathered the child. Miss Marden doesn't think she understands fully what is even wrong, although she did seek out Mrs. Wilson." Dr. Morton's voice was low and soothing. "Although I want to see justice done, right now I am more concerned about Amity. This is going to be very difficult for her, not only because of the horse injury but because she is only fourteen and still small. She doesn't seem to like my wife, and, as you see, I can be of little help. Mrs. Wilson hasn't delivered any babies this year because her age has made it difficult. And Amity's seizures complicate the situation."

"The seizures are in her head. The baby is in her belly. Why'd that make things complicated?"

"The process of birthing a child includes quite a bit of pain. I don't know why Amity has her seizures or what that much pain could do."

"Are you telling me my baby girl could die like her mother did?"

Tim moved back to his chair. "Each time a woman has a child, she walks in the valley of the shadow of death. We want to make sure your daughter has the best chance. So we have a plan."

"A plan?" Mr. Barns scratched his head.

Tim looked at the pained face of Dr. Morton and took up the conversation. "Amity needs to trust me like she does Dr. Morton. It would also help if she could start to like Mrs. Morton. Mrs. Wilson and Miss Marden agreed to invite Amity over for a few hours each day to visit, cook, and what all. During this time, Mrs. Morton and I will stop by for various reasons—borrowing sugar and stuff like that. Amity can get to know us better without us being there for her."

"It would do my girl some good to be around such nice folks as the widow and the teacher. And you would just see her for a few minutes each day?"

"Yes. I hope in time she will trust me enough to start talking to me. That way if I need to help with the delivery, it won't be so frightening if I am there."

"What will happen to the baby? I know my girl can't take care of it."

Tim's heart broke for the father's pain. "Reverend Palmer said he would look for a situation for the baby. There are those couples who just can't seem to get them on their own."

Mr. Barns nodded. "What do I tell my girl?"

"Tell her she isn't fat, so she will eat better. Widow Wilson can explain little by little what is going to happen. I suggest you leave that part to the women. I don't think men are very good at that sort of thing. Even doctors." Dr. Morton laughed a self-depreciating chuckle. "And this is something we need to ask Widow Wilson and Miss Marden about … but as Amity's time draws near, it may be best if she lives with them for a couple weeks. With working on the docks, you may not be there when she starts showing the first signs of labor."

A flash of relief interrupted the grief on Mr. Barns's face. "I think that is a right good idea."

"I will speak to Widow Wilson in the morning," said Tim.

"Doc, is there anything else I can do for my little girl?"

"Just keep loving her."

Mr. Barns nodded at Dr. Morton's advice. "I'd better go take her home. I'll tell her to go to the widow's in the morning. She doesn't remember too well."

Tim walked Mr. Barns down the stairs, and they found their way back to the kitchen, where the cook and the maid were helping Amity shape some pies.

Amity held up one. "Look-k. C-cook-k."

"Yes, darling. Are you ready to go home?"

Amity shook her head. "Bake first-t."

Mrs. Morton spoke up from the corner. "It is no problem if you both stay."

Mr. Barns took a seat at the table and gestured Tim over. "Amity, this is Dr. Dawes. He is Dr. Morton's helper."

Amity squinted at him as if she hadn't ever seen him before, then went back to her pies.

At least she hadn't run from the room.

Fourteen

*What do you think the reverend will preach on when
he learns the commandments you have broken?
Continue to avoid Dr. Dawes like you did after
church and we won't find out.*

SARAH STUFFED THE UNSIGNED NOTE in her pocket. The person
sending them must be watching her. What on earth would they
think when Tim started stopping by daily? Too bad she couldn't
respond. "Dear Watcher, he is here as a doctor and not for me."
But she doubted the anonymous writer would believe her.

"Something is wrong. It is too quiet. Where are my boys? Did
you see them when you came in?" Emma looked up from the pot
she was stirring.

Sarah set the egg basket down on the table. *Not today, Emma!*
"I didn't see anyone out by the henhouse."

"Well, my boys know better than to go sniffing around a henhouse. And why would you be there anyway? You're engaged."

Sarah breathed a sigh of relief. At least Emma recognized her, even if she was a few years off. "I gathered the eggs. I thought we could make a custard with Amity when she comes."

Emma took a mixing bowl out of the cupboard.

A knock sounded at the door. Sarah answered it. Amity shifted her weight from foot to foot. She wore a clean dress. "Da s-say see Mrs. Wil-il-son."

"That's right, Amity. We invited you over today for dinner. Mrs. Wilson is making custard. Do you want to help?"

Either Amity followed directions well, or she was just naturally a better cook than Sarah. There wasn't any need to pick a single shell out of the bowl she'd cracked the eggs in.

Sarah took the broom and swept the back porch. Through the open window, she monitored the conversation, which focused on cooking. Hearing footsteps on the front porch, Sarah hurried to answer the door first.

Tim carried his bag of instruments with him and took off his hat as Sarah opened the door. Due to the heat of the day, his hat had squashed his hair in a little ring. Longing to run her fingers through it to fix it, she found her hand had risen of its own volition. She covered the error by grabbing the door. "Dr. Dawes, come in. Mrs. Wilson and Amity are making custards."

She led Tim into the kitchen. Emma looked up. "Doctor, you are too early. These will need to bake yet. Amity, do you know the doctor?"

"He-e at D-doc-tor Mor. Hel-l-lo." Amity went back to stirring the contents of her bowl. Sarah felt her jaw drop. Amity had recognized Tim!

For a few minutes, Sarah and Tim watched as Emma helped Amity pour the mixture into the baking dish, then Tim tugged on Sarah's sleeve and pointed to the hallway. "See me out," he said in a voice meant only for her.

Sarah showed him to the door.

"Come out and talk for a moment."

Shutting the door behind her, she quickly looked around to see who might be watching.

"Dr. Morton told Amity's father yesterday of the diagnosis. He took it as well as he could. Reverend Palmer wrote a letter to the magistrate, so I don't think any fines will be levied."

Sarah continued to watch the street. A few children played over on the green, but none of them would write a note. Tim's touch at her elbow startled her.

"Are you listening?"

"I'm sorry. I just—" Sarah shrugged, unwilling either to lie or disclose her thoughts.

"Dr. Morton thinks it would be best if Amity moves in here the last couple weeks before her confinement. Do you think it would work with Emma?"

"Maybe. Emma seems to stay in the present when Amity is around. At least she has the last two times. Thomas Jr. is asking his sister-in-law to come help with Emma. If she comes, we will double up rooms, but it could work. It would be one more person for Amity to get accustomed to, but she is already acknowledging you after only one day."

Tim straightened his coat. "You know I do charm all the ladies."

Sarah rolled her eyes. "Go try your charms elsewhere. I need to get back in case Emma … I don't want her to frighten Amity."

"See you tomorrow." Tim jogged down the steps and to his little carriage.

Sarah looked up and down the street once more. Hopefully her letter writer hadn't been watching.

Tim wondered what had distracted Sarah. Mrs. Wilson had been in very good humor and even recognized him, though that could change in a moment. However, Sarah hadn't been looking at the house. She had been studying the street. Perhaps she did not wish to be seen with him. She had been rather abrupt after church yesterday.

He turned the corner to find Miss Page and Miss Brooks walking with their heads together. They waved him down.

"Oh, Doctor, we saw you in front of Widow Wilson's. Is she well? We worry about her so." Miss Page put her hand on the side of his carriage.

"I do not discuss my patients with anyone other than their families. If you wish to inquire about Mrs. Wilson's health, you will need to do so in person."

Miss Page blinked a couple of times. "Oh, that is good of you. Doctors shouldn't spread gossip. There is to be a men's choral concert across the river on Wednesday. Will you be attending?"

Miss Brooks shifted. Tim thought she might be trying to step on her friend's toes. *Good for her.* "I feel it is my duty to stay on the north side of the river while I see to Dr. Morton's patients. However, I am sure you will enjoy it."

"Oh." Miss Page looked at Miss Brooks to come to her rescue.

Miss Brooks obliged. "We must bid you good day, then. No doubt you are needed elsewhere. We must hurry off ourselves." She pulled Miss Page back up to the walkway.

Tim set his horse to a trot. He would need to remember to go around the other way when he came to Sarah's so as not to pass the boardinghouse. He didn't want to hurt one of his sister's friends with his rejection but feared he must soon make his preferences known.

Fifteen

Why does the doctor visit so often?
Mrs. Wilson seems to be healthy.

What would it do to her heart if she knew about
her son?
But maybe she already does …
Would that make her complicit?
Find another doctor.

THREE DAYS SINCE THE LAST note. Sarah studied the street. Whoever wrote the note was in a position to see Tim stopping by frequently. He brought his bag each time, so at least his visits looked medical.

Sarah slipped up to her room and added the notes to the others.

Mrs. Morton arrived just after nine, bringing a frosted cake for the noon meal. Sarah set a chicken to boil over the fire.

In preparation for the meal, Amity had agreed to a bath and having her hair washed. Sarah wasn't sure how Emma had coaxed her into such a thing, but it would allow the midwives to check the progress of the unwitting mother.

Sarah added more hot water to the tub they'd set up in Emma's room. Mrs. Morton followed with a bucket of cold water.

"N-no her! N-o h-her!"

Mrs. Morton quickly retreated to the kitchen.

Sarah helped Amity remove her boots, but once Amity stood in only her shift, she shooed Sarah away, too. Unwilling to leave Emma alone, Sarah pretended to straighten the room, dusting Emma's perfectly clean dressing table and watching Amity in the mirror.

Emma helped with the bath, washing Amity's hair.

As Amity stood to dry off, the baby kicked, stretching the girl's taut belly. Eyes wide, Amity touched her abdomen. "W-wrong. Fat. M-move."

Emma placed her hand where a foot pushed out. "This baby will be here mid-July."

"B-baby?" Amity tilted her head. "N-no, b-baby! Not Ma-ma!" She pushed Emma away. Emma lost her footing and fell against the bed.

Amity wrapped her arms around herself and wailed.

Sarah grabbed a quilt and wrapped it gently around the girl. "Mrs. Morton!"

Mrs. Morton rushed into the room.

Amity screamed and twisted out of Sarah's embrace and dashed for the door. Sarah made to follow but looked back at Mrs. Morton first. "Help Emma!"

As she turned back around, the screaming stopped.

Tim stood just inside the doorway and was holding the unconscious girl, the quilt pooled at their feet. His face was a color of scarlet not often seen on a male. "She's fainted."

Sarah hurried to wrap the quilt around Amity and said, "Bring her into Emma's room."

There, they found Emma sitting on her bed. "I'm right as rain. Now let me up!"

Mrs. Morton looked from Sarah to the doctor.

Sarah hurried to Emma's side. "Are you hurt?"

"Of course not. Can't raise a pack of boys without getting pushed now and then."

Sarah assisted Emma to her feet. "Perhaps if you take Mrs. Morton and Dr. Dawes to the parlor, I can get Amity dressed before she wakes up."

Tim shook his head "I'll help you."

"That isn't proper."

"As a doctor, I assure you I won't do anything improper, but she is bigger than you, and if she were to wake up ..."

Sarah nodded her agreement and retrieved Amity's shift from where she had hung it over the back of a chair.

"It looks like Mrs. Wilson was correct in her estimation of the pregnancy." Tim laid his hand on Amity's belly. "This one is active. He must have liked the bath better than his mother."

"*Her* mother."

"You think it is a girl?"

Sarah pulled the shift down to Amity's knees and started with the single petticoat. "Maybe."

"What happened?"

"Emma forgot she couldn't talk about the baby. Amity didn't take the news well. Can you lift her a little?"

They worked in silence for a moment, Sarah watching how gently Tim handled the girl. Every touch was professional and kind. Doctoring suited him. The thoughts swirling around Sarah's head came out unbidden. "You know more about expectant women than I thought you would."

Tim swallowed. Of course he did. There were more to treat than just the dying men on the front. "I am familiar with the process."

The spot between Sarah's brow furrowed. "I suppose there were not too many midwives around the camps."

He nodded. "Most people blamed the women, but it was the men too. I think Reverend Woods didn't address that as much as he should have in some of his sermons. I have no idea what Reverend Palmer's view is, but I wish everyone would just learn to live the sixth commandment. Then things like this wouldn't happen."

"It isn't Amity's fault." Sarah dropped the stocking she held.

"I didn't say it was. I do not blame the women who suffer because a man has taken advantage of them. But those women who are willing? I harbor equal disdain for them as I do the men."

Sarah buttoned the cuffs of Amity's dress. "Come now, you know a good portion of the women who marry are in the family way. Are you telling me you condemn them?"

He felt the conversation slipping into places as slippery as axle grease. "No, but I don't think a woman should let even her fiancé take liberties. That is why the Commonwealth has kept the fornication fine."

Sarah made a funny sound in her throat as she tied Amity's shoes. "I think she is coming around. You had better leave."

Tim took her advice but didn't shut the door. He knew most men his age didn't agree with his strict moral code, but he had always assumed most good Christian women did. What had he said to upset Sarah? Surely she didn't think he placed any responsibility on Amity. He replayed the conversation and was left feeling confused.

Low murmurs came from both the parlor and the bedroom. He peeked into the bedroom to see Sarah with her arm around Amity. He moved to the parlor, figuring it was best to leave before Amity realized he had been there.

Amity kept rubbing her belly. "B-baby?" she asked repeatedly. Sarah confirmed her answer each time, thankful Amity didn't ask the question everyone else would.

Amity stood up and took Sarah's hand, pulling her up, too. "T-tell Da." Without releasing Sarah's hand, Amity headed for the front door.

"One moment, Amity. We need our wraps. It is cold today." Sarah took a moment to stick her head into the parlor. "She wants me to go with her to tell her father."

Mrs. Morton nodded. "I'll let Dr. Dawes know where you went. Stay away from the docks." She slipped out the door.

Sarah understood. Amity's news was best shared in private.

Emma shuffled out of the parlor. "Why, dear, your hair is still dripping. Let Sarah braid it before you go out." Emma herded them back into her bedroom and directed Amity to sit at her table.

"Tell-l D-da."

"Yes, sweetheart, we will, but let's get your hair all pretty before we do." Sarah used Emma's brush and made a hasty braid.

As soon as she stepped outside, Sarah wished she had dried Amity's hair completely. The temperature had dropped twenty degrees since dawn. The closer they got to the river, the more Sarah felt like running back for her pelisse as her shawl did little to keep out the chill.

Somehow it was fitting the weather had turned upside down today too.

Tim slowed the buggy to a stop in front of the rundown building. He hoped Sarah had only gone as far as the Barns's small apartment. They had just reached the door when Amity burst out, dragging Sarah behind her.

"Where are you going?" Tim hopped down, unsure how to stop them from going to the docks.

"F-find Da."

"It is awfully chilly out here. Why don't you let me go fetch him and you stay in the apartment?"

"The doctor has a very good idea. With his buggy, he can go so much faster than we can." Sarah tried to put her arm around Amity, but the girl shrugged her off.

Amity pointed her finger at the center of Tim's chest. "G-go fin-nd Da."

"I'll be back as quick as I can."

He looked back to be sure Amity and Sarah had entered the building.

Driving along the docks, Tim occasionally stopped to ask if anyone had seen Mr. Barns. After three false leads, he found the man supervising the unloading of several barrels from one of his late stepfather's ships.

"Mr. Barns! Mr. Barns!"

"Hey, Barny, boss man's brother wants ya!"

Mr. Barns hurried over to Tim's buggy. "If it's Amity, make 'em think it's ship business."

"I've been asked to fetch you. Foreman, he'll be back soon. You are not to dock his pay!" It was probably going too far, but Mr. Barns needed all of his daily wages. He would pay it out of his own pocket if Ichabod had an issue with what he had done. Tim turned the buggy and set the horse to a trot.

"What is wrong with my girl?"

"She wants to tell you. She realized she is having a baby. She brought Miss Marden with her." They stopped in front of the apartment building, and Tim ran up the stairs after Mr. Barns.

Amity greeted her father with a hug. "B-baby." She pointed to her rounded belly.

Mr. Barns pulled her back into his arms. "I know, my girl. I know."

Amity pulled away and studied her father. Reaching up, she wiped a tear from his face, her head tilted. Tim had come to recognize the gesture. Amity did it often when she pondered. "S-sad?"

To his credit, Mr. Barns lied. When Amity took his hand and laid it on her belly, she turned to Sarah with a perplexed look. "G-gone?"

Sarah came over and laid her hand next to Mr. Barns's. "No, the baby is sleeping. Sometimes babies sleep. Then when you eat something or you want to sleep, they wake up and move again."

Amity nodded, then yawned. "I sleep-p t-too." She walked over to the corner and curled up on a little cot.

Tim and Sarah followed Mr. Barns out of the apartment.

"Should I stay with her?" asked Sarah.

"No, my girl be fine. I need to get back to work before they figure out I didn't go see your brother. I don't like lying."

"Then let me take you to the office. I'll tell my brother I needed you, and then you will have talked with him."

"What if he cuts me pay?"

"I'll cover it." Tim turned to Sarah. "Come with us, then I'll take you back. You shouldn't be down here alone."

Mr. Barns studied Sarah for a moment. "Docks ain't no place for a lady. Best you cover your head with your shawl."

Sarah did as Mr. Barns asked, and the three of them went over to the Morse shipping office. Tim explained as little as possible. Ichabod asked Mr. Barns into his office and closed the door.

Knowing his brother wouldn't fire the man, Tim hopped back into the buggy. Sarah kept her shawl tight around her head, shading her face, even as they drew close to her house.

"I hope you know I would never blame Miss Amity for what happened."

Sarah only nodded.

"Don't be upset at me for keeps."

"I'm not cross with you. Just thinking."

When he stopped in front of the house, Sarah hopped out of the buggy and ran quickly into the house. Clearly she didn't want him to follow.

Miss Page crossed the street in front of the green. Not wanting to have her quiz him, Tim didn't linger. As the buggy passed her, he met her wave with a brief nod but urged the horse onward. He'd had enough of emotional women today.

Sixteen

THE THIRD DAY OF JUNE. Sarah bit her lip. Surely she could tuck her woolen petticoat away for the summer. With Amity coming daily, she'd neglected to pack away her winter clothes, even if she had needed them only last week for her jaunt to Amity's. Too bad she hadn't worn them that day.

She opened the trunk, banging the wall. The first volume of *Pride and Prejudice* tumbled off the shelf, the papers inside it scattering. The note left Friday morning landed closest.

> *Hiding your face under a shawl?*
>
> *You know what they say about women who frequent the docks.*
>
> *How far have you fallen?*

Sarah tucked it back in the book. There hadn't been another note since. Knowing someone was paying such close attention to her sent chills up her spine. It had to be a single woman who'd written them, but narrowing it down to just one seemed an impossible task. Mrs. Webb's boardinghouse housed a dozen women at capacity. But she couldn't imagine any of the women there being the author of the notes. Sarah put the book back in place and prayed there would be no more notes to add since there hadn't been one for three mornings.

She placed her two warmest petticoats in the trunk and pulled out her lightest ones. Soon it would be too warm to be comfortable with these. Sarah couldn't wait. Like everyone else, she'd grown tired of the cold. What would it be like to live farther south? Lucky Miriam. Ohio must be warmer than the North Shore. They'd had only a moment to speak after church, but Mrs. Miriam Wells couldn't look happier.

Sarah would have talked longer, but Tim had joined them. Fearing she was being watched, Sarah made an excuse and left. It must have been enough because no new note awaited her this morning. She wished she could just respond. If people wouldn't think she had gone mad, Sarah would shout it from the front porch. "I don't intend to marry anyone. If you want Dr. Dawes, win him without my help!"

But that would lead to questions she could never answer.

The clock tower chimed eleven. Since he was the only one in the office, Tim decided it would be a good time to visit Miss Amity. Since learning of her condition last week, she had started to talk to him more and not avoid Mrs. Morton. Although not privy to the conversations, he knew Sarah had been doing her best to impart the information Amity needed to get through the delivery. No one talked about what would happen to the baby after. There would be pain enough then.

As always, Tim took his doctor bag into the house with him. Amity needed to not fear the bag like some of his young patients did. He found Mrs. Morton already there, teaching Amity some sort of sewing stitch for a small quilt. Mrs. Wilson sat on the other side of Amity giving encouragement. No Sarah.

"Dr. Dawes, how nice of you to come by. Would you like some chocolate?" Mrs. Wilson lifted her own cup. Chocolate wasn't his favorite drink, but having a cup would allow him to stay longer.

Amity looked up from her sewing. "My b-bab-by." She laid the few pieces she had sewn together over her rounded middle.

"Do you think spring is here to stay—or should I say summer?" Mrs. Morton started the conversation.

After ten minutes of discussing the weather and the next color Amity should add to her blanket, Tim finished the chocolate and a piece of shortbread. "Well, ladies, I bid you good day."

"Good-d b-b, Doc-c." Amity smiled at him.

"Good day, Amity. Say hello to your father for me."

She nodded her head and bent back over her miniature quilt.

Miss Brooks and Miss Page walked by as he exited the house. Miss Brooks raised her hand in greeting. There would be no good way to avoid her. "Good day, Miss Brooks, Miss Page. Are you enjoying the sun today?"

Miss Page answered. "Oh yes. I am! I think summer has just arrived. We are on our way to visit Sarah—I mean Miss Marden. She isn't ill, is she?"

Someday the two would earn their places as town gossips, providing the widows that occupied the front pew at church all contracted a case of the putrid throat. Tim tried not to smile at the thought. "I did not see Miss Marden today. I do not believe she is at home."

A door banged open behind them.

"Doct-t-or bab-by." Awe filled Amity's face as it did every time she felt the baby move inside her. Mrs. Wilson put her arm around the girl and took her back into the house.

Miss Page looked from the closing door to the doctor and back again. "Oh, is she—? Oh, the poor thing! How did that happen?" She covered her mouth as if trying to silence herself.

"As you see, that is my reason for visiting today." *And every day if that knowledge will keep you from questioning me daily.* "It is best

Miss Amity thinks of me as a friend for her lying-in, as it will likely be more difficult than most. Now, if you will excuse me, I have other patients to attend to."

"Oh, that is why you come so often. I thought—" Miss Page stammered.

Tim had no wish to know what the women thought, but he did need to attempt to quell any prospective gossip. "If you would please keep Miss Amity's condition to yourself ... I doubt it will remain hidden much longer, but she doesn't need everyone treating her any differently than they do now." Most people acted as if they didn't see her at all.

Miss Brooks fanned herself. "We wouldn't tell her tale. The poor child. But did she get herself into this mess? With her eye and head the way they are, she isn't even pretty."

"Miss Brooks, whomever is responsible for taking advantage of the girl wanted only easy prey. If he is found, he will be prosecuted. Miss Amity deserves only love, not your censure. Anyone can see she's done nothing to 'get into this mess,' as you put it. Now, if you will excuse me, I must go." It took great effort for Tim to hold his tongue as he drove away. Not pretty! Obviously no one ever had taught Miss Brooks that the type of beauty that mattered had little to do with hair or eyes or clothes.

Two pounds of sugar, two pounds of flour, and a ginger root. Sarah finished her purchases, then packed them in her basket. Today's outing to the store was a treat. Emma always seemed to stay in the present around Amity, but Sarah didn't dare leave them alone. Sarah took advantage of Mrs. Morton's visits, as the midwife and Amity were to the point Sarah no longer needed to carry the conversation. Mr. Swanson added a peppermint to the basket the same as he had for twenty years and gave Sarah a wink.

She heard the bell chime the half hour as she walked past the church. Tim was coming down the road ahead of her and slowed his doctor buggy to a stop just beside her. Sarah looked around. No one seemed to be watching, but she couldn't be too careful.

"I missed you at the house today."

"As you see, I needed to get a few things. We find ourselves baking more than we used to."

"I could give you a ride." Tim reached for the basket, but Sarah kept it away from him.

"No. It is a beautiful day, and you are headed the opposite direction. Good day, Doctor." Sarah nodded and walked on. There. If her note writer were watching, she would see nothing to threaten Sarah about.

Turning the corner, she nearly bumped into Parmelia. "Oh, pardon me."

"My fault. I thought you were teaching the summer term. Didn't it start today?" Sarah shifted the basket.

"Oh, Mr. Colburn has me teaching only on Tuesdays and Thursdays. He said he had a niece... Anyway, I am glad for the time off. I can get some sewing done before fall." Parmelia's smile didn't reach her eyes.

"How could he do that? Didn't he promise you the job?"

"Oh, it doesn't matter. Was that Dr. Dawes I saw you speaking to?"

Sarah looked back the way she had come, the buggy no longer in sight. "Yes. He stopped for a moment. He is very busy."

"Oh? We had a lengthy conversation this morning. He is such a perfect gentleman, but so busy."

"I suppose most doctors are."

"Oh, I've tried to get him to go to a lecture and a choral with me, but"—Parmelia sighed—"I guess one could get used to it."

"Mrs. Morton seems happy enough, so I guess one does." Sarah shifted her basket. "Nice talking with you, but I must get home with these."

"Oh yes. Good day."

Sarah couldn't help but wonder if Parmelia started every sentence with *Oh* when she taught as well.

As she locked up for the night, Sarah heard a scraping sound on the front door. She peered into the dark street but saw no movement, so she opened it. A paper fluttered in the breeze.

> *How benevolent of you, caring for little Amity.*
> *The perfect excuse to see Dr. Dawes so often.*
> *Does he know how much you and Amity have*
> *in common?*

Seventeen

Friday morning dawned, bringing with it a chill wind that fluttered the paper Sarah held. The third note this week. Besides the one she'd found Monday night, there had been another Wednesday morning, which was now folded in the pages of her book upstairs.

I see you read my notes. Why do you not listen?
That conversation was much too long to be
all business.
Encourage him to take someone to the concert
on Saturday.

Tuesday's conversation on the front porch had been all business—on her end at least. Tim had expressed concern about the date Emma had set for Amity's lying-in, as well as worries over Emma's condition. Although she didn't seem to slip away around Amity, she had called Tim by various names. Too bad the note writer wasn't a better eavesdropper.

Hoping to point Tim in the right direction—away from her—Sarah had tricked Tim into attending Saturday's concert yesterday, when Noah Larkin had come selling tickets, by feigning that she didn't have the fifty cents to cover the cost of one. She hoped the person writing the notes didn't realize he had asked her first. Using Emma as an excuse, Sarah had declined, assuming he would chose to escort one of the women from the boardinghouse after she'd pointed out that few of them could afford to attend on their own.

According to the note, Tim's second choice hadn't met with her unknown correspondent's approval either.

His mother? Try again.

Sarah laughed out loud. She'd had no idea he would ask his mother. How did that come about? He certainly hadn't told her of his choice. The note writer must have ways of gathering information Sarah didn't. Sarah pocketed the note. It would join the others upstairs.

John rode up in his wagon.

About time he visited Emma.

"Morning, Sarah. Is Ma here?" John didn't wait for an answer as he walked passed her and went into the house.

After looking up and down the street a couple of times, Sarah followed him in and found him with his mother in the kitchen.

John stood near the work table. "Can't Sarah take care of that? I really need you."

Emma continued stirring the contents of her bowl. "Sarah can't cook for company."

"But Lettie can't come help today."

Did he not listen during the family meeting last week? Emma was doing so well, with only minor lapses at night. She did not need to go out to the old house! Sarah balled her hands into fists. "John, can I talk to you for a moment? I think Piggy Peggy has a problem."

Emma waved him out the door. "Go help Sarah while I put this in the oven."

John stomped out the back door after Sarah. As soon as they reached the pigpen, she whirled around and looked him straight in the eye. It was hard to be intimidating when she was more than a foot shorter. "What are you doing?"

"I need Ma out at the house. Lettie sent a note saying she is ill, and it looks like it may rain, finally, and the south field is half frozen. I need to try to save the corn. I can't risk having the children running around if this infernal weather takes another turn for the worse."

"We agreed last week you would not take Emma out to the old house."

"I didn't agree to anything. All I heard was you telling tales about Ma not being in her right mind."

Sarah moved her hands to her hips. "They weren't tales. She has been so good this week. Helping Amity Barns has worked wonders to keep her in the present."

"Well then, helping her own grandchildren should be better." John turned back to the house.

Sarah fumed. Unless Emma refused, she had no say. If only Samuel were here.

Emma was just putting the cake in the oven when Sarah reached the kitchen. "Take this out at ten thirty and let it cool. To the beans, add yesterday's ham at the same time. You'll be fine without me. Mrs. Morton said she would be here the entire morning unless either Mrs. Holcomb or Mrs. Cobb started their lying-in early. Oh, good. You found my wrap." She said to John, then she kissed Sarah on the cheek and left.

Amity took Mrs. Wilson's absence in stride and worked on her next nine-patch square. Somehow Sarah remembered to remove the cake from the oven—only five minutes late. It didn't look burned.

By the time the clock tower rang out the noon hour, Sarah concluded from Mrs. Morton's absence that another citizen was about to come into the world. Tim knocked and came in—a pattern they had found less disruptive to Amity. He looked around the room. "Mrs. Morton went to assist Mrs. Cobb. Where is Mrs. Wilson?"

Sarah couldn't stop her frown. "John came this morning. I think the meal is ready. Amity, would you like to come eat?"

Amity sniffed the air.

"Don't worry. Emma made it before she left."

As they moved into the kitchen, Tim leaned low and whispered in Sarah's ear. "I don't believe the tales about your inability to cook at all. You just don't like to cook."

Sarah shook her head. "I assure you I only abhor cooking because I do it so terribly. The entire Wilson family wouldn't lie about it."

They sat at the table. Sarah searched for a topic of conversation. Amity always listened, though sometimes she would participate. "I understand you are going to the concert with your mother on Saturday."

"How did you hear that? I only told—My mother seems a bit miffed about it too. I am not sure why I invited her to go with me."

Sarah wished he'd finished the sentence regarding whether she knew whom he'd told, but then, Mrs. Dawes-Morse could have told any number of people. "I think your problem is you are the most eligible bachelor in town. You probably upset more women than just your mother with your choice."

"The woman I asked first wouldn't go with me."

"*Couldn't.* There is a difference." Sarah set three bowls of baked beans on the table.

"Yes, and when I must leave halfway through to attend to some emergency, my mother will forgive me. Name another woman who would do that."

"S-Sarah."

Tim laughed. "You are right, Amity. Miss Marden wouldn't be upset with me at all."

Sarah bent over her bowl and rolled her eyes. Tim thought entirely too much of himself.

The temperature dropped significantly while they had been eating lunch. The farmers were not going to like this, not after last night's rain and freeze. Tim's horse's breath formed pale clouds. In February he would predict snow, but in June this could only mean rain.

The cold sliced through him—and a feeling he hadn't experienced since the night before the battle at Plattsburgh overcame him. Something bad was coming, and he was not prepared.

He stopped by the livery to get an extra horse blanket. In this weather, someone was bound to need him, and leaving the horse cold and wet wouldn't help anyone.

Next stop—home.

The greatcoat he'd worn during the war might come in handy. He grabbed the muffler his sister had sent him last winter and a set of gloves. On the way out, he raided the kitchen. The cook frowned when he took half a loaf of bread and a large wedge of cheese, but she didn't complain.

At the office, he inspected his bag, adding a bottle of laudanum and some more bandages, as well as soap and a clean towel. He checked his bag again, then added a pair of forceps. With Mrs. Cobb delivering early, other women could too. There was supposed to be a lunar eclipse on Sunday, or maybe Saturday. At the moment he couldn't remember other than some farmers arguing about it over the newspaper last week. Who knew how that could affect things both with weather and babies? But he did know they came at the most inconvenient times.

He arrived at the Mortons just as Mrs. Morton returned.

"Join me in a cup of tea, or coffee, or whatever we can find warm in the house." She waited at the front door. "The Cobbs added one more boy to their family, well over seven pounds."

The maid took both their coats and told them she would serve them in the parlor.

Tim was surprised to find the doctor downstairs. Mrs. Morton frowned and immediately started fussing over her husband.

"Don't look at me that way. I couldn't stay one more day in that bedroom. Don't worry, dearest. They carried me like a baby. I didn't walk."

Mrs. Morton took the chair nearest the couch where Dr. Morton rested.

The doctor rubbed his splinted leg. "I always wondered what the old men complained about when they told me they could feel the weather changing in their bones. I am content to believe them now."

The maid came in with a steaming pot.

Tim took a cup from her and warmed his hands. "I can't say I ever wondered myself."

"Don't! It isn't worth it. But I don't like this weather at all. Tell me about your visits today."

Tim and the Mortons conversed about the few patients he had seen and went over Mrs. Morton's list of women set to deliver during the next three weeks—twelve in all. Only two were first-time mothers. Mrs. Morton had checked on both. Neither showed signs of early labor. Tim breathed a sigh of relief. He hadn't delivered a baby for over a year and wanted to avoid it if possible.

They were just finishing when someone pounded on the door. A boy of twelve brought news of a brother falling and breaking his leg.

"And so it starts." Dr. Morton raised his cup in salute as Tim pulled on his greatcoat.

As he trotted his buggy down the road, he thought he saw a snowflake in the fading sunlight. It had to be his imagination. It didn't snow in June.

Mr. Barns came to collect Amity not long after Tim left. Sarah wished not for the first time that she owned a thermometer. It felt like January outside, not June. Just before dusk fell, John returned with Emma. He only stayed long enough to mutter a goodbye.

Sarah helped Emma with her wrap, then led her into the kitchen.

"Oh, Mary, I am so glad you are here. Is Anna upstairs with the boys? I am sorry I took so long."

No. Not that night! Sarah would beg Samuel to punch his brother for taking Emma home. Sarah had only been mistaken for her aunt, who had been murdered by deserters during the Revolutionary war, a couple of times before. Getting lost in that day never ended well for Emma, as in the end she had to remember the death of her own child as well as discovering her dear friend's body.

"Emma, I am not Mary. I'm Sarah, her niece."

"Don't be ridiculous. Anna isn't married yet."

Direct wasn't working. Next up—distraction. "I made some baked beans. Why don't you sit down for dinner?"

"They smell just like mine. You girls are going to be excellent cooks. But you must go. Look how dark it is getting. It feels like snow."

"Emma, it is the 7th of June, *1816.*" She emphasized the year. "It is not going to snow."

Slap!

Sarah covered the side of her face and tried to rub out the sting.

"Don't you ever lie to me again. Your father is going to worry about you not coming home, and you are trying to tell me it isn't 1778? What is wrong with you?"

Tears stung Sarah's eyes.

Eighteen

A DRAFT WOUND ITS ICY fingers around Sarah's ankles as she descended the stairs. Hadn't she banked the fire properly last night? White powder covered the floor. Flour? Emma wasn't usually careless when she baked...

Sarah's foot slipped.

Snow.

Impossible. Snow didn't fall in June, and it shouldn't be inside even in January. Not in Massachusetts.

Wind blew more snow through the open back door. She hurried to close it and threw the latch. Sarah closed her eyes and tried to remember if she'd locked up last night, and then her heart dropped.

Emma!

She rushed to Emma's room. It was empty, the bed unmade. Then she hurried up to her room in search of her heavy boots. Needing extra light, she pulled back the curtain. The ice-covered window revealed a world buried in at least a half foot of snow. Was this some sort of odd dream—a result of last night's conversation with Emma? Sarah pressed her hand to the glass but pulled it back immediately as the frost stung her palm. No dream.

She pulled on her heavy woolen stockings and dug her wool pelisse out of the trunk, along with a pair of mittens. She tugged them on as she hurried back down the stairs. The snow in the hallway had already started to melt. Sarah took a moment to check the fire and added a log. The bark pulled a yarn from her mitten. She untangled it. Rushing made her sloppy. But Emma would be cold. Sarah forced herself to slow down. If the log rolled out of the fireplace after she left... Using her teeth, she pulled off her mittens and laid the fire properly.

Satisfied the fire posed no danger, Sarah grabbed her mittens and stepped out the back door, the wind whipping at the loose hairs around her face.

She cursed, then covered her mouth with a mitten. But the word fit.

There were no tracks.

The area between the house and the one behind it was devoid of human life. Sarah quickly made her way back through the house and out the front door, grabbing her shawl on her way and wrapping it around her head. Sarah looked up and down the empty street. Only a few people braved the cold. Horses churned up the snow, and boys were shoveling off porches and walkways. Snow blew off the rooftops, mingling with the few flakes still falling from the sky.

Sarah made her way through the snow as best she could.

The boy across the street looked up. "Hey, Miss Marden! Mama told me to clear the snow at your house next."

"So kind of you. Have you seen Mrs. Wilson?"

"No, you're the only lady I have seen out."

Sarah crossed the street and took the path Noah Larkin had cleared to his home. The front door opened before Sarah could knock.

"Miss Marden, whatever are you doing? Have you ever seen snow in June? I didn't believe those tales out of Canada, but here we are. Come in!" Mrs. Larkin held the door wide for her.

Sarah shook her head. "Mrs. Wilson is missing. She went out in the night. I started a fire. Can you send one of your girls to tend it for me?"

"Oh, my! What is she doing out in this? Verity! Verity!" Mrs. Larkin's twelve-year-old daughter came from the kitchen. "Get your cloak and run over to Mrs. Wilson's to mind the fire. Get some water boiling, too." Verity nodded and left the room.

Mrs. Larkin turned back to Sarah. "I'll come over as soon as I can. No doubt you'll need some warm soup when you find her."

Sarah cringed at the thought of Mrs. Larkin finding her larder lacking. "Do be careful. The door was open for a while, and I didn't have a chance to mop."

"Shall I send Noah with you?"

"No, I am going to go to the livery to see if I can get a horse. But if he and his friends could look around here..."

"A horse—you know Mr. Hood won't let a woman—"

Sarah didn't want to debate Mr. Hood's archaic views on a woman's abilities. "It is still worth a try. I really must hurry." With any luck, he'll have a small buggy with runners on it. He would be more likely to rent that out to a woman, especially if he learned she was searching for Emma.

Avoiding the deeper drifts as best she could, Sarah worked her way down the street, asking each person she met if they had seen Mrs. Wilson. No one had.

A hidden layer of ice lurked beneath the snow, threatening to topple her more than once. If Emma had left after most of the snowfall, she could not have gone far, but the amount of snow that had blown inside indicated Emma had been out for hours already.

There were several boys on the green preparing for battle, snowballs and barriers being prepared in earnest. Sarah recognized Davey Sloan, who'd terrorized her class two years ago.

"Davey!"

The redhead looked up and prepared to sprint away.

"Have you seen Mrs. Wilson pass this way?"

"The old woman you live with?" He dropped the snowball he was forming and came over.

She didn't bother correcting his rudeness regarding Emma. "Did she come this way?"

"Nah, you are the only lady I've seen." The other boys had halted their preparations and moved closer.

"Have any of you boys seen Mrs. Wilson?"

They all shook their heads or shrugged.

"If you see her, will you please walk her back to my house? I don't want her to slip on the ice." She didn't bother inquiring if they knew which house. She was a teacher. They knew.

Mr. Swanson was sweeping the snow off the walk in front of his store. He promised to keep an eye out and ask anyone who came by.

The livery door stood slightly ajar. The elder Mr. Hood looked up from the horse he was brushing. "Miss Marden, what brings you here?"

"I need our horse!"

"I already rented the buggy sleigh to the young doctor, and there is no way I am going to let a young girl ride in this snow."

Sarah bit back the retort. People always judged her by her size. "Mrs. Wilson is missing. I need to find her."

"Get some of the boys to go looking for her, and you go back and wait at home."

"Please, I think she may have walked to her old place or to Samuel's. If I can ride, I can be there and back so much faster."

The old man shook his head. "I can't be responsible for lending you a horse that could kill you. There is ice under the snow."

"Little Brown is sure-footed. I just need help saddling him." Unlike his father, Little Brown made an excellent carriage horse and didn't balk at being ridden sidesaddle, which was why Samuel had boarded him for her use.

The man crossed his arms. "You think your sister's husband would forgive me if you get yourself killed?"

"Please, Mr. Hood. I must find Mrs. Wilson."

"Then you better go find a man who can ride." He turned and walked away.

For the horses' sake, she willed herself not to scream. *Find a man.* She clenched her fists. If only it were that easy.

The tiny sleigh glided easily over the snow. Tim was lucky Mr. Hood had runners on any of his buggies in June. No doubt it would get more use before the day ended, but right now all he wanted was a warm fire and a warm drink. The baby he had been called out to deliver arrived before he had as they often did in the first storm of the season. If that was what one could call snow in June. Maybe the traveling minister was correct about it being close to the end of the world. Red and yellow snow in Italy, snow here in June, and Canada had gotten so much snow in May there were rumors of the Canadians not exporting any food this year. If it didn't warm up soon, Massachusetts wouldn't grow much to export either.

A woman ran out of the livery and into his path, and he reined in the horse. "Look out!"

She jumped back.

"Sarah?" He came to a stop in front of her. "What are you doing?"

She used her mitten to wipe at her eyes. "Emma is missing! I need to go out to Samuel's, and Mr. Hood won't help me saddle Little Brown."

"Climb up." Tim extended his hand. "Now, tell me again more slowly."

As her story lengthened, so did his concern. Mrs. Wilson could have been gone for hours.

"Let's go check your house quickly. We'll need some extra blankets when we find her." He didn't point out that Sarah was shivering and could use one now. He simply lifted his lap robe and spread it over her too. "Why do you think she went toward Samuel and Lucy's?"

"Last night Emma thought I was my aunt and kept calling me Mary. Mary died in 1778 during a snowstorm. Emma found her and my mother, who was badly injured. I think Emma may have gone looking for them."

He pondered her information for a moment. As illogical as Mrs. Wilson's thinking seemed to be, Sarah had hit upon a good explanation. He stopped the horse in front of her house. "Go get me some blankets, and I'll go look for her."

"I am coming with you. There is no telling where Emma thinks she is, and she won't come with you if she doesn't recognize you."

"What if she doesn't recognize you?"

"She always recognizes me, but as my mother or my aunt or a younger version of Lucy. At least I am always someone she knows."

Tim helped Sarah down. "If you are coming with me, you are going to need to get some dry socks on. I don't want to be treating both of you."

Sarah nodded and ran up the now-cleared path to the door, Tim following in her wake. Once inside, she became a model of efficiency, checking with the Larkin girl, then gathering several quilts, which she stacked in Tim's arms. "Ready."

"Not until you change your socks and boots, if you own another pair."

Sarah opened her mouth to argue.

He raised his hand, nearly toppling the blankets. "I don't want to treat you for frostbite." Sarah ran up the stairs. From what he could see of her skirt, she could do with changing it too. He yelled after her. "Add an extra petticoat or two!"

A gasp came from the Larkin girl in the kitchen. Likely she wasn't used to hearing men discuss such things. He nodded in her direction, and she blushed. He hoped she wouldn't carry any tales.

Nineteen

WISDOM OR NOT, SARAH SEETHED at the extra time it took her to change her stockings, add an old-fashioned quilted petticoat, and put on an old pair of half boots. Didn't he realize that Emma could be dying? It didn't matter if her feet were cold. He was wasting time treating her like a little girl.

She pulled the laces on her boots tight. Her feet were still cold but dry. Maybe he had a point.

Tim told her the hardest part of being an army doctor was performing amputations. She'd rather not have any toes amputated. She ran down the stairs, not wanting to delay a second longer.

Tim waited for her, a steaming mug in hand. He took a drink, then handed it to her. "Finish it and we'll go."

The chocolate in milk was bitter but welcome, warming her as it worked its way down her throat.

"Did you eat this morning?"

Sarah shook her head as she drank.

"Miss Larkin, do you see a bit of bread or cheese?"

The girl produced both. Tim took the empty mug and handed the food to Sarah. "You can eat on our way. I don't need you fainting, either."

A retort about his heavy-handedness came to mind, but she had already stuffed the cheese in her mouth.

Tiny snowflakes floated softly down.

"At least it is slowing. You should have seen it at three o'clock this morning. I couldn't see ten feet in front of me," said Tim as he handed her up into the bench seat. Sarah put the last of the bread in her mouth and replaced her mitten.

"You said between the old Wilson place and Samuel's farm. Do you know where?"

"Not exactly. Lucy showed me a place she thought Aunt Mary was killed. But she wasn't sure as Mama never spoke of it and Emma only talks of it when she is lost in the past. There is always the back trail between our farms too, but Lucy believes the attack happened in the woods along the north road." She hoped he wouldn't ask more about the history than she wished to tell. The deserters who'd left her mother for dead and killed her aunt had also fathered her sister. Among the women Emma's age, it was an unspoken secret but hardly one that needed to be brought to light now. Sarah couldn't stand it when someone treated Lucy poorly due to her origin.

"We'll stop at John's on the way. Mrs. Wilson may have stopped there, and he can help look."

With no other vehicles on the road and the runners gliding swiftly over the snow, they made it to John's in record time.

John came outside to meet them. As Sarah explained what had happened, his face grew increasingly red. She didn't need to wait long for the explosion.

"I told you something like this would happen! If Ma is dead, it's on your head. If you had agreed to my plan and married me—" He took a step forward, but Tim stepped in between them.

Sarah ducked under his arms and placed her hands on her hips. "If you had listened to me, she wouldn't have been here all day yesterday!"

Tim stepped in front of her. "Fighting is not going to find your mother. Sarah mentioned a back path to Samuel's. Take your horse and search there. We will stay on the main road."

"No. Sarah can stay here and watch after my children."

Don't talk about me like I am a child. Sarah stretched to try to reach a height she didn't possess. "Isn't Lettie here?"

"Of course she is here. Came down yesterday afternoon, so I took Ma back. Perhaps I shouldn't have."

"Then she can watch your children. I am going with Dr. Dawes." Sarah climbed back into the sleigh without assistance.

Tim walked around the vehicle and said to John, "If we are not at Samuel's, circle back around by the road. If you don't see us, we found her and took her home. If you aren't at Samuel's, we will do the same."

John glared. "Bring her here."

"Only if I must. The Larkins will have warm blankets and bricks ready. It will be easier to help her in her own bed." Tim didn't wait for a reply before urging the horse into a trot.

Sarah studied the side of the road as they went along. "This is the wooded area Lucy showed me."

Tim slowed the horse.

"Do you know what Mrs. Wilson is wearing?"

Sarah bit her lip. "I—I didn't look at her clothing carefully. Her shawl wasn't by the door when I got mine."

"What color is it?"

"Probably the blue one, but it has faded to a grayish color."

"Too bad it isn't red."

"Stop!" Sarah pointed to a place where the snow was disturbed. "It looks like somebody's walked here. I hope it's more than a deer."

She didn't wait for Tim to hand her down. The last thing she wanted to hear was that she should wait. The trees grew thick in this area, and snow fell from the branches in large dollops, making it hard to tell footprints from nature's snowballs.

"Emma?"

She felt Tim come up behind her. When she didn't turn around, he touched her shoulder.

"I'm not going back to the buggy."

"I know. I am going to go over there about ten yards. We can cover more area if we spread out. Look at the base of the larger trees. If she got tired, she may have sat down. Stop when you reach the creek, and we can choose a different area."

Sarah nodded, and Tim turned north. The wind moaned through the high branches, sending snow down on her head. Tim called for Emma, and Sarah did the same as she forged through the snow-covered trail.

"Emma!"

The only response was Tim echoing her call. A drift at the base of a tree caught her attention. Just a stump.

Sarah followed the trail around a boulder. There on the leeward side of the rock sat Emma. She appeared to be sleeping.

"Tim! Tim!" Sarah brushed the snow off Emma. She thought she felt Emma breathing.

"Where are you?" Tim's voice echoed off the trees.

"Behind the boulder!"

The strands of the knit shawl were frozen to Emma's face and hair. Sarah wasn't sure if she imagined the flutter of Emma's eyes or not.

Snow crunched as Tim came closer. "Sarah?"

She stood and waved her arms. "Here!"

Tim plowed through the snow and came to kneel by Emma's side. "I think she is still alive." He scooped Emma into his arms. "Walk in front of me. Tell me if there are rocks or branches to avoid."

Sarah nodded, praying all the way back to the road.

⊶ ✳ ⊷

Mrs. Wilson's half-frozen body was heavier than he expected. Tim didn't dare voice his doubts or the need for a miracle. He stumbled a few times but managed not to fall, now feeling the absence of every missed moment of sleep. Oh, to be as strong as the Wilson men. Intent on just the next few steps, he focused on Sarah's back. If he fell or dropped Emma, he knew he didn't possess the strength to lift her back up.

Voices called out, and shortly after Sarah answered, Samuel Wilson appeared, blocking his way.

"Let me." Samuel took his mother from Tim's arms.

Free of the weight, Tim followed them back to the road. Samuel laid Mrs. Wilson in the back of his wagon, which was lined with blankets. "Sarah, climb up here and help me."

Tim noted Sarah's frozen skirt hem. While they cared for Mrs. Wilson, he'd need to make sure she got warm and dry. Especially her feet—those flimsy boots were not made for snow.

Samuel turned to face him. "Doctor, my Lucy is heating water and blankets. Since my home is closer, I suggest we go there. We can send word to the Larkins."

"We should probably get this sleigh back to the livery as well. No doubt others will need it today."

Samuel nodded and jumped into his wagon. Tim climbed into the converted buggy and only then noted John's presence. Not sure how to read the man's expression, Tim called to his horse to trot and followed Samuel to the farm.

Twenty

Sarah heard Emma groan as the wagon hit a bump, and she tightened her grip to keep them from rocking too much in the wagon bed. When the wagon slowed and Samuel pulled up to the porch, Sarah sat up, pulling off the blanket covering her.

Lucy threw open the door. "Our room is ready. Sarah, I had Louisa lay out dry clothes for you behind the screen. Change and come help me."

"I can help now." Sarah hopped out of the wagon.

Lucy put a hand on her lower back, which made her growing belly seem larger. "You'll be of no use if you are standing there shivering. Hurry now. The doctor will want to see Emma, and I can't have you changing when he is in there."

Sarah flew into her sister and brother-in-law's room and was still shrugging out of her wet dress and shoes when she heard Samuel and Lucy enter.

"Let me get that. I don't want her to burn herself on the warming pans," said Lucy.

"A knife, please? It will be easier to cut these frozen clothes off her."

At the sound of Tim's voice, Sarah's hands froze, unable to finish undoing the ties of her petticoat.

"My scissors are in my sewing box. Sarah, the box is back there. Can you hand them out?"

Lucy's head appeared around the end of the screen. "Heaven's! Aren't you done yet?"

"Sorry, my fingers…"

"Allow me." Lucy made quick work of the strings of the corset and petticoats, tossing them on top of the wet dress.

"Give me back my corset," whispered Sarah.

"You won't need it under Louisa's dress." At least her sister hadn't pointed out how Sarah didn't need the corset at all. Lucy dropped a dry shift over Sarah's head and tied the laces of the petticoats before helping Sarah into the dress minus the corset.

"Pass me my scissors and hurry. You are shivering. I must get back to Emma."

The dry clothes felt good. Sarah hadn't realized how cold she was until now. She didn't bother putting her wet boots back over the new stockings. Eventually her feet would thaw.

Tim hardly spared her a glance when she emerged from behind the screen. He was bent over Emma with Lucy helping him. "Sarah, can you get some hot water in the basin? Some of Mrs. Wilson's clothes are so frozen we can't get them off."

Her hands shook as she poured water from the kettle into the basin, some of the water splashing out.

Tim looked up. "You are shivering!" He took a quilt off the end of the bed and wrapped it around her, his fingers grazing her neck. The shiver that went down her spine had nothing do to with the cold. "Go get warm. We'll call you when we need you." He gave her a push toward the door. Sarah glanced back, but he was already helping Lucy with Emma's frozen clothing.

Her sister looked up. "There is some stew. Eat while you warm up, then you can trade me."

The promise of being needed warmed her almost as much as the quilt. Sarah ladled herself a bowl of stew and was scooting her chair as close to the fire as she dared when the door banged open, nearly causing her to spill the contents of the bowl in her lap.

Samuel appeared to be arguing with John, but both men quit talking when they saw her.

Samuel spoke first. "How is Ma?"

"They are still trying to get her frozen clothing off."

"Why aren't you helping?" John crossed his arms and glared at her.

"They—"

Samuel turned on his younger brother. "As you see, Sarah is half frozen after spending the morning looking for Ma. Lucy and the doctor don't need two patients."

"If she had stayed at my house like I told her to—"

"Then we would still be looking for Ma. Dr. Dawes told me Sarah was the one who knew where to find her."

"What I don't understand is why she couldn't watch Ma in the first place." John's hands were balled into fists, and he took a step toward Samuel.

Sarah stood. "I did watch her! I locked the house like I do every night. I hid the key. I told you how much I hate that, but I did it anyway! I don't know how she got out or if she found the other key or something. I didn't hear her leave." Tears started to run down her cheeks.

Samuel came around the table and pulled her into his arms. For a moment, she didn't mind being small. She could almost pretend he was holding her like he did when she was little. "And you found her." He placed a kiss on top of her head and released her. "Brother, let's not fight about this now. All that could be said on the matter was discussed two weeks ago. None of us could guess we would get a half foot of snow in June or plan for such a danger." Samuel turned back to Sarah. "Did Ma act oddly last night?"

"She kept calling me Mary and searching for you and Thomas Jr. as well as her baby. I finally lied and told her you were all sleeping upstairs and that Mama was watching them. I said Emma needed to get some rest so she could get better and see them. She went to bed but kept wanting to go see her children. I stayed awake until I was sure she was asleep, then I banked the fire, locked the house, and went to bed." Sarah took a bite of her cooling stew.

John hadn't moved from his spot by the door. "You are sure you locked up?"

"I think I did. Since I do it every night, it is hard to remember one night from another."

"You think?" John pushed off the wall.

Samuel glared at his brother. "Not now." He turned back to Sarah. "How long did Ma think you were Mary last night?"

"Close to two hours. None of my tricks worked. She got angrier than she has ever been when I wouldn't let her see you or the other children." She raised a hand to cover the side of her face.

Samuel pulled her hand away and touched her cheek. "How did you get this bruise? Did Ma hit you last night?"

Sarah looked at the floor, not wanting to answer.

John studied her face. "That is ridiculous. Ma never slapped us, even as children."

Samuel didn't reply to his brother. He lifted Sarah's chin with his finger and locked gazes with her. "Was this the first time?"

"No." Sarah tried to step back, but the chair was right behind her.

"Why didn't you tell me?"

"I tried to last Sunday." She shrugged and looked in John's direction.

"I shouldn't have brought her home last night."

Samuel dropped Sarah's chin and turned to his brother. "Ma was out at your place yesterday?"

"Of course. With Lettie ill, I needed someone to help with the children before the storm hit. As it is, I probably lost the south field. Sarah protested, but Ma did just fine."

Samuel groaned.

Lucy appeared in the bedroom doorway, rubbing her back. "Sarah, can you come assist the doctor?"

Sarah was glad for an excuse to leave the room.

Samuel stopped her with a hand on her shoulder. "Tell the doctor I sent the boys back to the livery with the sleigh. They'll bring Little Brown back here so he can leave when he needs to."

Sarah nodded and crossed the room.

Samuel's voice stopped her. "Sarah, thank you for finding Ma. I know you tried your best."

Sarah didn't look back at him, afraid he might see her tears.

Lucy shut the door once Sarah had entered, then hovered over her younger sister for a moment, talking in hushed tones, before addressing Tim. "Well, Doctor, it seems my replacement is here. I need to go take care of some other things."

"What you need to do, Mrs. Wilson, is to lie down. I don't believe the baby is due quite yet, but the way you are rubbing your back makes me wonder if he is not considering an early arrival. This bed is large enough. You can lie down here if you wish, or perhaps in one of the children's rooms."

"I promise I will go lie down as soon as I take care—" Lucy's face pinked.

Understanding dawned. Most likely she needed the chamber pot stashed behind the screen where Sarah had changed earlier. But he doubted she would want to use it with him in the room. "Very good plan. A least a half hour of rest. Sarah, can you take over here? The shawl is almost off Emma. I don't want to rip her hair out or get her too wet."

Sarah took the cloth from him and worked at separating the yarn from Emma's hair. Tim checked Mrs. Wilson's feet. Frostbite. If she lived, he might end up having to amputate part of the foot.

He moved the flannel-wrapped bed warmer closer.

"Is there anything else I can do?" Sarah held the shawl away from the bed as it started to thaw.

"Could you make some type of tea? We can try spooning some into her."

"Would you like some? Or some stew?"

"Yes, please, and check that your sister really did lie down."

Sarah left the room with the wet clothing, shutting the door behind her.

Tim checked to make sure the door was closed before falling to his knees. As a doctor, there was little more he could do at this point. He had seen miracles in his battlefield hospital, but he had also seen weeks in which there were none. Emma's life rested in the Almighty's hands now. Part of him was tempted to let Emma slip away if he had a choice. Her apparent frustration that her memory played tricks on her would only worsen. Surely she would not be any better after nearly freezing to death. Yet, for Sarah's sake, he hoped Emma would live, mostly so the brothers wouldn't blame her for the death. Words wouldn't come for the prayer he wanted to utter. He didn't know what to petition for, so he muttered the Lord's prayer and hoped God would understand.

Beyond the door, he heard voices. John was ranting again. Tim stood. If he couldn't help Emma, maybe he could help Sarah.

Twenty-one

LADLE IN HAND, SARAH WHIRLED to face John, who stood over her. "Please stop. I am not a child, nor am I a soothsayer. I took every precaution for your mother's safety. Other than sleeping in her room last night, I don't know how I could have prevented her leaving. You don't understand the state she was in yesterday. I've never seen her so bad."

John crossed his arms and looked down on her. "It wasn't enough."

"What would be enough? Locking her in her room? Tying her to her bed? Sending her to some asylum in Philadelphia?" The angry words tumbled out. No one had ever discussed sending Emma away, but ever since she had read they were building an asylum near Boston, Sarah wondered if it might be an option.

"I told you my plan. If you had only listened months ago, we could have brought Ma home, and she would be right as rain."

"I don't think so." Both Sarah and John turned to face Tim. "There is very little research on the madness of the elderly, but in all, I find it escalates. Mrs. Wilson has had more frequent lapses. I witnessed several myself. Usually the person becomes violent. Miss Marden never confirmed it, but I am certain this is the case as evidenced by her bruised cheek. None of the doctors I've spoken with have ever seen a patient this age whose madness decreases. It always grows worse."

"But if Ma came back home, she would be better."

Tim shook his head. "Sarah has told me she is always worse after being at your place. Perhaps it is because the memories come more easily there. Upsetting memories. Last night, for example, she remembered the death of Sarah's aunt and possibly one of your siblings. I've had her mistake me for Mark or Daniel more than once, and then she lives through finding out they are dead or missing at sea all over again as the memories come back. Do you understand what type of heartache that must cause your mother?"

Or me? Sarah blinked back tears.

Samuel had entered the room at some point. "John, I asked you to let this go for now. Blaming Sarah will not change things. Why don't you go sit with Ma for a spell? I am sure Dr. Dawes needs a moment to eat the food Sarah is dishing up."

Sarah felt John's glare as he went into the bedroom, but she didn't look up to meet it.

Samuel came around the table to Sarah's side and addressed Tim. "Have you had a chance to look at Sarah's feet? Her fingers are still red, and she is walking clumsily."

"I am not!" No way would Tim examine her feet.

"How are your feet?"

There was no good answer. "Cold?"

"Sit down and let me see." Tim gestured to the rocking chair.

Sarah shook her head. "Samuel can look. He studied to be a doctor too. Maybe he should check your feet first."

Tim shook his head. "I am wearing a perfectly sturdy set of fur-lined boots made to keep the cold out."

Samuel and Tim held a silent conversation consisting of a couple of shrugs and a nod. Why did men do that?

Finally it ended, and Samuel spoke. "Very well, but if I feel the need, I will ask for the doctor's opinion. Remember, I failed at Harvard, and that was twenty years ago. I have not seen any frostbite since." Samuel escorted her to the chair.

Tim turned to the table while Sarah untied the garters and removed the borrowed socks. Samuel's touch hurt near her ankles but not so much as he continued feeling the rest of her feet. He looked up from where he knelt and whispered. "Pumpkin, I think I need another opinion. I don't like the feel of your left foot especially."

The childhood endearment sent a shiver down her spine. Samuel wouldn't use it in front of the doctor unless he were truly concerned.

Sarah chanced a glance at Tim. He was bent over the stew with his back to her. "Must he?" she whispered back.

The man who had been more father than brother nodded and stood. "I'll stay here."

Samuel stood and went to the table. The two men had a whispered conversation Sarah strained to hear, but she caught little. Both men rose and came to kneel at her side. Tim's hands on her feet and calves did not feel much different from Samuel's, but Sarah could still feel the heat rising in her face.

"Tell me if this hurts." Tim kneaded her foot.

"Ouch, that pinches."

Tim stood. Another whispered conversation passed between the men. Samuel went out into the lean-to and returned with the washtub.

Tim pulled the bench forward and sat. "Sarah, there is some frostbite, but I am not sure how bad it is. We are going to warm your feet by having you soak them in water. You need to tell us how bad the pain is and where. If it makes you more comfortable, I'll ask Samuel to check on your progress as often as possible."

Samuel filled the washtub using some water from over the fire as well as out of the bucket. Tim tested it. "That's it. Not too hot. Her feet need to warm gradually."

"They feel like they are burning."

Tim swirled the water with his hand. "No warmer than a hot bath."

The bedroom door opened. "Ma is shivering."

"That is a good sign." Tim hurried into the bedroom.

Samuel positioned the washtub. "Pull your skirts up a bit more so they don't get wet."

"What if Tim comes back?"

"I am sure he has seen more than a woman's feet during his career." He smiled. "Let me go see if I can find a board and some paper. You can draw while you wait, unless you'd rather work on the mending."

"I am not sure I could hold a needle or pencil. My fingers feel huge."

"Why didn't you say something sooner?"

"Emma needed more help, and Lucy doesn't seem to be doing well."

"This child has been more difficult on Lucy than even the twins. I hoped Ma could help when it came time, as well as you, but I have had my doubts about Ma these last few weeks." Samuel tested the water again.

"My feet feel like I am standing in a thorny bush."

"Then they are defrosting."

"Emma misses being a midwife most, I think. It is the one place she seems to remember everything. You should see her with Amity. But with the consensus being that I, as a spinster, can't aid her…continuing to deliver babies isn't feasible."

"Lucy has never complained about your help before."

"Yes, but both doctors forbade Emma to practice, and I can't imagine they would allow me to help in anything short of dire need."

Samuel added another cupful of the hot water. "Even Dr. Dawes?"

"Especially him. Most likely he suffers from suspicious husbands because he is unwed. Can you imagine if I were to help him?"

Samuel chuckled. "Old Reverend Woods would have had you married by sundown to prevent the gossip."

She cringed at the memory of the overly pious minster of her youth. "Not by sundown, but he would have had our intentions read, even if he had to hold a special meeting to announce them." Sarah kicked to make the water splash. Samuel moved back, laughing.

The bedroom door slammed.

"What is your problem, laughing while Ma is dying?" John's face reddened with anger.

Samuel stood and laid a hand on his brother's shoulder. "We are not being disrespectful. You know Ma would prefer we found something to laugh about."

Four-year-old Stella came down the stairs. "Papa? Mama says she needs you."

Samuel was across the room immediately, taking the stairs two at a time.

Why hadn't John returned with the warming pan? Tim stuck his head out the door to find Sarah and John in a staring contest. "Did you refill the warming pan? It is essential we keep her warm."

John grunted and moved to the fireplace.

"Wish that there was more I could do other than suggest earnest prayer and—"

Samuel and Lucy lumbered down the stairs, ending whatever Tim wanted to say.

Sarah paled at her sister's distraught face. It was all the confirmation Tim needed to know today was going to be much more eventful than it already had been.

John turned with the full warming pan. His face also fell.

Lucy spoke first. "Doctor, we would be obliged if you could stay for a while. This little one is not going to wait another three weeks, and, to be honest, something doesn't feel quite right."

Clang! The warming pan fell to the floor, scattering the coals. John wavered as if he might faint.

Sarah stood, the water in the basin at her feet sloshing about.

Samuel helped Lucy to the other rocker and took control. "John, the baby won't be here for several hours yet. Get those coals back in the pan before you burn down my house. Sarah sit back down. We are going to need you, so you'd better get those feet defrosted now."

To Tim's amazement, John and Sarah complied immediately. He turned to Lucy. After eight children, she would have a good idea of when this one would arrive. He didn't need to ask.

"I think two to three hours. Samuel, if you can take the little ones to Maryanna, Louisa can help Sarah and the doctor. John, unless you feel you need to be at your mother's side, you may as well go home. I would like to have Lettie here. When the boys get back from town, they can do the chores. In fact, John, it would be better if you would take the children to Maryanna's." Lucy stopped as a contraction moved over her.

Tim suppressed a smile. Lucy was one of those women who took charge during a birthing. So much easier than the ones who whimpered in fear.

John crossed his arms. "You know Samuel is no good with childbirth."

"No, but he will be good with Emma. Now get the warming pan in where it needs to be. Timmy, check Sarah. I need her help, but not until her feet are out of danger." Tim didn't laugh at the use of his childhood nickname. A birthing mother could call him anything she pleased.

Sarah didn't balk when Tim lifted one foot out of the water. Her eyebrows and lips pinched together as he tested her cold flesh. "Does that hurt?"

"Of course it does," said Sarah through gritted teeth.

Tim tested the other foot with better results. He added more hot water to the tub. "They are thawing out nicely. There is no reason why Sarah won't be ready to assist in the delivery." He did not add that although most of her foot seemed to be recovering, the smallest two toes on her left foot were not. He prayed he was wrong, but an amputation could wait until another doctor could perform it.

Twenty-two

WHEN LUCY STARTED PACING BACK and forth, Sarah knew it wouldn't be long. Tim had given her permission to get out of the water as long as she kept her feet warm. Lucy had produced three sets of stockings. Emma's condition had neither markedly improved in the past two hours nor deteriorated. After some debate, they carried Emma to the narrow bed from what had once been Sarah's room, having moved the table so the bed could be placed near the fire. Sarah changed the linens and prepared Lucy and Samuel's room for the arrival of her newest niece or nephew, then offered her arm to Lucy and began to pace the room with her. With the exception of Maryanna, Sarah had helped with the delivery of all Lucy's children, even if it had only been entertaining the children.

As they made the turn, her sister's grip tightened unbearably. Lucy breathed heavily. After a minute, Lucy whispered one word.

"Bed."

Sarah could only remember Lucy trying a birthing stool once and declaring she did not like that position. Sarah helped her sister remove her over robe and climb into her bed, then went through the mental checklist Emma had taught her to go through.

Tim knocked on the door. "May I come in?"

Sarah nodded. Talking about what happened during a birthing with a man, even the father of the baby, was embarrassing, but discussing it with Tim? Much worse. How could Lucy not be mortified? Tim walked over to Lucy, bent over her, and spoke quietly with her.

He stood and turned toward Sarah as the next contraction took Lucy's body. "She is close, but she is worried. She has agreed to let me examine her. Hold the lantern, please."

"The cord should not be there." Tim's eyes met Sarah's. "Your hands are smaller than mine. Did Emma ever teach you how to move it?"

Sarah couldn't speak, so she nodded and rolled up her sleeves.

Tim spoke to Lucy in a calm, low voice. Sarah faced the difficult choice of which way to move the cord. The wrong way could strangle the baby. As soon as the next contraction passed, Sarah worked as fast as she could. Emma's voice echoed in her head as she labored against nature to move the baby back and release the cord. The next contraction came while her fingers were still around the side of the baby's head. How could such a small baby survive such squeezing? As soon as it ended, Sarah completed her job.

Tim slipped Lucy's hands around the rope tied to the headboard. "Try not to push until I say." He changed places with Sarah and took a wicked-looking instrument from his bag. He shook his head at Sarah.

Sarah kept her mouth closed. Forceps. She had only ever heard of them. She couldn't watch, even if it would be the fastest way to get the baby out.

Tim gave her no such option. "Hold your sister's leg. That little one needs to come out now. We don't know if the cord is wrapped around—" He left the sentence hanging as the next contraction built. "Push now!"

Lucy's scream filled the air. Sarah struggled to keep herself from joining in as Tim clamped the instrument around the babe's head and pulled.

The cord was wrapped under the child's arm and across its chest. Sarah gasped. She had moved the cord in the wrong direction! In one motion, Tim cut it, freeing its strangle hold, and told Lucy she could push with the next contraction. As soon as the baby was out, he worked quickly, rubbing the child's back until it mewed a tiny sound. "There you go, little one. Get some more air in you."

He turned the baby over, and the quietest cry escaped.

Lucy reached for Sarah. "Is he—?"

"She," corrected Tim as a lusty cry filled the room.

Sarah released a breath she hadn't realized she'd been holding. The forceps had saved her niece. If they had waited for Lucy to push the baby out naturally, the cord could have strangled her, all because Sarah had guessed wrong when she'd moved the cord.

Tim turned to her. "This little angel isn't as big as I would like. I need you to keep her warm while we finish. We can wash her later."

Lucy reached for the baby, but Tim shook his head. "Not yet. You can't keep her warm enough while you finish."

Sarah walked to the place where the sun came through the window. Not that it was much warmer there, but holding the baby tightly wrapped in soft flannel seemed to work. The baby hiccupped.

A knock came at the door. Sarah opened it to Samuel's pale face. She scooted him out. "Sit before you faint."

Samuel crumpled into a chair. "Ma's gone."

Lucy breathed in sharply, then looked down at the little bundle in her arms.

Samuel held out his hands.

"I haven't washed her yet."

"I don't care."

"There is blood."

"I don't care."

Sarah transferred the baby to Samuel's arms. "Keep her warm. She is too small."

Samuel nodded, then unbuttoned his shirt and slipped the baby inside. He looked at Sarah, his gaze steady but his voice wavering. "Ma said this works with mothers. Maybe it works with fathers, too."

Sarah studied him for a moment. He appeared steady enough. He wasn't as excited as he had been when the other children were born, but with Emma... She sighed. Nothing would change that. It was better to focus on the baby and Lucy. "Do you feel faint?"

Samuel shook his head, his eyes on the tiny child on his chest.

"I'll let Tim—I mean Dr. Dawes—know." Sarah returned to the bedroom but stopped in the doorway.

Tim held another bundle in his arms. "Another girl. Go put her with her sister."

The baby whimpered as they transferred her. "She is smaller, isn't she?"

Tim nodded. "Hurry back."

Sarah was out the door before she realized she hadn't shared the news of Emma's passing.

Samuel rocked slowly in the rocker, whispering to the baby on his chest. He looked up when Sarah approached. He blinked, and his eyes grew wide.

"Do you have room for another one? Ti—Dr. Dawes said to put them together."

Samuel uncovered the first little girl, who seemed to be sleeping. "Twins? Help me set her here."

Sarah partially unwrapped the tiny baby and positioned her next to her sister. The older one moved her arm as if trying to draw her younger sister to her. Samuel scooted them closer, then covered them with the flannel. "Can you get me a warmed blanket from the chair by the fire?"

Sarah chose the smallest one from the pile, but it was almost half as big as the new father. Sarah checked once again to be sure the blood was not bothering her brother-in-law. "I need to go back in. Will you be all right until I can come back and wash them?"

Samuel nodded.

Sarah hurried back to her sister's bedside. Tim was rinsing his hands in the wash basin. "I assume Emma taught you the massage techniques?"

Sarah nodded, then whispered, "Emma passed a few minutes ago."

A curt nod indicated he'd heard her. "I'm sorry, Sarah. If you can take care of your sister, I will go look at those baby girls."

"I didn't wash them." Sarah pointed to the pitcher, large wooden bowl, and toweling she'd set up on the dressing table near the window.

"I'll take care of that. Come get me if there is anything amiss. I'll be back in a few minutes." Tim grabbed the toweling and empty bowl along with his bag and left the room.

Sarah sat next to Lucy. "Another set of twins."

Lucy gave her a weak smile. "For a moment I thought I saw Emma standing in here helping with the second baby, but ... she passed, didn't she?"

Sarah nodded.

"Then maybe she was here."

"How are they breathing?" Tim gently pulled back the blanket to look at the babies.

"It may sound odd, but the older one is breathing better since her sister joined her."

"Then they aren't going to like me separating them to wash them."

Samuel looked up. "I thought you asked Sarah to do that."

"She is helping Lucy. Your mother taught her well. It is too bad she was not accepted as a midwife due to being unwed. She knew exactly what to do when the first one tried to come a bit too fast."

Samuel traced a semicircular bruise on the first daughter's head. "You used forceps." There was no question in his voice.

"I felt it was best given the difficulty." Tim didn't know what Samuel had learned years ago when he'd studied to become a doctor, and he didn't want to overwhelm the new father with details he didn't need to know.

"I am glad you were here, then. Hand me a cloth, and I will clean them as much as I can, then you can count all their fingers and toes and we can take them in to my wife. I am surprised she is not calling for them."

The men worked in silence for several minutes. Sarah came out of the bedroom and crossed to the fireplace. "Lucy is shivering."

"May I go in?" Samuel asked Sarah rather than the doctor.

"There is still blood. I have not finished cleaning."

Samuel handed the babies to the doctor. "I don't think it will bother me today."

"Then I have no objection. Dr. Dawes?" Sarah asked.

Tim nodded. Samuel grabbed another warmed blanket and followed Sarah into the room.

Tim needed to check on Lucy, but he was holding both infants.

"I'll hold them." Louisa said from the rocker her father had just vacated. Tim had forgotten she was here.

"Keep them warm and close together." Tim checked the infants' breathing before hurrying into the bedroom.

Samuel sat at the head of the bed, whispering to his wife and brushing her hair. Tim felt like an intruder as he checked Lucy's pulse. Sarah cleared the afterbirth and cleaned up most of the blood. Lucy's shivering diminished, and her color remained good. When they finished, Sarah brought the babies in, and she and Tim left the new parents alone.

Louisa ran upstairs holding her handkerchief to her mouth as soon as Sarah and Tim exited the room.

A lamp sat in the center of the table. Tim lit it. "I've never seen a husband brush his wife's hair."

"Samuel's father used to brush Emma's hair. It's one of the things I do—did—to calm her at night. What am I going to do without her?" Sarah wiped the tears from her eyes before Tim could follow through on his instincts to do it himself. "I love her so much. She has been—"

This time a sob racked Sarah's body. Tim pulled her into his arms and let her cry. A hundred thoughts crossed his mind about what he could say. Most of them would be less than helpful—pointing out that if Mrs. Wilson had lived, she would not ever be the same or that he would most likely have had to amputate frozen fingers and feet. So he just held her until the tears subsided.

Tim's relief at not needing to perform an amputation on Emma brought a new worry to his mind. "How are your feet?"

Sarah shifted her weight but didn't answer.

He stepped back, holding Sarah by the shoulders. "Sit down and let me look at them."

For a moment he thought she would argue. But like him, she must be too tired to protest.

He set the lamp next to him on the bench. "Are they still painful?"

"Mostly my toes and left ankle. I am glad you insisted I change my stockings earlier or I fear they would be worse. I was angry we weren't searching instead, but it wouldn't have mattered, would it?"

"I am glad you listened. I spoke harshly this morning. And, no, finding her even a half hour earlier most likely would not have saved her."

"Was it only this morning?"

Tim wasn't sure. He had been on his way home to sleep when Sarah had asked for help. A wave of tiredness washed over him. He released her left foot and picked up the other one. "Your toes are going to blister. Keep them wrapped, and see if you can borrow some bigger shoes."

"That shouldn't be hard. Everyone has bigger shoes than I do."

"Not so. Just yesterday I set the leg of a seven-year-old boy, and I am almost positive his feet were smaller than yours."

"I think I am too tired to care that you are teasing me about my size."

Tim brought her foot up so he could inspect the bottom.

"Will you need to amputate my toe?"

Tim shook his head. "I don't know yet. Only time will tell. It may only be partially bruised. I can't say."

"Emma did step on my foot last night."

"Step or stomp?"

Sarah pulled her foot back. "Does it matter?"

Tim turned to give her some privacy as she put her stockings back on, then walked over to the bed where Emma's body lay. Samuel had covered his mother's head with the blanket. Tim realized he had never confirmed the death. He lifted the blanket, then replaced it. Going to where his bag still sat on the table, he reached in and took out his book and pencil. "The girls were born at 5:47 and 6:08. Do you know when Emma died?"

"Samuel knocked on the door not long after the first baby came."

"I am going to write that Emma passed at the same time, then."

Samuel exited the bedroom. "They are all sleeping."

A frown crinkled Tim's brow. "Sarah, will you bring the babies in here? I am afraid they will be too cold, even with Lucy."

Sarah took two flannel squares warming on the back of a chair with her.

Lucy stirred as Sarah lifted the larger girl from her arms first. "What?"

"Don't worry. I am going to put them near the fire. They are so tiny they need to be extra warm."

Lucy nodded. Sarah wrapped the second baby and returned to the great room, where Tim and Samuel sat at the table and Louisa ladled stew into bowls.

"Should I give some to Mama?" Louisa's eyes were rimmed with red.

Samuel took the offered bowl. "If she wants it. If not, try to get her to drink some of the peppermint tea or cider, if there is any left from the fall."

"I think it is all gone, but I can make apple-peel tea." Louisa opened the cupboard and pulled down a crock.

Sarah turned to the men. "Doctor, did you still need to look at the babies?"

"No, I am just worried about their size. Let me help you get them into the cradle." Tim took one baby and partially unwrapped her before laying her in the cradle, causing her to protest. He did the same with the other, placing her as close to her sister as possible. Both infants calmed, and he covered them.

Samuel watched in awe. "Benjamin and Bessie never did that."

"Do you know if John and Joe did?" asked Sarah.

Samuel shook his head. "I don't remember. I could ask—" He looked at the bed at Emma's still form. For a moment Sarah thought he might break down, but he squared his shoulders. "I guess I can't. I think we need a plan."

The front door opened, and Lettie came in. She looked at the cradle and then to the bed where her grandmother lay and burst into tears. Samuel went to her and wrapped his daughter in his arms.

Plans would wait.

Twenty-three

Instead of immediately heading back to town on the horse he'd been provided, Tim chose to stay for a few more hours. If the babies made it through the night, they had a good chance of survival. He wasn't as experienced as Mrs. Wilson, but he felt he owed it to her to make sure her tiny granddaughters had his attention.

Samuel Wilson was a master of handling crises. Tim watched as he calmed one daughter, then the other, giving them both helpful tasks. Several times he consulted with Sarah in whispered conversations. From her expression, she didn't always agree with him, but in the end they both seemed happy.

Tim helped Samuel move Emma's body into the parlor.

"I need to go talk to John, but I think we will send the body back to Ma's little house. It will be more convenient for the funeral, and I don't want everyone coming here with the new babies." Samuel shut the door to keep the room cooler.

The girls had the narrow bed stripped by the time they returned. Samuel carried the tick outside before having Tim help him remove the bed frame from the room.

After another whispered conversation with Sarah, Samuel left the house. Sarah joined Tim at the fireplace with Lettie in tow.

"Lucy wants to try feeding them again." Sarah lifted the largest baby from the cradle and carried her to Lucy, then came back and took the smaller one, carefully wrapping it in a warmed cloth before she went into the bedroom.

A quarter hour later, Samuel returned with the rest of his children, including Maryanna and her husband, who carried Seth. The two-year-old studied the room in bewilderment. James gulped a couple of deep breaths, Benjamin and Betsy looked as they may have been crying, and Stella clung to Maryanna's hand. Philip hovered over his new bride.

Benjamin ran over to the cradle. "Where are they?"

"They are in with your mother," said Tim.

Samuel went to the bedroom door. "Wait here, children."

Louisa produced a wash basin. "Grandma would have insisted you wash up before seeing the babies."

Maryanna supervised the hanging of coats and took charge of the little ones.

Tim watched, mesmerized. With only two siblings and servants to care for most things, he had never seen a family working together like this. The oldest Wilson boy, James, who couldn't have been more than eleven, took one look at the wood box and filled it without being asked. The only person who didn't seem to know what to do was Maryanna's husband.

Samuel came out of the room with Lettie, and the children gathered around him. "Mama says she will show you the girls in a half hour or so. Sarah will let you know when it is time. Boys, if you'll take care of the chores, I am going to ride to Uncle John's. He doesn't know Grandma died." He turned to Maryanna's husband. "Philip, can you ride to Carrie's and find a messenger to ride to Thomas Jr.'s?" Samuel pulled some money from his pocket. "Hopefully that will cover the cost. Don't go yourself."

Phillip nodded.

Samuel looked across the room. "Dr. Dawes, do you need a horse now too?"

"I would like to keep an eye on those babies for at least a few more hours—if you don't mind me staying."

Relief filled Samuel's face. "I would be much obliged. Things are bound to be a bit topsy-turvy around here, and I feel better knowing you are watching out for my girls." Samuel's gaze drifted to the closed bedroom door. "I'll be back as soon as I can."

Tim retreated to the corner, where he felt he wasn't in anyone's way, and watched. What would it be like to be the father of a family like this?

Sarah caught her eyes drooping as she waited for Lucy to feed the baby in her arms. Shaking her head, Sarah tried to clear the cobwebs. "Do you know what you want to name them?"

"Samuel still isn't sure. He wants to talk with John, Carrie, and Thomas Jr., but I really want to name the second one Emma. He may not believe me, but it really did feel like she was here, telling me to breathe calmly, before Dr. Dawes realized that I was having twins. I thought it was my imagination, but knowing Emma just passed, I wonder. I can't believe she is gone. I want to cry, but I look at my babies and want to laugh. So, I can't do either. I want to name the other one Anna, but it may be too close to Maryanna, and I want to ask her."

Sarah understood. She herself had been able to cry, but holding her niece cut the sadness in half. "Emma and Anna, I like that. I doubt Maryanna will mind. What if someone objects to Emma?"

"I had been thinking of the name Jerusha. But I was so sure this would be a boy the way they kicked me. This pregnancy is so different than the one I had with Benjamin and Bessie. I never guessed. I just thought it felt different because I am so old." Lucy turned her attention to the baby at her breast.

A longing filled Sarah. If only she had a baby of her own she could hold in her arms. But that dream had died with Mark in some tent as he'd lost his battle with dysentery. He didn't even have the chance to fight the British. If only they had gotten married, at least she would be a widow. Somehow that sounded more appealing than a spinster.

"Switch me." Lucy held up the bundled baby. "I can't wait until they are a little bigger and I can nurse them both at the same time."

Sarah nuzzled the child she held under her chin. "Is that easier?"

"No, but it is faster."

"How long would you like me to stay?"

Lucy studied the babe in her arms for a moment before looking up. "I think I'll ask Maryanna to stay. Where she and Phillip are living at his parents' home, it won't be that big of a change. And she needs to learn a few of the things you or Emma always took care of. Besides, you will be needed to dress Emma, and then there is Amity."

Sarah had forgotten about Amity. She didn't usually come on Saturday, so there was no worry she would find the house empty. With Emma gone, would she trust the rest of them when her time came?

"Where shall we have Emma's funeral?"

"Samuel thinks her little house is best because of the weather and the proximity to the church. John will want it at his place. So we will see."

Sarah didn't need to wait to know. Thomas Jr. would side with Samuel, so it would be at her house. But it wasn't her house. The baby burped, and Sarah put her thoughts about the future out of her mind for now.

In any other circumstance, Tim would love the position he found himself in, gliding over the icy road in the Wilson's old sleigh, with a beautiful woman at his side under a starry sky. But on a June night with a body in the back seat and Sarah sitting ramrod straight a good foot away from him, the moment was far from enjoyable. If Sarah moved any farther, she would fall out the side. Tim had wondered for several days if she wasn't trying to put distance between them. He had his answer.

She hadn't been happy when Samuel had returned from John's with his parents' old sleigh. Tim hadn't understood the jokes about Mr. and Mrs. Wilson's love of the sleigh or how if Emma had a choice she would choose it to be her last conveyance, but it wasn't until John left grumbling about the dangers of sleighs and snow-drifts that Sarah lost her smile and begged Samuel to let her stay the night. Her requests to take Louisa, James, and even Benjamin or Bessie home with her were also met with rejection.

And then she'd stopped talking.

But only to him. She wouldn't look at him or allow him to carry her to the sleigh when they left, though neither he nor Samuel wanted her feet in the snow again. And so Samuel had done it, though Tim wished it could have been him.

He had asked Samuel what was wrong, but the whispered answer made no sense. "My parents were married in that sleigh." Tim studied the sleigh as he drove. It was at least fifty years old but in excellent repair. But people didn't get married in sleighs, and what did that have to do with Sarah ignoring him?

Here and there lights shined out of a few windows as they entered town, but most people were tucked safely in their beds.

As expected, Mrs. Wilson's house was dark. He hurried around the sleigh and lifted Sarah out, carrying her to the porch before she could protest. He set her down inside the front door. Word-lessly, Sarah lit a lamp and carried it into the parlor, then set it on the table.

"I need—"

She looked at him for the first time in nearly an hour. Tears stained her cheeks. She had been crying on the way back. Had he known, he would have comforted her.

"You need to leave. Go find someone to help with Emma, Dr. Dawes. You can't be here with me." She turned her back to him and started to push one of the chairs closer to the wall—to prepare the room for the funeral, he surmised.

Tim laid his hand on her shoulder.

She shrugged it off. "Please, leave me."

If he turned her, he knew there would be more tears. But she didn't want him. Someone knocked on the door, and Sarah hurried to answer it. Tim finished moving the chair.

Reverend Palmer stepped into the room. "Samuel Wilson sent me a message about his mother. Is the funeral to be from this house?"

Sarah answered. "Yes, Samuel will bring the coffin in before church. Can you help the doctor with ... if you would put her in her room, then ..." Sarah took in a deep breath. "Then I can prepare the body."

"Mrs. Palmer will be over to help you as soon as I let her know you are back. I noticed the light in the window just as we were going to bed."

Sarah shook her head. "It's late. Your wife can sleep if you'll just bring in—" Again Sarah had to pause before continuing. If the reverend hadn't been there, Tim would have taken her in his arms. Sarah needed to be held and to be able to cry. Sarah was as close to Mrs. Wilson as any of her own children.

A lighter knock sounded at the door. Mrs. Palmer didn't wait for it to be answered but came in, took one look at Sarah, and pulled her into her arms. "There, there, dear, it will be better soon."

Sarah pulled back. "My father used to say problems always looked better in the sunlight." She turned to the men. "If you would please bring her in. I am sure Dr. Dawes needs sleep worse than I do. He was already out and about when he stopped to help me."

Reverend Palmer clasped Tim's shoulder. "Good thing you did

too, I understand we lost Mrs. Wilson but gained two more in her place."

Tim really didn't need the minister to help him bring in the body, but it did solve Sarah's worries about them being alone.

Tim left as soon as they were done. He would return the sleigh early in the morning before the remaining ice and snow melted. He looked back to the house to see Sarah in Mrs. Palmer's arms again.

How he wished she trusted him enough for it to be his arms around her.

Twenty-four

THE SUN HOVERED JUST A pinch above the skyline when Samuel
knocked on the door. As soon as Sarah opened it, he pulled her
into a hug. "You don't look like you slept much, pumpkin."

"Neither do you."

"It's been a long night."

"Did the babies?"

"They were both fussing when I left. Dr. Dawes brought Mrs.
Morton out with him when he returned the sleigh just before
dawn. So everyone is in good hands." Samuel waved toward the
wagon, where James sat. The boy climbed down and hurried into
the house.

Samuel walked into the parlor. "Who helped you move all the
furniture?"

"Reverend Palmer moved most of it last night while Mrs. Palmer
helped me." Sarah didn't tell Samuel she'd rearranged most of it
before dawn after an unsuccessful attempt to paint a memorial.
She had been unable to sleep. She had not handled the jokes about
being in the sleigh alone with Tim well, though she knew they
were just something to relieve the stress of the day. Perhaps had
she cared for him less, she could have laughed more. Crying in
his arms yesterday had been as disturbing as it was comforting. It

would do neither of them any good for her to follow the path her heart begged her to explore.

Two straight-backed chairs stood alone in the center of the room. "If you will hold the door for us..." Samuel and James went back out to the wagon.

When they returned with the coffin, Sarah adjusted the location of the chairs to hold up either end. She ran her hand over the smooth stained wood and traced the carvings on top. "How long have you been working on this?"

Samuel pinked. "I started on it the day I built Pa's. I wanted to use the same wood. Ma was so distraught when Pa died, I thought she might go any day because of a broken heart. Over the years I added to it, either on the anniversary of Pa's death or when I was worried about Ma."

"You truly outdid yourself. Now all the ladies in the widows' pew are going to beg you to make one just like it for them."

"I'll tell them it took me ten years. I think that will stop them." Samuel smiled and turned to his son. "Do you think you can help me place grandma's body in here? I can get someone else..."

The boy straightened to his full height, causing Sarah to tilt her head up. "We already talked about this, Pa. I can do this."

Sarah ran and got Emma's old wedding quilt to put under her body. It was the one thing Emma would want to take with her.

When they were finished, Samuel took his leave. "I'll see you at the church. Lucy wants all the children to come in. What I think she really wants is some silence. Seth runs around the house holding up two fingers and shouting 'Two!' every time he sees the twins. Benjamin and Bessie keep arguing over which one is theirs. One of the girls will stay home. Carrie's and Thomas Jr.'s families should be here by the time church starts. So it will be a crowd."

Sarah covered her mouth. "I don't have anything to feed everyone!"

"Don't worry. Maryanna thought of that last night with today being the Sabbath and all. It is only beans and cornbread, but there will be enough for everyone, and you know that once the reverend announces Ma's passing, food will just start to show up. By tomorrow morning after the funeral, there will be more food in this house than the entire Wilson family can eat in a week." Samuel hugged her one more time before he left.

Sarah wandered into the kitchen. It needed a good sweeping. Sabbath or not, she needed to tidy things up. At least cleaning would keep her awake until church started.

The last bell's echo faded as Tim slipped into the back of the church. His breeches were splattered with mud, and he was late—two very good reasons to slide into one of the back pews. He should pay more attention. The entirety of Widow Webb's boardinghouse sat in the row in front of him.

"She looks exhausted."

"She should be. Got in his buggy alone … was gone all day … parlor light on about ten thirty … just the two of … bold as you can be."

"… could be another explanation."

Tim tried to discern which women were speaking, but their bonnets hid their identities.

Reverend Palmer stood. "Before we begin, I would like to announce the death of Mrs. Emma Wilson last night."

One of the women in front of him jumped a bit and gave a little squeak.

"Told you."

As he suspected, they had been gossiping about Sarah. Her fears about being alone with him had some foundation. He would try to be more careful. Gossip like this could stain a lady's reputation.

Tim missed the rest of the announcements and didn't remember singing the hymn. These women were supposed to be her friends.

Halfway through the sermon, Sarah stood with little Stella in her arms and exited the building. Tim waited a few minutes before following, certain no one had noticed since he already sat by the door.

Sarah stood near one of the privies, rubbing her arms to keep warm.

"If I were twenty years younger, I would take advantage of finding a pretty girl behind the church."

Sarah turned to face him. Judging by the dark rings under her eyes, if she had slept last night, it had been a poor sleep, indeed. The black mourning dress robbed her of all color. "And I would hit you like Samuel taught me. Please go before someone realizes we're both out here."

"Do they gossip about you often?"

"Who?"

Tim shrugged. That had been the wrong question.

"I am a poor spinster teacher. You are a doctor from one of the wealthiest families in town. Of course they gossip. Please go."

The tremor in her voice hit him harder than her fist ever could. He heeded her request, but instead of returning to the church, he got on his horse and left. If she returned and he didn't, the gossips would be less likely to talk. Besides, he needed to change his soiled clothes.

At least the day warmed up enough that people could move out to the porch to talk. The house was filled to overflowing. Seth came over and asked to be lifted up again. When she complied, he immediately laid his head on her shoulder and stuck his thumb in his mouth. Sarah took him upstairs, where Stella already slept next to John's children on her bed. Tucking him in next to her pillow, she hoped he had been to the privy earlier. Too late now. She moved her pillow to the top of her trunk.

Neighbors continued to come in. Considering Emma had probably delivered half of the population under the age of twenty, there would be more to come. Sarah found Louisa in a corner, studying her boots. Her niece had never been one for crowds or talking with strangers.

Sarah whispered in her ear. "The children are sleeping in my room. You can go up and watch them if you wish. I may have a book you haven't read on my shelf."

Louisa brightened and hurried from the room. Samuel gave her a smile. It wasn't until Sarah spoke to Mrs. Larkin that she remembered the notes stuffed between the pages of *Pride and Prejudice*. Hopefully the complete set of Sense and Sensibility Mark had given her as an engagement present would be more enticing. Of all her nieces, Louisa didn't need more proof that the world could be a cruel place.

Widow Webb and her boarders arrived together. There were a couple Sarah didn't recognize. She nodded to each of them and didn't bother remembering the names of the new women who were going to work in the bindery in town.

"Oh, you poor thing. It seems like you just got out of mourning. But then, you were not really related, so you don't need to stay in black forever."

Sarah bit her tongue. Parmelia would never understand how close she had been to Emma from her childhood—not quite mother, not quite grandmother, nearly mother-in-law. In Sarah's mind, coming out of mourning in anything less than six months was disgraceful.

"Thank you for your condolences. I will miss Mrs. Wilson very much." Sarah turned to the next person, who handed her a heavy crockery. Thank goodness—a reason to escape to the kitchen.

"Benjamin Wilson, get your finger out of the pudding right now!"

"But, Aunt Sarah, I'm hungry."

"We all are, but it would be rude to eat in front of our guests. You know your mother would have you mopping the floors first thing in the morning if she caught you."

Benjamin looked at his twin. Purple discolored her upper lip. "I see both of you tested the pudding. Perhaps instead of the kitchen you should go sit in the parlor, where you won't be so tempted."

Bessie looked at her with pleading eyes. "Please, Aunt, we are very hungry."

"There is this jar of beets. If you want, you may take them on the back porch."

Both children made a face. "We are not that hungry."

"Then scoot."

A wail came from the parlor, followed by a crash. Sarah and everyone else in the house rushed to see what had happened.

Amity lay on the floor, shaking and thrashing about. Her father stood guarding her.

"Benjamin! James! Go find Dr. Dawes!" Sarah did her best to clear the area. "Give her a bit of room."

When Amity finally lay still, Mr. Barns looked at Sarah.

"Bring her in here." Sarah led the way to Emma's room. When they gained entrance, Sarah shut the door against any prying eyes.

"I'm sorry, Miss Marden. When Amity heard Mrs. Wilson passed, she kept asking to come. I didn't think she would get so upset." Mr. Barns wrung his hands.

"Don't worry. How long does it usually take her to come around after one of these episodes?"

Mr. Barns shrugged. "Ten minutes. You mean she hasn't had one here yet?"

"No, but Dr. Morton told me what to expect. Did she hurt herself when she fell?" Sarah put a light quilt over Amity. Someone tapped on the door. Sarah opened it to find Dr. Dawes. "Doctor, do come in." Sarah left as he entered. As much as she wanted to know how Amity would fare, being in the room with the doctor and Mr. Barns could lead to another note.

Several heads turned when she returned to the parlor, but no one asked any questions.

Twenty-five

THE FUNERAL HAD CONCLUDED HOURS ago, the neighbors had returned to their normal Monday routines, and the younger children had all been either sent home or out to walk around the green.

Thomas Jr. stood next to the window. "In all the commotion, we forgot to mention that Dorcas is supposed to be here tomorrow. We were planning on having her stay here with Ma and Sarah. I am not sure what we should do now."

"Sarah can't stay here. It wouldn't be proper." John crossed his arms. "She should move home."

Carrie opened her mouth, then closed it.

Samuel rubbed the back of his neck. "With the new babies, there really isn't room. Besides, it is too far for Sarah to go to the school each day."

Sarah waved her hand. "I am in the room. Has anyone considered asking me what I want?"

Everyone looked at her.

"I'll be twenty-four this fall. I still have Amity to help, and as Samuel has pointed out, his house is on the crowded side, which, to be honest, is hardly conducive to grading papers." She held up her hand. "John, don't think it, and don't say it. I am not inclined to marry anyone. I would say I could take a room at Widow Webb's, but she had new boarders today, and it didn't work out too well for me years ago. If the intention is to sell this house, it may take a few weeks. I assume from what Thomas Jr. said that his sister-in-law Dorcas has few other options now. Is there a problem with the two of us living here for the next month or so?"

Thomas Jr. looked around the room. "Sorry, Sarah, I think we forget you are so grown up. I don't have an objection. Samuel, what about you? This is your house, isn't it?"

Sarah looked at Samuel. His house? He just shook his head at her. "Yes, it is, and selling it doesn't help me much as Louisa and Lettie will be attending Bradford this fall and I rather not pay to put them in a second-rate boardinghouse. Carrie, wasn't one of your daughters planning on living here too?"

"I'd hoped to send both Prissy and Cornelia."

Thomas straightened. "Our Beth won't start for another term. But having her live here is better than trying to get one of the boarding spots above the school. Any objections?"

John opened his mouth, but Samuel glared at him, and John sat back with his arms folded.

Sarah breathed a sigh of relief. She could not endure another half-hearted proposal. "It sounds like I am running a boardinghouse. I hope Dorcas can cook."

"I can't guarantee she will stay very long once the rest of the siblings find out our need for her is no longer dire. Someone is likely to claim her to come help at their house." Thomas Jr. frowned. "I feel a bit sorry for her—always passed from house to house. Well, I had better gather my family. I'd like to get home before sunset." He hugged each of his siblings, as well as Sarah.

Samuel left last. "You can come with me if you'd rather not be alone tonight."

Sarah shook her head. "I don't think I've slept more than two hours since I woke up Saturday morning. At least here I will get some sleep."

"Anna and Emma don't cry loud enough to keep anyone awake."

"Maybe so, but Lettie kicks in her sleep. Why do you think Louisa volunteered to share a bed with Bessie?"

"Ah, that makes sense now. Bye, pumpkin."

Once everyone was gone, Sarah looked around the empty house. How should she rearrange it with so many nieces coming this fall? She didn't want to give Dorcas Emma's room, but it felt wrong to take it for herself just yet. The bed would need new ticking. If she emptied the mattress, that would be a good enough reason to put Dorcas in the room Maryanna and the other girls had used during their stays at the house.

Sarah had the old straw out before she realized she didn't have any new. She would need to get word to Samuel or John that she needed some.

Hunger finally drove her to stop her preparation of the rooms. The bottle of beets sat on the table in the same spot as yesterday. Sarah wondered how many times the bottle had been gifted at a funeral or birth. She lifted it to move it to a side shelf, and a paper fluttered to the floor.

Your secret didn't die with Mrs. Wilson.

Sarah sunk to the floor and cried.

Twenty-six

"I can't believe it snowed here two weeks ago," Dorcas Smith said as she fanned herself. "Today it is hot enough for the devil himself to come dance on the street."

"I think you have it just about right. I don't think I have ever lived in such an upside-down year." Sarah pulled at the fabric of her dress and bent back over the silk she was painting. After seeing the memorial Sarah had painted for herself depicting the story of Ruth and Naomi, Samuel had requested one for himself. She couldn't resist portraying Hannah leaving Samuel at the temple.

Amity continued sewing her nine-patch squares. Already she had enough squares for a child-sized quilt. Her seizures had come frequently over the past two weeks, but Sarah didn't send Noah after Dr. Dawes unless Amity hit her head. Mr. Barns asked if she could stay with Sarah until the baby came. Amity was a welcome addition, and putting her in Emma's room seemed natural.

Unlike the heat.

Amity found a scrap of paper to fan herself with. The writing looked familiar.

"Sweetheart, can I trade you my fan for that paper?"

"Fan-n." The smile on Amity's face told Sarah the fan would never be hers again.

I gave you two weeks to mourn.
But I grow tired.

Who shall I tell first?

Two weeks ago, Tim had worried about his littlest patients dying because they were too cold. Today he worried about his oldest patients dying due to the excessive heat. Fortunately, most of them had family to dampen their clothing and keep them in cooler parts of the houses or out in the shade. He worried about the farmers out in their fields, desperately trying to make up for the crops lost in the snowstorm.

His rounds were taking him past the Samuel Wilson farm. Sure of his welcome and of water for his horse, Tim rode into the yard.

Lucy and several of the children were working in the garden. Everyone shouted, "Dr. Dawes!" at once. Benjamin came for Tim's horse and led the beast in the direction of the barn.

"Come, sit." Lucy told him. "James has already gone to get a fresh bucket of water. I think we are all tempted to jump in the well today. I told the children if they helped me for a half hour they could go play in what is left of the creek. You rode up at the twenty-five-minute mark. Thank you. I couldn't stand out here another minute." Lucy fanned herself. Summer had come with a vengeance, and despite the late snow, the crops still didn't have enough rain to see them through.

"I'm surprised you are out here at all. I thought you would still be resting." Tim took a cup of water from Bessie.

Lucy laughed. "I did with Maryanna, but by the time Stella came along I got up and made supper that night. Well, I cut the bread I made the day before and set out some apple preserves. But still, I wasn't in bed."

"All the same, I do wish you would take it easy, especially in this heat."

"I can live with that order. No more hard work today."

"Really, Mama?" came a chorus of voices.

"Yes, off to the creek with you. James, watch Seth and Bessie, and keep Stella where you can see her. And everyone mind Louisa!" Shouting the last part was necessary as the children were already halfway across the nearest field.

"Where is Mr. Wilson?"

"Samuel and Lettie are down at John's. I don't know if it is possible to save the crop, but after last year's drought, John is desperate. He is talking about slaughtering all but his best two milk cows if he doesn't get a crop growing. Can't run a dairy without fodder for the cows."

"I had no idea things were that bad." Tim finished the last of his water. "How about I take a look at those two little angels of yours and I'll be on my way."

The girls slept in a basket near the door in only their diapers. They reminded him of a drawing he had seen of a sea creature with eight arms. "I hate to wake them. They both look like they have grown, I think."

"They always sleep like knotted yarn. But I believe they are both more than five pounds now when I weigh them against my flour."

"I am not sure if babies experience as many problems with the heat as the elderly, but do watch them."

Lucy smiled the smile of a mother who knew more than the doctor, which, in this case, Tim willingly admitted she did. "Don't worry, Doc, I got them this far. I am not going to let a hot day defeat us."

Tim took his leave. Unfortunately, the visit only made him think of Sarah, the only girl on the north side of the river who seemed to be avoiding him.

Half the women in Miss Webb's boardinghouse had come to the

office in the past two weeks complaining of some fictitious ailment, then again to bring food to thank him. Miss Page hadn't overstated her cooking abilities.

Sarah, on the other hand, managed to be "out" all but twice during his daily visits to Amity. He was tempted to see just how long he could keep her hiding in the privy today. But in this heat, that would be cruel.

The sweltering heat in her bedroom nearly drove Sarah downstairs, but she lay on her bed and waited for Tim to leave. She had been coming downstairs after adding the latest note to her collection when he rode up. At least her bedroom smelled better than the privy.

Amity's laughter drifted up the stairway. Sarah wiped the perspiration from her brow. Why was she hiding, anyway? Dr. Dawes was visiting in a professional capacity. Anyone who saw her in her last-summer's dress could see that.

She wiped her damp handkerchief over her face again before heading down the stairs and to the porch.

"S-sarah. Doc-c." Amity beamed. Next to her father, who came nightly to visit, they had become her favorite people. Mrs. Morton continued to be tolerated, though somewhat less since Emma's passing, having been replaced by Dorcas.

Tim stood from the chair he occupied, studying Sarah long enough to have her questioning her choice to come down.

"Miss Marden, do you not own a dress of a material more suited to the weather?"

"Of course she doesn't. At least she isn't wearing the dress made of bombazine." Dorcas fanned herself as if she were wearing the wool-and-silk hanging in Sarah's room. "At least the crepe is somewhat lighter."

"Could you not dye a lighter fabric, like the dress Amity is wearing, black?"

Sarah shook her head. "At best, it comes out a deep gray, or the die rubs off on everything and the wearer ends up with hands as dirty as a chimney sweep's."

"And I suppose wearing half mourning would not be appropriate. However, your sister was not in black when I saw her earlier today, so there must be some room for common sense."

"I suspect Lucy was not expecting company. One of the advantages of living so far out is that one can dress practically unless coming into town. To dress the children in black all the time would be expensive as well. When Emma's husband died, she declared anyone under sixteen need only wear mourning to church or school. She couldn't stand having them sit around stiffly for months, afraid to ruin their clothing. Living here, I cannot step out of my house without observation, so I will wear my black dress."

"That is the stupidest reason to overheat one's self I've ever heard!" Tim picked up the half-full bucket of water sitting on the porch and dumped it over Sarah's head.

Sarah sputtered as Amity and Dorcas burst into laughter. "Why did you do that?"

"Because you've dampened your face three times since you've been out here, compared to Miss Smith's one. Your face is a color of red that comes from being too hot, not embarrassment, and being drenched will force you to go put on one of those hideous gray dresses you wear all the time."

Sarah balled her fists and stood up straight. How she wished she had Lucy's height, so her glare would have more power. But her hair fell in her face, and words failed her. She stormed into the house.

Tim caught up with her as she reached the stairs. He caught her elbow. "Sarah, I'm sorry."

She climbed onto the first step and turned to face him. Rather than put distance between them as she supposed, it brought her closer to eye level. "How dare you pour water on my head where everyone can see? What must people think now?"

"I don't care what they think as long as you don't make yourself heat sick because you are wearing that black dress."

She had never before noticed the little flecks of gold flashing in his eyes or how they danced. "And why do you care about that?" The words came out funny.

Tim suddenly leaned forward and brushed his lips across hers. Fire danced through her. She blinked, and he stepped closer, his fingers smoothing her wet hair off her cheek. The second kiss started just as soft, but the fire it kindled forced her to respond. Too soon, he broke the kiss, then rested his forehead against her wet one. "Now, go change. And if you come down in anything made of wool or silk, I will take you to the river and drop you in. So help me, Sarah Marden, I will."

Sarah ran up the stairs before he could kiss her a third time. For a man who worried about her overheating, he had a funny way of showing it.

Sarah kept on her damp petticoat and corset as they were wonderfully cool, and pulled on a deep-gray muslin—the experiment gone bad from her mourning for Mark.

Mark.

Sarah pressed her hand to her mouth. She had just kissed another man and enjoyed it. A man Mark would thrash if he knew.

Holding the dress to her chest, she sat down on the bed and cried.

Miss Smith claimed Sarah had fallen asleep. The odd look she gave Tim caused him to wonder at the truthfulness of the statement. He began the walk back to his office, pondering his actions. He'd looked forward to kissing Sarah for twenty years.

The moment had eclipsed his expectations. She'd returned it, but still, he'd managed to scare her away.

He didn't notice Miss Brooks and Miss Page until he ran into them.

He apologized and walked on. A block later, he realized he'd left his doctor bag on the porch. He took the long way back, keeping an eye out for any of Miss Webb's boarders.

Twenty-seven

A chaperone is not enough. She isn't with you all the time.

Sarah touched her lips. How could anyone possibly know about Monday's kiss? Dorcas might have deduced something, but the notes had started long before she'd arrived.

Sarah had stood at the bottom of the stairs a half dozen times. No one outside of the house could have seen the kiss. And if Amity had seen it, she would have said something.

Someone was very good at guessing.

Sarah pretended to be sick for the next three days, telling Dorcas it was her woman's complaint.

Tim sat next to his mother in the family pew and waited for the last bell to chime before the meeting started. Sarah sat with Samuel and the children. And Lucy was keeping the babies away for another week, though no illness circulated in the community.

Sarah was the only congregant who had been in bed with any type of illness this week. And the only single female who refused to see a doctor, it seemed.

Seth made a run for the door. Sarah hurried after the little boy, easily catching him before he exited the building.

Amazing recovery.

Perhaps Mother was right. He needed to enlarge his social circle.

Reverend Palmer started off with the announcements—two weddings, one death, one birth. He hadn't heard about the death. Must have been one of Dr. Norris's patients.

During the hymn, he leaned over to his mother. "I'll come to your musical night. When is it?"

"Wednesday the third."

As little Emma yawned, Sarah closed her eyes and breathed in the baby smell. This was her favorite part of being an aunt. She had discovered this over seventeen years ago with Maryanna. For years she had dreamed of holding her own baby. She could be content to live the life Dorcas did, being passed from family to family to care for children, as long as there was an infant at hand. But it would not be an easy life.

Dorcas had little money or anything else to call her own. Even servants received some recompense for their work. The woman she called friend had little love for children and hinted she would be needed back in Billerica by the end of the month. Sarah suspected her departure had more to do with not wanting to be present when Amity delivered. Dorcas had mentioned spending the rest of the month at Thomas Jr.'s home, although she had rarely stayed there.

Coaxing her to stay became a daily conversation. Sarah needed Dorcas as a buffer between her and Tim. There couldn't be another kiss. Dr. Morton had the splints removed, but according to his wife, he continued to complain of pain and asked Tim to stay through the first of August. Thirty-one days, give or take. She could avoid him that long if Dorcas stayed.

The kiss had either been a terrible mistake or a gift. Either way, she wanted to repeat it. Mark's kisses had been warm and comfortable, like reading next to a fire on a winter's night. She touched her lips. Tim's had been more like what a moth must feel like near a flame—the need to draw close regardless of the risk.

A risk she could never take. Not with Tim, not with John, not with any man. The price was more than she could ever pay.

The role of spinster aunt suited her. Little Emma fussed for Lucy, so Sarah reluctantly gave up her charge to go join in the Sunday-afternoon chaos in the parlor. Even surrounded by her nieces and nephews, her empty arms magnified the hole in her heart. She let out a deep sigh. Maryanna snuggled next to her new husband on the couch, reading a book to Stella. They had been married for three months now. There would be another baby next year.

Maybe a grand-nephew could soothe her soul better than twin nieces.

The Misses Garretts both played rather well, and Miss Brooks's voice was unexpectedly sweet. Mother had pulled together a fair amount of people, including a few other bachelors, and the sweltering heat from a week ago had reverted to unseasonably cool weather. Halfway through the evening and it was not as disastrous as he thought it would be. A half hour of mingling over refreshments, another hour of music, and everyone would go home.

As the last notes of the pianoforte faded, Tim started his circuit of the room. Both of Miss Webb's boarders were seventeen and were much more interested in Ichabod.

Dr. Norris and his wife were there, but as Tim approached, the other doctor turned his back. Tim made a quick turn—right into Miss Page and Miss Brooks.

"Oh! Dr. Dawes, your mother is so gracious to start the holiday off this way. I can't wait for the reverend to read *Defense of Fort McHenry*. It is such a stirring poem." She would find it stirring. The first stanza started with her favorite word.

"I am sure it will be. Miss Brooks, I enjoyed your selection." Tim's nod was met with a blush. "If you'll excuse me, I believe my mother needs me." A little white lie. His mother tried to communicate something else with her fan, but he chose to ignore it and joined her anyway.

She frowned at him. "I thought you were going to make an effort."

"I'm mingling with all the guests."

"That is not what I meant, and you know it. Go sit. The second half is about to start." His mother started for the front of the room. Already people were taking their seats, choosing places different from their previous locations. Only a few spots remained. Widow Webb must be giving her boarders advice on how to sit by prospective suitors. There were obvious seats and four bachelors still standing, each empty seat flanked by young women desperately seeking spouses.

A straight-backed chair from the dining room had been moved into a corner. Ichabod made a beeline for it, narrowly beating a young man Tim had not met before tonight, from New Hampshire. Soon the only seat left lay between Miss Brooks and Miss Page.

It was hard to tell who smiled more when he took it—his mother or Miss Page. Miss Brooks wore a funny little smirk as well.

A fiddler and a couple of older men stood. One was missing an arm, curtesy of a musket ball fired by a redcoat at Bunker Hill. The first notes of the "Massachusetts Liberty Song" began to play, and it wasn't long before many in the room joined them in singing:

We led fair Freedom hither, and lo! the desert smiled;
   A paradise of pleasure now opened in the wild:
Your harvest, bold Americans, no power shall snatch away;
   Preserve, preserve, preserve your rights in free America...
Lift up your hearts, my heroes, and swear, with proud disdain,
   The wretch that would ensnare you shall spread his net in vain:
Should Europe empty all her force, we'd meet them in array,
   And shout huzza! Huzza! Huzza! Huzza for brave America!

The words of the late Dr. Warren filled the room. Tim closed his eyes. Images of men lost in the battles of the Second War of Independence filled his mind. Would that his children never need fight. It had been such a useless war. Men died, property was destroyed, and all because of the British blockade. More than fifteen thousand men could be building their lives, homes, and country, but now they lay buried for the cause of Mr. Madison's war.

Only the threat of what his mother would say kept him in his seat. Reverend Palmer stood next and recited Mr. Key's poem, penned after the battle at Fort McHenry. If Tim's thoughts hadn't been so poignant, he might have laughed at Miss Page's quick intake of breath at the first line: "O say can you see..."

Tim had only read the poem once in a well-worn newspaper. The words of the last stanza flowed over him, erasing the melancholy embracing him.

O thus be it ever, when freemen shall stand
   Between their loved homes and the war's desolation.
Blest with vict'ry and peace, may the Heav'n rescued land
   Praise the Power that hath made and preserved us a nation!
Then conquer we must, when our cause it is just,
   And this be our motto: "In God is our trust."
And the star-spangled banner in triumph shall wave
   O'er the land of the free and the home of the brave!

A rousing applause filled the room. Next to him Miss Page predictably commented, "Oh! That was glorious! Oh! Have you ever heard such a recitation?"

Tim bit back a smile lest she think he meant it for her. People swarmed around his mother. She had put on the most triumphant of evenings for the night before Independence Day.

Instead of joining the throng as Miss Page and Miss Brooks had, Tim moved to the back of the room and counted down the moments until he could escape.

Twenty-eight

"INDEPENDENCE DAY SHOULD NOT REMIND one of the crossing of Valley Forge." Dorcas added a log to the fire. "Do you think your sister will still come into town with the weather like this?"

"She has been looking forward to it, so unless one of them is ill, I am sure she will. Don't worry. When Samuel and Lucy arrive with the family, this house will warm up fast. I am glad that Amity could spend the day with her father. I worried that a dozen extra people would upset her."

Dorcas ground coffee beans for her preferred morning beverage. "Did I tell you one of the women I sat with at church has invited me over for the day? They are going to host a little dinner and play a quiet game of cards. I think I shall enjoy my time much better there."

"I hope you don't feel like I am chasing you off." Sarah set two bowls on the table.

"No, nothing like that, but with Amity at her father's, I would feel like a green apple in the bushel. If my sister was coming I might stay, but…"

"But there are far too many little children for your taste?" Sarah hoped her smile conveyed her teasing.

Dorcas poured the beans into her coffee pot, one of her few possessions. "Only a few weeks and you understand me well. It is not so much the older ones as it is the little ones. I just don't think I can be in the same house as month-old twins. I am sure they are adorable, but I ..." The sentence faded off.

"Was facing spinsterhood easier when you were my age, or has it grown more difficult over time?"

"Why would you ask that? You haven't reached your twenty-fifth year. And the doctor looks at you as if he would skip courtship and go straight to marriage if you would allow it. I realize you are in mourning, but you were not really related to Mrs. Wilson."

Sarah shook her head. "Emma would have been my mother-in-law had Mark not died. My own mother died shortly after my fifth birthday, and Lucy raised me, but Emma filled the gap when I needed a mother. But I decided I couldn't marry long before she died. It has nothing to do with mourning."

Dorcas sat at the table and motioned for Sarah to do the same. "Dead men don't come back. It took me years to learn that. I gave more than a quarter of a century to loving a man who could never love me back, caring for my siblings' children as my heart yearned for my own. When he died, another man wanted to court me. He waited for my time of mourning to pass. He wrote me letters as I chose to spend much of it in seclusion at my aunt's home in Brattleboro, Vermont. When I returned, I still could not betray my beloved, and eventually the other man married another. For the first few years, I didn't mind being a spinster so much, but then my parents died. I never learned to write well, nor was I educated beyond the dame school. My sewing skills are mediocre at best. At first, taking care of my sister's and brother's children was the perfect answer to my problem. But as each child grew and never thought of me more than they did the household cook, a new emptiness filled me. I am useful, and my sister's families treat me well enough, but I don't belong to anyone, and no one belongs to me. If I had it all to do over again, I would accept the suit offered me. I may not have loved him as much as my first, but I could have loved him more in time, as good marriages seem to grow in love. Instead, I walk around feeling like there is always something I miss."

For a moment, no words came to Sarah's mind, then understanding filled her. "That is why you don't like to be around young children. It hurts too much to long for something never to be yours."

Dorcas nodded and stood to pour herself some coffee. "That is part of it. I fall in love with them way too easily, but when they are sad, they never want me. I reached the age where love is a liability, a longing for things I will never feel. I don't know what is keeping you from accepting the doctor, but in twenty years, you will wish you had." She set her cup in the dry sink and went upstairs.

The fire popped. A combination of bright light, heat, and ashes, it danced a fine line between life and death. Somewhere in the flames lay the perfect metaphor. Too bad her life was already full of ash, or she might be tempted to hope for the flame.

A festering splinter caused Tim to be late to see the parade. Technically, since he was now a veteran, he could join them, but he'd left his uniform tucked in his trunk. The battle he'd fought, and often lost, had not been against the British but against an unseen foe stalking the lives of soldiers before and after the cannons' blasts. Men missing an arm or a leg passed in front of him. Their lives had been spared, but at a terrible cost. These men would not want him marching by their side.

As he followed the crowd to the green, he wished he had thought to bring his greatcoat. At least they would all be standing close together for the reading of the Declaration of Independence, forty years old today. The Wilson clan stood off to the left of the temporary stage. Tim chose to move to the right. Too late, he realized he stood behind many of the women who boarded at Widow

Webb's. He stepped back so as not to be too easily noticed, but the conversation still reached him.

"Do you think it is proper…in mourning?"

"…Independence Day…betrothed died in war…"

"Oh, what are they doing…they belong at…"

"Girls don't…the fallen women…"

Tim tried to move back farther, but as the mayor started to speak, the crowd moved in and his way was blocked.

"Most of them live near the docks…"

"Unless they live…"

"Oh…Mrs. Wilson never really married…"

"…*if* Samuel Wilson married his wife…"

"Of course, they'd take in Amity…just like the rest of them…"

"…no better than they ought to be…"

Tim turned and made his way out of the throng. He'd rather stand in the cold wind than listen to the gossip. Old gossip, too. The standoff between the old minister, Reverend Woods, and Thomas and Emma Wilson had become a local legend. They'd claimed they were married, and he'd said it wasn't legal. But in the end, actions spoke louder than words, and the Wilsons had lived happily as a couple for more than thirty years. Now they lay side by side in the cemetery, both under the name Wilson. As far as Lucy and Samuel Wilson went, he didn't know the whole story, but he remembered the day the intentions were first read. That was the day he'd decided to marry Sarah and tell her so behind the church.

He tried to focus on the words of the Declaration. But from his new vantage point, he could see the Wilsons clearly. Sarah stood in front with the children who were still shorter than her. She had expertly avoided him for a week now. If the women of Widow Webb's house put as much effort into catching him as Sarah did avoiding him, one of them would have caught him by now.

The wind gusted, and Tim headed home. He would need his greatcoat before the day ended. Firecrackers would be lit, and someone was likely to get hurt.

Pounding on the door woke Sarah. She pulled a quilt off her bed and wrapped it around her shoulders. Dorcas stood at the top of the stairs.

"What on earth?" Dorcas handed her candle to Sarah when the pounding started again. "You answer it."

Sarah hurried to the door. "Who is it?"

"Sarah, it's Amity and me!"

Tim? Here in the middle of the night? She set the candle on the table and opened the door.

Tears coated Amity's face. Tim supported the girl's weight as if standing was more than she could bear.

"D-da-d-d-da-d." Amity fell into Sarah's arms, nearly toppling her.

Sarah looked to Tim for an answer as she tried to pull Amity fully into the house.

"Mr. Burns is dead." Tim slowly mouthed the words.

Dorcas appeared, fully dressed and with a lantern.

"Help me get her into her bed, please."

Dorcas put an arm around Amity and took some of the girl's weight off Sarah.

"I need my bag. I'll be right back." Tim shut the door behind him.

"I'll get her in bed. You'd better get something on over your shift," said Dorcas.

Sarah hadn't realized the quilt had come off. Grabbing it from the floor, she ran up the stairs. The black bombazine would be handy tonight. The thick material wouldn't show if she didn't wear her corset. Sarah reached the bottom of the stairs just as Tim did. "What happened?"

"I'll tell you after we get Amity settled. She hasn't had one of her seizures yet, and I would like to see if we can prevent that. Can you make—"

"Sarah? Help me!"

Sarah beat Tim to the bedroom. With her dress partially off, Amity's arms flailed wildly, striking Dorcas. Sarah hurried to Amity's side and pulled her into a hug. "There, there."

Amity sobbed into the black bombazine. Sarah managed to get her to sit on the bed. "Let's get this dress off you." Sarah finished lifting the dress over Amity's head.

Blood.

"Ti—Dr. Dawes?" Sarah tried to use a calm voice.

Tim came to stand beside her. "It isn't hers. Miss Smith is getting some water so you can help wash her. Does she have something you can change her into?"

Sarah nodded.

Tim left the room. Dorcas came only as far as the doorway with the kettle. A bruise had formed on her cheek. Sarah touched her own cheek as she took the kettle. "How bad?"

"I think I shall retire. I can't help you with her anymore." Dorcas went upstairs without looking back.

Tim leaned against the doorjamb. "Shall I run for Mrs. Morton, or perhaps Mrs. Larkin?"

"No, Amity is calm now. I'll change her. You can leave."

"No, once she is changed, I want to give her a drop of laudanum so she can sleep. I am worried about a seizure. When you are washing her, can you check to be sure the shock of what happened is not starting her labor?"

"Of course."

Amity didn't speak as Sarah cleaned her; rather, she sat like a rag doll, which worried Sarah almost as much as if the girl had fought her. Sarah's ministrations were met with the kick of a little foot but no signs of imminent change of residence for the babe Amity carried.

Sarah tucked a quilt around Amity before gathering the soiled garment and going to the kitchen. Tim sat at the table drinking a cup of Dorcas's rewarmed coffee. Two cups sat nearby. One smelled of peppermint tea, the other stood empty. "I didn't know what you would want. I've already put a drop of laudanum in the tea for Amity. I hesitate to give it to her under normal circumstances, but the longer she can sleep, the better."

Tim followed Sarah as she took the cup to Amity. The girl drank her tea but still didn't speak.

Sarah waited until they were out of the room to ask the question her mind was shouting. "Will Amity ... I mean ... she is just starting. Is that ..." How could she describe what she wanted to know?

"Just a moment." Tim grabbed a straight-backed chair from the kitchen and took it into Amity's room, setting it next to Emma's old rocker. "I don't think she should be alone, and if we talk quietly, we won't disturb her." He motioned for Sarah to sit in the rocker.

Sitting next to Tim in a semidark room, even with a patient, wasn't the best of ideas. Sarah needed a bit of distance. "I need to put her clothes in cold water to get the stain out."

The water bucket stood empty, so Sarah went to the well she shared with the neighbors and drew out a bucketful. There had to be another way to delay being with Tim. She poured herself some of Dorcas's coffee and nearly spit it out. At least it would keep her fully alert. The only way to get Tim to leave would be to talk with him. Sarah had watched him enough over the last month to know he wouldn't leave a patient without knowing they were in capable hands. The sooner she went in, the sooner he would leave.

Sarah was avoiding him. He sat back and watched Amity. He had only seen the aftermath of what had occurred on the dock tonight and heard her father's final words. "I said I'd kill the man who hurt my girl. Keep her safe, Doc."

Witnesses confirmed what Tim had guessed. One of the other dockmen had come out of the pub already in his cups. Mr. Barns and Amity were returning home after the fireworks.

The dockman had started talking about Amity in such a way as to leave little reason to question he had been the one, or perhaps one of a few, who had taken advantage of Amity while her father worked. The man's friends had laughed. A fight might not have occurred as Mr. Barns had only walked faster toward home, but the dockman ran to catch up and pulled Amity from her father's arms and kissed her.

Amity had hit the man first. Then Mr. Barns did what any father would do and knocked the man senseless. One of his drunken friends stepped in. At some point, a knife was introduced, perhaps two. By the time Tim arrived, the first dockworker had died, the second was injured, and Mr. Barns lay in his daughter's lap, struggling to breathe. Amity held one of the knives and was slashing it at anyone who came too near.

The weeks of letting Amity get used to him had paid off. Tim got her to drop the knife and let him touch her father. Little could be done.

Sarah came in and sat in the rocking chair, moving it an inch or two away in the process.

"How is she?"

"I wish I knew."

Sarah turned to him then. "What do you mean?"

"She witnessed a fight between her father and the man I assume took advantage of her. Both men are dead. Since she hardly speaks, it is impossible to know what she is thinking or feeling. Soldiers who saw horrific things in battle would sometimes do what she did tonight—simply stare and not move. If someone could get them talking, sometimes it helped." He didn't tell her about the ones who never talked or ate or slept.

The chair creaked as Sarah changed positions. "What do you need me to do?"

"Stay with her. You can probably lie down on the bed with her. I'll come by first thing or send Mrs. Morton."

"What about a funeral? I don't think she'll survive if many people visit."

"I'll talk to Dr. Morton. I think a small one tomorrow, just at the cemetery, no visitation." Tim consulted his watch. "I mean this afternoon."

Sarah hid a yawn. "I'll show you out, then."

As Tim stopped in the kitchen to gather his bag, Sarah waited near the front door.

There were things he needed to say, but it was late. Maybe too late. And so he left, keeping all the words inside for another day.

Twenty-nine

A week passed. Amity ate and slept, but nothing else. Sarah had never believed in ghosts, but if she did, Amity could be one. The farthest she could coax the girl was to the rocker. There, Amity would rock and hum and rub the child when he kicked her. There had been nightmares but no seizures. Mrs. Morton said they should thank God for a miracle.

It wasn't the only miracle that week. There had been no new notes, even though Tim had been in several times a day. Perhaps the writer had some compassion on Amity as others had quietly dropped by food, clothing, and money.

Dorcas volunteered to clean out the small apartment where the Barns had lived and attended a session of the women's relief circle to discuss Amity's future. In fact, Dorcas was very helpful as long she wasn't asked to sit with Amity. The extent of Dorcas's interaction with her was to stand in the bedroom doorway when Sarah needed to run to the privy.

Someone knocked on the door. When Sarah didn't hear Dorcas's quick step, she went to answer it herself.

"Thomas Jr.? Come in."

Thomas Jr. took off his hat and looked around the parlor. "Good day, Sarah, is Dorcas ready?"

"Ready? For what?"

"She sent a note around on Wednesday saying she was no longer needed and asked if she could come visit." Thomas Jr. rubbed the back of his head just like Samuel did when he was worried.

Footsteps echoed on the stairs. Sarah turned to face Dorcas. "You are leaving? I thought you were happy here. What am I going to do without you?"

Dorcas handed a small crate to her brother-in-law. "I just can't be here when … I was hired to help you with Emma, not this." Dorcas waved her hand in the direction of the room Amity occupied. "I stayed a month, but I cannot honestly ask to be paid when I can't do the work Thomas Jr. hired me for."

"What? You were paid to be here?" Sarah tried to process what was happening.

Thomas Jr. shifted the crate to his other arm. "Samuel and I agreed Dorcas deserved a wage when she came to help you with Emma."

Dorcas disappeared into the kitchen and Thomas Jr. took the crate outside, as well as a chest sitting next to the front door."

"I can't leave my coffee pot. Here, I made this for you. I am not good with goodbyes, especially when I like a person. That is why I didn't tell you sooner. I made fresh bread, and a roast chicken is in the warmer. Someone from the relief circle will be bringing in food every other day. I told them watching Amity doesn't leave you with time to cook." Dorcas handed Sarah a small package wrapped in paper and tied with string.

"But what am I going to do when the doctor comes? I need a chaperone or people will talk!" Sarah wished her voice didn't sound so panicked.

"Perhaps what you really need is to not have a chaperone so you can finally say what needs to be said. I know you don't want to hear it, but this old spinster has seen enough to know if you keep putting him off, you will regret it. The way he looks at you … I wish either of my beaus had looked at me with that much love and concern. You are brave in so many things. Be brave in this, too." Dorcas kissed Sarah on the cheek and was gone.

Sarah watched Thomas Jr.'s coach drive down the road until it was past the church. She ripped open the package. Two new handkerchiefs embroidered and trimmed with lace.

"But I am not brave," she whispered as she dried her eyes.

Sarah smiled, but Tim could tell it was forced and that she had been crying.

He stepped in the door and wished he had permission to take her in his arms and hold her until her smile became real.

"Miss Smith left today, and she won't be back. I don't know if Dr. Morton is up to making these calls, but until there is someone else here..." She shrugged.

"Dr. Morton is not up to making calls. Even a few steps with his cane is still difficult. If you are worried I will take liberties again, I won't. Your avoidance of me is enough to let me know they are not welcomed." Not what he wished to say, but it was what she needed to hear. He would not touch her again, even if she did welcome his touch when they were alone in the house. Not exactly alone, but Amity couldn't chaperone.

Sarah nodded, and new tears glistened but did not fall. "She is sleeping. I think she is experiencing some early signs but is probably days away still." She left him in the bedroom and went out the back door.

"Well, Miss Amity. Will you talk with me today?"

Silence answered him.

Sarah returned a few minutes later.

Tim went to meet her in the hall. "How many hours is she sleeping a day?"

"Sixteen to twenty."

"Is she eating any better?"

"She will eat anything I spoon into her mouth."

"What about you? Are you getting enough sleep?" The darkening under her eyes told him the truth. Would she?

"I get as much as I can. Amity dreams at night, and they often wake her."

"You are still sleeping in here, then?"

Sarah nodded. "She hasn't had a seizure since her father passed, but the dreams upset her so much, I don't dare be too far away."

"Would it help if I hired someone to be here?"

Sarah looked at her hands as she twisted a handkerchief around her fingers. "It is so much money. I can handle it. Some of the women are sending in food, so I don't need to leave her side to cook."

Tim lifted her chin with his finger and for a moment forgot what he wanted to say. "That isn't what I asked. Would it help if I hired someone to be here?"

Sarah tried to look away.

"Shall I take your refusal to answer as a yes?" He dropped his finger, afraid if he didn't step back he would break a promise not a half hour old.

"It would be helpful, but I don't have the money. I didn't know Miss Smith was paid to be here." A tear finally escaped.

Tim resisted the urge to wipe it. "Don't you worry about that. I'll talk with my mother and Mrs. Morton. They may know of someone."

Sarah half turned and used the handkerchief. "Amity will need to like her."

"I don't know if it will matter much at the moment or if we will even be able to tell. I will try to find someone who has experience with the sick, or at least midwifery."

For the first time since he arrived, Sarah willingly looked at him. "Thank you, Tim."

He left before he did anything stupid.

To say Mrs. Duncan had saved Sarah's life was an exaggeration. But not by much. Sarah walked by the church green, which was much browner than it should be this time of year. Sadly, the late snows and the few rainstorms were not enough to end the drought. The calendar in the post-office window told her it had been twenty days since Mr. Barns died. Each day seemed much the same to Sarah, some cooler than the others but the same.

Ahead of her, Miss Brooks, Miss Page, and a young woman Sarah didn't recognize laughed as they read a news sheet. Good news? Samuel had left a copy of the *Merrimack Intelligencer* last week. The front page had urged farmers to try to plant again after the early July frost. Sarah hadn't realized it had gotten so cold.

"Oh, Sarah, have you seen this? It is the most hilarious thing!" Parmelia moved to the side so Sarah could read the column.

"I can't think any woman of quality would answer him," said the unknown woman.

Miss Brooks looked up. "I am sure he will get many inquiries, all highly unsuitable. Even Parmelia's coffee wouldn't meet this standard."

Poor man. He was doomed to be the laughing stock of all who knew him if newspapers nearly four hundred miles away were mocking his advertisement.

"I shall be glad I am too old for his age requirement." Sarah gave them all a smile and walked on.

At Swanson's she found the price of flour had risen sharply. Without her even asking, the clerk apologized.

"With the drought this year and last and the untimely frosts killing most of the crops again and with Canada begging for imports, our supplier raised his price. We are very sorry, miss."

Sarah wondered if the more valid article was the short one she'd seen next to the ad. There may well be those who went hungry this winter. Starvation. The thought made for a ponderous walk home.

Mrs. Morton accompanied Tim for this visit. Not that he doubted Sarah's skills, but she lacked experience. Amity's lack of communication didn't help him in gauging the situation.

Mrs. Duncan showed them into the bedroom, where Amity sat in the chair, rocking and humming and clutching the nine-patch quilt Sarah had completed. "Miss Sarah went to the store. Do you need her?"

Tim looked to Mrs. Morton for confirmation before speaking. "It would be best if she were here. While we are waiting, I'll see if I can get Amity to talk with me." Mrs. Morton sat on the chair next to Amity and started to hum along. Amity seemed oblivious to anyone in the room.

"Amity?" Tim reached out and touched the back of Amity's hand. Still, there was no response. Tim walked out of the room.

Mrs. Duncan stood in the doorway to the kitchen. "Dr. Dawes, would you fancy a bit of cake?"

"No, thank you. I think I will sit in the parlor for a minute. I had one of those early morning calls, and now I want to sleep."

With the window open, the parlor was neither too hot nor too cold—a rarity this month. Tim sat in the largest chair and shut his eyes.

A rustling on the porch woke him. He sat up and straightened his coat. No one came in or knocked. He looked out the window and saw a woman hurrying away from the door. He'd seen that bonnet someplace before…

Sarah straightened her shoulders and prepared herself to open the door. A paper, the same as the others, was stuffed next to the doorknob.

Answer this ad. Oh, but he probably won't want a fallen woman. And you are too old!

A clipping from the July 24th *Worcester Gazette* was attached. It was the same one she read yesterday in the *Baltimore Federal Gazette*.

WANTED

A Young Lady, about 17 or 21 years of age, as a wife. She must be well acquainted with the necessary accomplishments of such; she must understand washing and ironing, baking bread, making good coffee, roasting beef, veal, &c. boning a fowl, broiling a fish, making tarts, plumb-pudding and deserts of all kinds, preserving fruits and pickles, expert with a needle, keeping a clean and snug house; must know reading writing and arithmetick. Never have been in the habit of attending ball-rooms; she must have been taught true and genuine principles of religion, and a member in church of good standing; must not be addicted to making too free use of her tongue, such as repeating any report that is injurious to her neighbor, or using taunting language to any person about her house. A Lady finding herself in possession of the above accomplishments, will please address to Alphonso. It will not be required that she should exercise all these requisites, unless a change in fortune should take place the which time it will be necessary, in order to live with such economy as to prevent a trespass on our friends, whose frowns and caprices we otherwise must endure—what every man of noble mind will despise. At present she shall have a coach and four at her command, servants in abundance, a house furnished in first modern style; shall always be treated with that tender affection which female delicacy requires and nothing shall be wanting that will be necessary to contribute to her happiness.

Sarah crumpled it in her hand and opened the door.

Tim reached for the basket. "Do you need some help?"

She handed him the basket with the flour and sundries and hurried up the stairs, hoping he hadn't seen the note.

Thirty

THE FIRST WEEK OF AUGUST seemed frightfully normal as far as the weather. Sarah donned the gray muslin and vowed to stay near the house. Amity seemed no closer to her lying-in than she had a month ago. Mrs. Morton thought it was because she wasn't very active. Today's goal? Convince Amity to walk past the bedroom doorway.

Sarah failed twice. Each time they reached the door, Amity would scream and thrash about. Mrs. Duncan tried once and got the same response. Amity returned to her bed.

"You should take a minute and get out of the house."

Sarah rubbed the spot on her arm where Amity had hit her. "So should you."

"Nonsense. I have been out already today."

"Hanging the laundry on the line doesn't count."

Mrs. Duncan laughed. "Still, it is more than you have been out. Go take the slop to that pig of yours. Then you won't need to change your dress."

Sarah took the bucket and went out the back door. With all the sheets and things hanging on the lines, she walked a maze to the pig pen. "Hey there, Piggy Peggy. I brought you some food."

The pig snorted.

"Don't worry. I didn't cook this week, so it is all edible. Well, other than the cake someone brought by the other day." *I've been reduced to talking to a pig.* The loneliness that settled around Sarah's heart the day Dorcas left had grown. Knowing the only reason she had been a friend was because she had been paid stung. Perhaps that was why Mrs. Duncan remained simply a kind person who worked in the house.

"Sarah? Sarah?"

"Maryanna?"

Maryanna made her way through a set of sheets. "There you are! Come offer me a drink and let's talk."

"What are you doing in town? Are you alone?" Sarah led the way back to the porch.

"Philip and Papa are with me, but they are off to the blacksmith's. And I just came from Mrs. Morton's." Maryanna sat on the porch step.

Sarah looked her niece up and down. "There are only a few reasons for a woman of your age to visit a midwife. Are you saying?"

"In February."

Sarah hugged Maryanna, aware that at the same time her heart overflowed with love and congratulations, the little hole hiding in the back had just grown deeper. "I can't believe it! Your own baby. What did Lucy say?"

"Mama has been smiling for a week. Although she does find it odd Anna and Little Emma will be practically the same age as her first grandchild. Papa said they could have one younger, too. Mama told him to move into the barn and—"

"Don't tell me he started to talk like a pirate!" Sarah had always thought Lucy and Samuel's banter endearing, even if it was a bit silly.

Maryanna closed one eye. "Are ye sayin' me bonny wench is a'feared of a wee grandbaby?"

Sarah hadn't laughed so hard in weeks. "And I bet he isn't in the barn either."

"Never. Besides, Mama says the girls are still not sleeping through the night, and she needs the extra hands. But that is not the only reason we are in town." Maryanna twisted her skirt, a sure sign she had another secret.

"You may as well tell me. Papa won't have you clean the floors anymore."

"Uncle John is also here. He says if there is one more freeze before October, he is out of here. Uncle Joe sent him a letter from Indiana last week, and he wants to move. They are trying to decide what to do with the farm since Daniel still owns part of it. Uncle Joe isn't coming back, and he said to sell off his part. I think Uncle John will leave either way. His Indian corn is coming in nicely, or at least as good as anyone else's. I think he is looking for an excuse to leave."

"What does Samuel say?" Sarah fanned her skirts.

"He thinks Uncle John and Uncle Joe should just rent the farm in case they decide to come back. I don't think they'll come back to where Remember is buried, not when they are talking again."

Maryanna was probably right. Joe had brought Remember from Boston to meet the family before declaring himself. If only he had married her before the visit, John would not have kissed her, and Joe would not have left. "At least the farm isn't mortgaged, but who wants to rent a farm now?"

Maryanna laid a protective hand over her abdomen. "We do."

"It would be nice to live in your own place after living with Philip's parents, wouldn't it?"

"I'm afraid if we don't move soon, he won't love me anymore. Mother Gardner is always pointing out what I do wrong. She even objects to the way I kiss!"

Sarah's jaw dropped. There was no other response.

"Mama and Papa always kiss and hug in front of us, but in her house, it isn't proper."

Sarah handed Maryanna a handkerchief. "Does she know you are in the family way?"

Maryanna nodded. "I don't want Uncle John to leave, but I want our own place."

They felt the vibrations of the footfalls before they saw the men.

"So, this is where my girls are hiding."

Sarah stepped into Samuel's welcome hug.

"Did Maryanna tell you all the family secrets?" he asked.

"I am not sure."

Maryanna stood next to her husband. "Yes, I did." The couple blushed in unison.

John stepped forward. "Sarah, I've asked Samuel's permission to ask you something, and he said you are a grown woman. Can I get you to walk with me for a minute?"

Sarah sighed, but she could endure one last proposal. "Only as far as the back fence. I am not dressed in the proper black to walk to the green." She led the way, stopping at the stable, empty but for the nanny goat.

"I'm not asking you to marry me. Joe says there are more men than women out there because some of the soldiers didn't go back home, like him. I know you feel you have no prospects around here, and if you want to go, you can come with us as my sister. I plan to leave in the next week or two. So you have a little time to think about it. I promise I'll wait for Miss Amity to have her child if that is what's keeping you here."

It was the longest speech she'd heard out of John without him grumbling since Remember died. "I don't know. I need to think on it."

"You should probably pray too. Let's get back before Samuel thinks I kidnapped you." John didn't wait for her.

Indiana. Miles farther than Ohio. If she left, her tormentor would stop and Tim would never learn the truth about her heart.

Going west was brave. Wasn't it?

"She hasn't eaten all morning?" Tim questioned Mrs. Duncan again before trying to find a pulse.

"She threw her porridge at Miss Sarah. And when she tried again, Amity got her across the nose."

"Is Miss Marden injured?"

"Not bad." Sarah entered the room and sat on the opposite side of the bed. "She has been rocking backward in the chair, but I only counted a couple of contractions in fifteen minutes."

"Should I send for Mrs. Morton?"

Sarah brushed a hair away from the sleeping girl's face. "Not yet. She has hours and hours to go. Don't worry. I'll send one of the Larkin boys long before she is needed."

There was nothing more for Tim to do. The biggest concern with the birth was a seizure, though it had been more than a month since Amity's last one. "Miss Marden, will you see me out?"

Sarah followed Tim out to the buggy.

"Let me see your face." Tim reached for her, but she tilted her face up before he could touch her. Her nose was slightly swollen but not enough that anyone who hadn't studied her face would notice.

"See, I told you. Nothing to worry about." Sarah lowered her face.

"We need to discuss what happens next with Amity. Come walk around the block with me. It is going to be a long night, and you could use a minute of fresh air."

"My hat. I'll be right back."

He hated the black hat she wore to church during mourning and hoped she would wear the bonnet instead. No such luck. Sarah appeared in the church hat with the veil over her face. "If there wasn't a breeze, I would be tempted to forbid you, as your doctor, to wear such a thing. Can you breathe under there?"

"Quite well, Doctor. But if I am seen walking with you, I must wear this."

Tim offered his arm, and she took it. "I discussed the matter with Dr. Morton, and we agree that if Amity remains in this state, the best place for her will be the Friends Asylum in Philadelphia, run by the Quakers."

"I've heard of it. They will at least be kind to her. What of the child?"

"The orphanage we had hoped to place the child with wrote that they are full at present. Most of them are. Already the poor are feeling the effects of the drought. Though there is meat on the tables now as so many farmers are selling ... by winter?" Tim shrugged. "You know this, but the few families who'd expressed interest in Amity's baby have all given the drought as their excuse for backing out."

The wind caught Sarah's veil as they crossed to the green. "More than likely, now that the father is known, they are afraid the child will be a bad seed."

"Mrs. Morton advises we keep the baby here for a week or so as there are a few other women who are expecting, and sometimes when they lose one, they are willing to take another." Tim moved them to the shadier side of the street.

"That's ... that's ... I don't have the word for it!"

"I know, but it happens. If there is no one who will take the child, then we send it to Philadelphia with Amity and hope one of their orphanages will take it."

"How are you going to get her all the way there?"

Tim swallowed. "There is a rumor John Wilson is leaving for Indiana in the next week or two and you are going with him. I thought you could see Amity safely there."

Sarah stopped, pulling her hand from Tim's arm. "Where did you hear this?"

"John told me Sunday after church."

Sarah moved her hands to her hips. "I only learned of the plan three days ago on Monday."

"You mean you're not yet decided?" Tim held his breath, praying she wouldn't leave.

"No, I am not. There are so many things I am loath to leave. But there is no reason I couldn't teach out there."

"John would let you teach?"

"Why wouldn't he?"

"Married women don't teach school."

Sarah stopped again. "I don't know what he told you, but if I go out, it will be as his sister, not his wife."

Relief filled Tim. "I just assumed since he has proposed before..."

Several women came out of the boardinghouse. In unison, Tim and Sarah turned the other direction.

"I should be getting back. Mrs. Duncan will be worried."

"And you have no desire to be caught in a conversation with me."

At Sarah's nod, Tim quickened his pace.

Amity still slept, so Tim didn't linger. He hurried to his buggy, but he wasn't fast enough to avoid Miss Page, Miss Brooks, and their new companion.

"Oh, Doctor! Is everything well? We saw you walking with Miss Marden, and she looked upset."

"Miss Page, Miss Brooks, and Miss ... ?"

"Oh! Do excuse our poor manners, this is Miss Long. She moved in just over a week ago." Miss Page gestured to the newest boarder. "You were walking with Miss Marden, weren't you? Is all well?"

"Yes, I was walking with Miss Marden. As you may know, she has a patient of mine living with her. I needed to discuss a matter privately. If you wish to be of help, you can pray for Miss Amity. Good day, ladies." *Insufferable gossips!*

Near dawn, Amity sat up and began yelling.

Sarah ran across the street and woke the Larkins. On her way back, she saw the paper on the porch.

You did not try hard enough.

I see it in his eyes when he says your name.

At least she knew the writer was a liar.

Thirty-one

The sun was hanging low in the west when a knock came at the door. Mrs. Morton was conversing with a boy of about six or seven years. When they were finished, she asked him to wait. "Sarah, that was Mrs. Oakes's son. And Widow Potting is already with Tilly Smyth. This is Mrs. Oakes's fourth, and her last one came in just a couple hours, so I should be back. I'll send Dr. Dawes over." Mrs. Morton left muttering something about the full moon the night before.

Sarah tried to coax Amity into walking again or at least sitting in the rocking chair. But Amity just lay on her side and moaned.

Mrs. Duncan wrung her hands, her calm exterior with Mrs. Morton having dissolved. "She can't birth a baby that way. She needs to be in a birthing chair, and Mrs. Morton took hers." Not that it mattered. Amity wouldn't open her eyes to even look at a chair.

"My sister Lucy didn't like the birthing chair and delivered most of her babies on her side." Sarah spoke before she thought and received a disdainful glare. "However, I think Emma's old birthing chair is in the attic." She ran to look before she could upset Mrs. Duncan again.

The narrow space didn't much qualify for an attic, but in the ten years it had been in use, it had managed to fill up. Pushing aside a couple of crates, Sarah managed to pull the chair out of its spot. She stopped in the kitchen to wipe the dust and a cobweb off, the spider no longer in residence.

"Here we are. Look, Amity, Emma's chair."

"Emmm." Amity looked around for the first time in hours.

"This is the chair Emma sat in when she had a baby."

"Emmm." Amity raised up on one arm, then collapsed back in bed.

Sarah wondered if talking about Emma would help. "Emma used to walk when she felt like you do. Would you like to walk like Emma?"

This time Amity tried to sit up. Sarah hurried to her side and helped her.

"Emmm."

"Yes, sweetheart, we are going to walk like Emma." Sarah helped her to stand.

Sarah found that as long as she talked about Emma, Amity would walk. She even walked into the kitchen. Sarah thought Amity might be looking for Emma, but if it got the baby to move, it would be worth it. They paused every few minutes to let a contraction pass. A knock sounded at the door.

Mrs. Duncan answered it.

"How did you get Amity out of bed?" Tim asked, his face registering surprise.

"Emmm."

Sarah supported Amity through another contraction as she answered. "I told her Emma walked when she had her babies." Sarah led Amity back to the kitchen and waited for another contraction to pass.

"Two minutes. I'd say she is closer than Mrs. Morton thought."

"Then, Doctor, I suggest you get ready. There is clean water to wash in the kitchen."

"Wash?"

"Emma would have insisted on it."

"Emmm."

Tim washed up, then went and set his bag next to the things Sarah had prepared.

"Don't get them out unless you must." Sarah stared at his bag and hoped he knew she meant the forceps. He nodded.

"Amity, sit in Emma's chair. I want to see if I can see the baby yet." Sarah positioned Amity in the three-legged chair. "Mrs. Duncan, will you please support her back?"

The housekeeper paled. "Not me! I'll go see if the water is boiling."

"Doctor, can you support her back?"

"How?"

"Just do what I am doing now." Sarah traded places with Tim, then knelt in front of Amity.

After she finished, she washed her hands in water Mrs. Duncan brought in. "Amity, do you want to walk like Emma or sit like Emma?"

Amity leaned back. "Emmm."

Tim raised his brows. "So, how long do I hold her up like this?"

"See if she can take her own weight. I can feel the baby's head, but she isn't quite ready yet."

Over the course of the next hour, Amity walked, rocked, sat in the birthing chair, and then pointed to the bed. Mrs. Duncan brought in coffee for both Tim and Sarah. Tim found himself looking at the clock, hoping Mrs. Morton would return soon.

Sarah rubbed Amity's back and spoke soothing words. The contractions brought louder and louder moaning. One brought on a scream.

"Tim!" Sarah moved to hold the shaking, thrashing girl.

Like her other seizures, this one ended in a faint, followed by a contraction that didn't wake her up.

"Can a woman give birth if she isn't conscious?" Tim wondered aloud.

"I was going to ask you that, Doctor." Sarah held Amity as another contraction caused her back to arch. "Help me get her on her side, like Lucy."

Twenty minutes later, Tim had his answer. It was possible to deliver a baby and not be conscious. Mrs. Duncan took the baby from Sarah and cleaned her while Sarah waited for the afterbirth. Tim cleaned his instruments, then put them back in the bag.

An involuntary scream came from Amity, and the convulsions started again. Sarah tried to keep her from falling off the bed. Tim dove from the other side to help. Finally, Amity stopped shaking.

Sarah pointed to Amity's mouth. "Blood."

"She bit her tongue." Tim wiped the blood away. "She should stay in the faint for a while. I am going to go check on the baby."

Mrs. Duncan sat in the corner of the kitchen, staring at the baby on the table. "That baby isn't right, Doctor. The best thing to do is to bury it in the garden."

Tim looked at her in astonishment. "Why do you say that, Mrs. Duncan?"

"She has the mark of the devil on her back."

Tim picked up the baby girl and turned her over to see a faint purplish stain covering half of her back.

"Don't make me look at it!"

"Perhaps, Mrs. Duncan, it would be best if you went to bed. I'll take care of the baby." Tim examined the little girl. Other than the unusual mark, nothing seemed amiss. He finished washing her and wrapped her in the cloth Sarah had set out. "Shall we go meet your mother?"

Sarah sat unmoving at the side of the bed.

"Sarah?"

"I think something is wrong with her breathing."

"Can you hold this little one?" Tim handed Sarah the baby and put his ear to Amity's chest. He closed his eyes and listened. He knew the sound all too well.

When he opened his eyes, he looked to Sarah. Her eyes were filled with tears. She knew it too.

As dawn crept over the horizon, Amity slipped away, and her daughter, wrapped in the nine-patch quilt and in Sarah's arms, took her first meal of goat's milk sucked from a cloth.

Thirty-two

"WHAT IS *THAT* STILL DOING here?" Mrs. Duncan's shrill voice woke Sarah.

"Dr. Dawes went for the undertaker. I suppose he hasn't come yet." Sarah sat up in the rocker and rubbed the sleep out of her eyes.

"Not her, the child. It has the devil's mark!"

The baby, sleeping in a basket at Sarah's feet, woke and began to cry. Sarah picked her up. "Mrs. Duncan, this baby has no such thing."

"I saw it with me own eyes. She is marked for the sin of the awful man." Mrs. Duncan backed out of the room.

"You mark my word. No child born that way can come to any good. That is why I told the doctor to bury it in the garden."

The baby in question cried harder. Sarah moved to the table, where she had prepared dry clothes. "Mrs. Duncan, it is nothing but an angel's kiss. It isn't as large as some I've seen."

"But those children be born of godly parents. The man who hurt poor Amity has given us the devil's own child. The baby be no good because she was forced on the mother. That kind always turns out bad."

Sarah's mind cleared. Mrs. Duncan wasn't as concerned about the baby's mark as she was her parentage. Sarah thought of Lucy.

What if some backward-thinking woman had buried her in a garden because the man who'd sired her was a murderer? Her temper flared. "Seeing this child's mother was as close to being an angel as any of us will ever meet, I think you are premature to doom her because her father was among the vilest men we know. How can you do that to a baby?" Sarah lifted the newly clothed infant to her shoulder.

Mrs. Duncan stepped farther away and turned her face. "I won't stay in the house with that devil child! Either she leaves or I do."

"I will not turn a baby out, so I suggest you pack your bags."

"I need me wages. The doctor hasn't paid me this week."

Sarah didn't believe it. Tim had been paying a week in advance each Monday morning. "Please gather your belongings."

"I get two dollars a week, and I'll need a reference."

If Sarah wasn't holding the baby, she might have walked the woman to the door and tossed her out. "Dr. Dawes hired you, so you will need to see him about a reference. As for the money, I watched him pay you a dollar each Monday since you have been here. I will not pay you a penny more."

"Then I'll get my things." Mrs. Duncan stomped upstairs.

After Emma died, Sarah had moved the jar they kept their money in from the kitchen shelf to the chest in Emma's room. Sarah put the baby down on the bed and retrieved the key from Emma's dressing table. Sarah waited for Mrs. Duncan at the bottom of the stairs.

The corner of a book stuck out from Mrs. Duncan's bundle. Sarah pulled it out. "You told me you don't read. Will you explain what you are doing with my copy of the second volume of *Pride and Prejudice*?"

"It's mine!"

"Let me see what else you're taking."

"Only my own things."

Mrs. Morton and Tim entered the house without knocking.

Sarah acknowledged them with a nod. "If it is yours, why is my name inside the cover?"

"I got it mixed up. Mine must still be in me room." Mrs. Duncan tried to step around Sarah.

Sarah stood her ground. "Mrs. Duncan, I insist you let me see the rest of what you are taking."

"You got no right." Mrs. Duncan tried to push past Sarah and succeeded only to turn the corner and run into Mrs. Morton and Tim.

"Why are you leaving, Mrs. Duncan?" asked Tim.

"Dr. Dawes, Mrs. Morton, I didn't know you was here."

Once again Sarah attempted to block the ornery housekeeper. "Mrs. Duncan has taken exception to being in the house with Amity's child. We were just having a discussion over some of her belongings."

"So I heard. Mrs. Duncan, I believe you were protesting Miss Marden's right to check your bundle. However, since I employed you, I do have that right. Set the bundle on the kitchen table, and let's make sure no other books with Miss Marden's name have been inadvertently packed among your things." Tim herded the woman into the kitchen.

The baby began to fuss again. Mrs. Morton left in the direction of the sound.

Tim picked up a handkerchief edged in fine lace. "*S. M.* Mrs. Duncan, I do not believe this is yours." He handed it to Sarah. "Do you recognize anything else?"

Sarah claimed a doily, a lace fichu, and another volume. When she reached for a pair of embroidered silk stockings, she felt her cheeks warm and tried to hide them behind her book. "Miss Marden, might I suggest you go check your room for anything else you might be missing so we can ascertain if we need to check Mrs. Duncan's person as well?"

Sarah hurried up the stairs. Mrs. Duncan was not a good thief. Sarah's drawers stood open. Papers littered the floor—the notes tucked in the first volume. Thank goodness the woman was illiterate! Inside a carved box, the two letters Mark had sent before he died remained in their ribbon, as did the letters her father had written her mother so long ago. The yards of ribbon Tim had given her after his sister's wedding lay in a tangled web. But the leather pouch that had once been filled with Spanish coins was gone, as was the broach Mark had given her the day he'd proposed. She had been foolish to leave her mother's box unlocked.

Sarah couldn't see anything else missing, but tears were starting to cloud her vision.

Mrs. Duncan kept shifting her weight.

"You are either hoping Miss Marden will miss something you took, or you are late to an appointment. If you have something else about your person, I suggest you place it on the table before she comes down and I find it necessary to send for the sheriff." Tim crossed his arms and waited.

From someplace inside the folds of her dress. Mrs. Duncan produced a leather pouch, a broach, and a cameo.

Hearing light footfalls on the stairs, Tim turned to allow Sarah into the room. She immediately picked up the cameo. "How could you paw through my things and take them?" Sarah examined the broach, then looked inside the bag.

Tim heard coins clink. "You may want to count that."

"I didn't have time to take any out. It be all there." Mrs. Duncan crossed her arms.

Sarah studied the interior of the pouch again. "I don't need to count it. The contents have not been rearranged."

Mrs. Duncan gathered the clothing she'd come with and added an apron from a hook near the door. "What about me pay?"

"I paid you on Monday in advance for this week. You are fortunate I don't ask for it back. I advise you leave before I change my mind."

The woman slunk out the back door.

Tim moved to the window. "Should I watch to see she doesn't take your eggs?"

Sarah shook her head.

"More goat's milk? This tiny one is hungry." The baby let out a belch twice her size, spitting up a bit on Mrs. Morton's shoulder.

"No, but I need to go milk the nanny anyway. Let me go put these away." Sarah lifted her full hands.

"It may have been a few years, but I can do it." More than a few, more like a score, but Tim was sure he'd remember how.

"Doctor, let me. Nanny tends to kick," Sarah said as she held her treasures close.

The baby yawned and snuggled into Mrs. Morton. "No rush on her account, but we do need to—"

A knock interrupted the conversation. "Sar—Miss Marden, go put those away. I'll answer the door."

Mrs. Larkin and Mrs. Palmer stood on the doorstep. He ushered them in. Mrs. Palmer scrutinized him. "Doctor, we didn't think you would still be here. You look like you had a very long night."

Tim nodded, unable to come up with a more coherent answer. Sarah and Mrs. Morton soon joined them in the parlor.

Mrs. Larkin took off her bonnet. "You all look like you could use some sleep. I heard there were three babies born last night."

"Four, if you count the Oakes baby, but he never took a breath. Mrs. Oakes is having a hard go of it, but her mother is there. Widow Potting presided at two deliveries. Tillie Smyth had a boy, and Mrs. Girl had a Pollard. I mean Mrs. Pollard had a girl." Mrs. Morton yawned.

Mrs. Palmer produced an apron Tim hadn't noticed before. "We came over to prepare Miss Amity. Why don't you all try to sleep. We can watch the baby or get Mrs. Duncan to."

Sarah tried to hide a yawn. "Mrs. Duncan has left our employ."

The visitors exchanged glances.

Sarah didn't elaborate, and Tim saw no need. "I think Mrs. Larkin has had a very good idea. I am going to go home and get some sleep before someone needs me again. Mrs. Morton, would you like a ride?"

"Definitely. Sarah, you get some sleep too. I'll look for a wet nurse, but the goat's milk will suffice until we get one." Mrs. Morton handed the baby to Mrs. Palmer.

"Nanny! I forgot I need to milk her."

Mrs. Larkin stopped Sarah with a hand on her arm. "Noah can come do it. You get some sleep."

"There isn't a cradle, but I made a bed out of a baske—" Sarah couldn't hide her yawn.

"That's it. All of you go get some sleep." Mrs. Larkin chased everyone out of the room. Tim mounted the buggy before he realized he hadn't bid any of them good day.

Thirty-three

AN UNHEARD-OF AUGUST FROST COVERED the ground the four days after Amity's funeral. Sarah would have put off her chores if it hadn't been for the baby she had dubbed Rose for the shape of the mark on her back. It may have been her imagination, but Rose seemed to cry more than her nieces and nephews did. Sarah shivered in the old gray work dress. Rose had spit up twice on the black bombazine, and it waited to be washed.

Sarah set the milk and eggs on the table next to the crock Mrs. Larkin had left. Maybe she would have an idea on how to calm the baby. She checked to make sure Rose was still sleeping before dashing across the street.

Another paper fluttered to the ground as she opened the front door.

Enjoy playing the mother while you can.

The school board is meeting tomorrow.

Sarah stepped back inside.

Tim yawned, interrupting Dr. Morton.

"And there you have the evidence that I am right. I see too many patients to handle these days, and Dr. Norris has the same problem. I've been back in the office for half days for the past week, and you are still run off your feet."

"But if many of the farmers move west, like John Wilson, your patient load will be reduced."

"If that happens, you may want to consider doing the same thing. There would be plenty of call for a doctor out in the wilds of Indiana."

He couldn't go to Indiana if Sarah went there. Or could he? Part of him was willing to follow her twice that far if she would just give him a chance. Following that line of thought was not helpful. "I get the feeling Dr. Norris rather I not join the two of you."

"He thinks I can come back like before I fell. But the pain and the late nights …" Dr. Morton rubbed his leg. "I just can't do it anymore. If I had been up all night with house calls, my wife would put me in bed and spike my tea with laudanum again."

"I think she is just as busy." Tim had helped her with a breech birth late last night. Or was it early this morning?

"That she is. But you are not going to change the conversation that easily. Think about it, and give me an answer by the end of the month. If you say no, I need to start looking for someone else."

"I'll be honest. I don't have any other offers, but I would like to take the next two weeks to think about it."

Dr. Morton leaned back in his chair and gave Tim a fatherly smile. "I probably shouldn't ask this, but does part of your answer lie in the hands of a certain school teacher taking in orphans this summer?"

Tim stopped at the doorway before answering. "I think it may."

He ignored the laughter coming from Dr. Morton as he left the building.

Sarah's head nodded in rhythm to the breathing of the infant. Try as she might, she was no replacement for the child's dead mother. Neither was the goat's milk. She couldn't remember any of her nieces or nephews fussing so much, but then, she had always been able to pass the child off to Lucy when the time arose.

The baby needed a wet nurse. Why hadn't Tim or Mrs. Morton been able to find someone willing? Even with Mrs. Duncan's wild stories, some woman must want the pay. A goat and a spinster were no replacement, although Mrs. Morton maintained the baby could suckle directly from the goat "quite satisfactorily." Orphan homes in London did it all the time. The nanny goats had been trained to stand over the cradles.

Sarah tried to picture her goat standing over Rose's basket. Every time she did, the goat ended up eating a prized quilt or running around the house, knocking something over. The alternative of taking Rose to the shed was not as chaotic in her mind's eye. But if Nanny kicked while Rose ate … Sarah shuddered. No goat was going to kick Amity's baby.

Whenever Rose slept sweetly, like now, Sarah relished the feeling of a tiny one in her arms. It had been years since she had let herself dream of motherhood.

The baby squirmed.

Sarah tensed, waiting for the cry she knew would come. Instead, a loud burp filled the room, and Rose snuggled back into her shoulder. Sarah knew she should lay the child down in the basket and try to get some sleep too. They had been up hours before the cock crowed, and the church bell had already announced the noon hour. Her stomach grumbled. Breakfast consisted of a wedge of cheese and stale bread as there wasn't much else prepared in the house, and there wasn't much of that. Some mother she would make.

Sarah stood, intent on finding some food for herself, when a knock interrupted her. Whether it was the knock or her sudden jump, the result was the same. The baby began to wail.

There would be no chance her caller would leave with the racket. Sarah opened the door. When had it started raining?

Tim looked as haggard as she felt. Without a word, she opened the door wider and let him in. She hoped the letter writer was avoiding the downpour and staying inside.

"I come bearing a gift." Tim handed her a pewter baby bottle. "It was mine when I was little. Mother says I was one of those babies who could never eat enough."

Sarah took it in her free hand and shook it, hoping to distract Rose. "Look what Dr. Dawes brought you. Ever so much nicer than using a rag."

Rose stopped crying. For a moment.

"Shall we try it?"

Sarah swayed with the baby. "Anything to get her to calm down."

Tim took the bottle out to Nanny and filled it. He brought it back with a scrap of cloth. "If you think the end is too hard on her mouth, you can cover it with a cloth. But it is pretty smooth."

Sarah sat in the parlor rocking chair. Greedy sucking sounds filled the room. "You may have saved my life. Rose and I were just discussing what a terrible mother I am. She can't rest, and I have no food in the house. It is a good thing this is only temporary."

"I think you would make a wonderful mother. You aren't old enough to be on the shelf yet."

"I can't ever be a mother."

Tim watched as tears collected in Sarah's eyes.

"You could if you would give me a chance. I know you are still in mourn—"

"Stop! Just stop!" The tears poured unchecked down Sarah's face. "I can't have children, so there is no reason to give you or anyone else a chance!"

Tim scooted to the edge of the chair. "What do you mean you can't have children?"

"When I lost—" Sarah spoke through her sobs, only some of the words intelligible. "So much blood... Emma said... I shouldn't ..." Sarah gasped, her eyes wide.

For a second Tim thought she would bolt and drop Rose. He knelt in front of them to prevent either from happening and covered the hand holding the bottle with his.

Sarah took several deep breaths. "I guess I'd rather you heard the truth from me and not from whatever happens at the school-board meeting."

Tim took a handkerchief from his pocket and wiped the tears from Sarah's face. "What is going to happen at the meeting?"

"She... someone... is going to tell... that I carried Mark's child. We were supposed to get married, then the war came and... ten dollars a month. Mark said he would only be gone for a while. Four months passed and... he died. All I got was a letter with his forty dollars." Tim raced to put the pieces together from her half-finished sentences. Mark wasn't the only one to join up for the ten-dollar monthly pay offered by the militia. The long goodbyes of a couple already engaged could naturally lead to a child.

Tim caught the new tears as he absorbed what she said. How could the girl of his dreams have carried another man's child? Pain filled him, but he didn't move, couldn't move.

"He was going to come home and marry me. But I lost him and the baby on the same day. Emma promised no one would ever know... so sick for so long. I wanted to die with them. But I didn't. I kept the forty dollars... in case." Sarah moved the baby to her shoulder and blew her nose in her own handkerchief. "The irony—he sent me just enough to pay the magistrate. I hid it for so long, and now everyone will know. I can't teach anymore. John will be furious, and I won't be able to go to Indiana and start over. If I am fortunate, Samuel and Lucy will take me in and I'll live the rest of my life pining for the two men I loved and can never have."

Rose burped, and milk dribbled onto Sarah's shoulder. "I'm sorry, Tim, I shouldn't ... I should have never spoken ... but now you know the truth." For the first time in days, she looked him in the eye. "I need you to know the truth. Whatever is said at the meeting will be worse. And by the time the gossips are done, I'll be lucky if Samuel and Lucy will talk to me. But at least someone will finally take Rose since I am unfit. I hope they will love her."

Tim stood. The only thing he could concentrate on was the sour milk running down the sleeve of Sarah's dress. "Let me hold her while you go clean up." He reached for Rose, but Sarah refused to give him the baby.

"You need to go before there is another note and your reputation is ruined because of me."

"Note?"

"All summer someone has been sending me notes, telling me to stay away from you. If she is watching now ... us, alone in the house, you kneeling in front of me. Then I don't know that she will wait. This morning I made up my mind to tell the truth to the people who would most be hurt—you, Samuel and Lucy, and maybe John. Then I'll pay the fine. I just want a chance to talk to Lucy before..." Sarah sniffled, "before everyone knows."

The notes had been about him? Sarah's initial revelation was more than he could process, but someone who would use her past to manipulate her? That he could try to stop. His last bit of goodwill. "Do you have these notes?"

Sarah nodded.

"May I see them?"

Sarah crossed the room and reached for a book with several papers stuffed in it. Rose squirmed, and Sarah brought her hand back to support the child. "They are all in there other than the first one, which I burned."

Thirty-four

SARAH LEFT TIM IN THE parlor and went to put Rose down. Maybe she would sleep for a couple hours. She used the cloth from the wash basin to clean her dress.

The pain she expected to come from confessing to Tim hadn't come. Yes, he was lost to her, but he had never been hers, really. Now he knew why, and something inside Sarah felt less heavy. She had been brave. She would rent a buggy and go out to Lucy's tonight. Teaching wasn't the only job in town. The bindery hired several women.

She washed her face and returned to the parlor, where Tim sat staring at her notes.

"You see? You need to leave."

He pulled one from the stack. "Is this why you tried to get me to take someone to the concert in June?"

"Yes."

"And this one with the newspaper clipping—did you find it in the door when you came home from Swanson's near the end of July?"

"How did you know?"

Tim shook his head. "Just a hunch."

"Before you go, I need to say something else. I'm sorry I didn't tell you earlier. If I had, you would have never shown any interest in me, and we would have never have k—" The word wouldn't come out, so Sarah pointed to the stairway. "I've been so afraid all summer that for years someone would find out or tell about my past. But now that I've been honest with you, I don't hurt so much. As soon as Rose wakes up, I am going to rent a buggy and go tell Lucy."

"The truth shall set you free?"

"Something like that. I know how you feel about the camp followers, and I don't blame you for thinking the same of me. I just hope someday you can forgive me."

"Sarah, I—" Tim took a step toward her.

Sarah held a hand up. Her bravery only went so far. "Please don't. Just say goodbye." Stupid tears were forming again.

"Don't rent a buggy. I'll be back at four. I need to go see the twins today and weigh them. Mrs. Morton is still with someone, and we are a week overdue."

"You don't need to do that. If the person who writes these notes sees..." Sarah waved her hand helplessly.

"You are still my friend. If nothing else, tonight may be quite upsetting. I wouldn't want you driving the buggy back when you are upset or with Rose upset."

Sarah bit her lip. She shouldn't accept, but it would be safer. "I'll accept your offer for Rose's sake."

"I'll see you at four." Tim put on his hat and left.

Sarah shut the door and went to join Rose for a nap.

No wonder Sarah has been in mourning for four years. He should have guessed. Maybe because they had been friends, or maybe because of all the good he had seen, his heart kept telling his mind the same thing. *Jesus didn't condemn the woman taken in adultery.*

He turned onto High Street. Rose and Sarah were not the only ones who could use some sleep. Several women stood outside the milliners. Tim slowed his horse and parked the carriage. Letters in hand, he hurried down the walkway.

"Miss Page, may I speak with you?"

"Oh, Doctor, how good of you to stop."

The rest of the women stayed near the window. It didn't afford him much privacy, so he kept his voice low. "Why did you send these to Miss Marden? Did you really think I would want to court a woman capable of blackmail?" Tim held the notes in front of her.

"Oh...I...oh..." Miss Page fanned herself. "What are you talking about? I don't understand."

The women were inching closer, so Tim moderated his tone. "I don't understand how you could have written 'Forty dollars is a lot of money. Stay away from Dr. Dawes,' and left it on Miss Marden's doorstep."

"Oh! I would never do such a thing!"

"Don't play the fool. I recognize your hat. I saw a woman with that hat drop off this note. I sat behind you in church when you gossiped with your friends—again, in this hat. Just what do you hope to accomplish at the school-board meeting?"

"Oh, this hat isn't mine. I borrowed it from Miss Brooks."

"Do you often borrow Miss Brooks headwear?"

Miss Page touched the brim. "No, this is the first time I've ever had the occasion. It went so well with my new dress. But she was wearing it in church."

"Miss Brooks?" Tim called to the group of women. "Could you help us sort out a conundrum?"

Miss Brooks left the other women and came to Miss Page's side. She paled when her eyes locked on the papers Tim held. "Where did you get those?"

"You are familiar with the contents?"

The color came back to Miss Brook's face. She lifted her chin and looked him in the eye. "So, you finally know your precious Miss Marden is not a bit better than she ought to be. I was going to wait to show my evidence at the meeting, but that may not be necessary."

Tim gritted his teeth. "What evidence?"

Miss Brooks opened her reticule and pulled out a folded paper. "A letter in her own hand and signed by her, addressed to a Private Mark Wilson. Shall I read it to you? It will be read tomorrow evening. Miss Marden declares her love and confesses they are in the family way. So cute the way she did it. She begs him to come home with all haste so they can stand before Reverend Woods as one."

The other ladies had joined them, making no secret of listening in.

"I believe that is enough, Miss Brooks." Tim reached for the letter, but she tucked it into the bodice of her dress.

"That's not the best part. It took me forever to find out what she meant when she told him they should not have spoken their vows like his parents. Did you know Mrs. Emma Wilson never truly married? Yet she is buried in the graveyard next to her *supposed* husband. Then there is Sarah's half sister. That marriage is also cloaked in scandal. You should thank me, Doctor, for saving you from an importune match. The only thing I can't figure out is where her baby went."

"Saving me? Just how should I thank you? Should I fall at your feet and beg for your hand?"

"Me? I think not. I did it for Parmelia. No one sees her for what she is worth."

Miss Page clawed at the hat, untying the ribbons. "Oh, Clara! How could you! I couldn't court Dr. Dawes now, and Miss Marden was always nice to me."

"We were never going to get better teaching positions with her there. You said—" Miss Brooks couldn't complete her sentence as Miss Page flung the hat in her face.

"Oh! I never want to see you again, Clara. I hope Widow Webb tosses you out."

"Why would she do that? *I* always pay my rent on time..." Miss Brooks turned and walked back past the milliners.

Miss Page gasped and turned to Tim. "Sarah must hate me if you thought I could..."

"Miss Page, it was not until I saw the hat that I suspected you, although I did assume it was one of the widow's boarders."

"Oh, poor Sarah. Will you tell her I'll sit with her at the meeting? I don't know what I can say to help her, but I will try."

"I will tell her when I see her. My apologies for assuming you were responsible."

Miss Page shook her head. "I gave you reason to doubt my character, or you would not have. Miss Long pointed out to me that I have been far too forward."

"Still, I hope you forgive my trespass. Good day, Miss Page, Miss Long."

Miss Brooks. Tim shook his head. Never in a century would he have thought of her. For the most part, she was so quiet and rather mousey. There was the one vicious remark about Amity ... had it been Miss Brooks he had overheard gossiping?

Wanting solitude, he took the road west, past the farms, mentally replaying his conversation with Sarah. *Jesus didn't condemn the woman taken in adultery. Neither should I.*

A line of their conversation came to mind. "I'll live the rest of my life pining for the two men I loved and can never have."

Who was the second?

Thirty-five

ROSE SLEPT PEACEFULLY IN HER basket. Sarah carried it out to the front porch as Tim drove up. She had no idea what to say, so she just handed him the basket and went back for the bottle. Tim helped her into the buggy, but he didn't speak either.

They were more than halfway to Lucy's before she broke the silence. "Thank you for the bottle. Rose slept for three hours. I think she wasn't getting enough the other way."

"My mother thought of it. If Rose likes it, it is hers."

"I am going to miss her."

Tim nodded his head.

They didn't speak again until they reached the house and then not to each other.

Tim made short work of checking Anna and Emma. "Eight pounds, and seven pounds twelve ounces. Mrs. Morton will be very pleased. She had intended to come, but she was needed elsewhere."

"Can you stay for supper? If not, Samuel can return Sarah to town."

"I'd be pleased to. I'll just go take care of my horse." Tim left the house with Benjamin trailing after him.

"Sarah, why don't you bring the baby into my room. I need to feed these two while the girls get supper on."

Lucy scooped both babies into a hammock she'd made of her apron. "I don't think I can do this much longer."

"Do they still sleep all tangled up?"

Lucy changed Anna's clothes. "They seem to prefer it. And thank heavens they will eat at the same time."

Sarah wondered how to begin. Tim had been easier because she hadn't planned on saying anything. She waited until Lucy had the girls settled.

"I've needed to say something for a very long time, and I would appreciate it if you would let me get it out."

The tale Lucy heard was much more coherent than the version Tim had.

"So, do you think I need to confess to Samuel and John? By tomorrow night, the whole town will know some version of it."

Lucy moved one baby to her shoulder and patted her back. "Do you feel you should?"

"I do, but getting them alone is so much harder." Sarah lifted Rose from her basket.

"If it makes it any easier, Samuel and I suspected as much."

"Why didn't you say anything?"

"You were nineteen, a woman grown. There was nothing to say unless you said it first. We wondered if we had been wrong to coerce you into postponing your wedding. But like everything we see in hindsight, we couldn't change things. Do not give up hope of having a child of your own. Besides the three you know I lost, there were two more, very early on, that I could not carry."

Sarah nodded. "Still, I cannot have children if I can never marry."

Lucy placed her sleeping daughter in the cradle. "I think I hear everyone gathering. Come to supper."

"One moment. Rose is sopping."

"Welcome to my world. I don't think I've had more than three bites of warm food at any meal in almost eighteen years, maybe longer. But I'll ask Samuel to wait on prayers."

Tim checked the horseshoes for the third time. With the Wilson's ten children always underfoot, it seemed he might never get the opportunity to speak with Samuel.

"Either you have a grave problem with your horse, or you want to speak to me."

Tim dropped the hoof he was pretending to inspect and looked around to make sure they were alone before he spoke. "I would like a private moment if you have the time."

"Come into my woodworking shed. The children know if the door is closed and I am in there, they are not to come in."

The word *shed* was inadequate to describe the building they entered. Sawdust, pine resin, and the lingering odor of stain filled the air. A set of half-finished cabinets took up a portion of the room, and a cradle sat on the table. Tim ran his hand down the smooth surface.

Rose needed something like this. "I heard you were the best furniture maker in the area, but I've never seen your work in progress. I must say I agree."

"I'm building this for Maryanna. My first of several, I suspect. Did you want to commission something, or is there another reason you had for making your horse nervous?" Samuel leaned against the table.

Tim shifted his weight. "I'm not sure how to approach this, as some of what I need to say involves a story I have no right to share."

"Then share what you can."

"For the last several months a Miss Brooks has been blackmailing Sarah. I haven't told Sarah the identity of her tormentor as I only discovered this today after Sarah revealed more than she probably intended to tell me."

"I take it that is the part you can't share."

"Yes, sir. Anyway, this morning Dr. Morton offered me a partnership again. Part of my answer to him revolves around

Sarah. Even though she is in mourning, I had planned to ask her if I could court her. But then—" Tim traced the carving at the foot of the cradle as he searched for the right words. "My heart and my mind are unsettled. But I wanted your blessing if I should try to seek her hand."

"When I start a carving, I need to know what I want it to look like in the end. For Maryanna's cradle, I know I want wild strawberries. If I had just picked up my tools and started using them without a plan, I'd end up with something like this." Samuel picked up a randomly gouged board. "Benjamin is trying to learn the tools, so his carving isn't planned. I think you need to decide on a plan for a relationship with Sarah. I suspect she won't be much easier to convince than her sister. Had I not known what my heart wanted and continued to follow it, I don't think I would be building this cradle today." Samuel wiped the cradle with a rag and started to laugh.

Tim looked around. There was nothing in the story to laugh at and certainly nothing in the room that was comical. In fact, he was fairly sure Samuel was denying his suit.

Samuel put a hand on Tim's shoulder. "I'm sorry. I just realized I have become my father." He worked to catch his breath before continuing. "He often gave me lectures in the form of woodworking metaphors. Then he would set me to work. One of his sermons probably saved my marriage before it was a month old." Samuel pulled out a handkerchief and wiped at his eyes. "Fifteen years ago I warned you not to try to kiss my Sarah until she gave you permission and told you that better not happen for a decade. The decade is over, and my brothers are no longer standing in line to blacken your eye if you try."

Samuel paused and looked Tim in the eye. Tim was being measured and hoped he wasn't found as lacking as he felt.

"If you leave this building and decide to pursue Sarah, I expect you to see it through to the end. You can't quit if she tries to brush you off, because we both know she will. After four years, mourning is a habit with her. But if you leave here still unsure, I will ask you once again to stay away."

"There is something else you should know; the black mailer's game isn't at an end. Miss Brooks intends to slander Sarah's reputation in front of the school board tomorrow night. I intend to be there. I know it won't stop Miss Brooks, but I hope it shows Sarah I intend to stay regardless of the consequence."

"Then I think we both have our answers. And just in time. I hear someone calling for us to come eat."

Tim looked at the half-finished carving. Did he really know his answer?

Thirty-six

THE FANCY HAIRSTYLE SARAH HAD configured would be hidden by her hat and veil, but knowing she was as presentable as possible made her feel brave.

She tucked her resignation letter in her reticule and went downstairs. She hoped Samuel and Louisa would come before Rose woke up, as the black silk showed every little stain. She paced back and forth. If she could speak first, then perhaps she could escape without being revealed by Miss Brooks. She could hardly believe quiet Clara had done such a thing but had spent enough time questioning Tim on the way home last evening she was sure he wasn't mistaken.

At least she'd solved part of the mystery of how Miss Brooks had come to be in possession of the last letter Sarah had written to Mark. One of Mark's tent mates had been Joseph Brooks, Clara's older brother. Joseph had died at Fort Sullivan in the summer of '14. Somehow the letter had been among his belongings. Sarah had always assumed Mark had received that letter. Had he never known about their child?

Sarah placed her hand on her abdomen. It felt as if she'd swallowed a hummingbird. She could do this. Her talk with Samuel last night had gone much better than she'd hoped. He'd opened the Bible he kept in his shop and read the words of Jesus to the woman who was to be stoned. Then he'd showed her a piece of lumber. "I was going to make a chair out of this, but see this scar? It would make the chair weak. Recently, someone commissioned a chest for a wedding gift." Samuel turned the board over and traced the grain where a natural heart had formed. "This would not be here if not for the scar. The father has offered to pay me extra if I use this for the top. It is the scar that makes it beautiful, pumpkin. And you were never meant to be a chair."

Sarah envied the woman who would own the chest. She had not spoken to John, as Samuel had offered to ask his brother if she was still welcome to travel west with him next week.

A knock on the door caused her to jump. It was less than fifteen minutes until the meeting. Samuel was late. She opened the door, ready to censure him for his tardiness, and found Tim there instead.

"Dr. Dawes, what are you doing here?"

"I came to accompany you to the school-board meeting. Dr. Morton has asked me to attend in his stead."

"But … you … but—"

At that moment, Samuel and Louisa arrived. "I am going to go with Samuel." She didn't want Tim there to witness her humiliation. Before she could explain, Samuel and Louisa joined them.

"Aunt Sarah, where is Rose?"

"She is sleeping. Come, and I will show you where her bottle is." As Sarah took her niece into the kitchen, she noted a few unspoken words pass between Samuel and Tim. The hummingbird flapped harder than it had all day. Even more than when she'd sat in Reverend Palmer's office and confessed to him. She concentrated on the moment the fluttering had stopped when the reverend told her he doubted she would have to pay any fines or be sent to jail.

Sarah replayed his words in her mind while Louisa filled the bottle. "Some of the purposes of the law are to encourage couples to marry and to provide funds for those children who are abandoned by women who ply their trade in such immorality. Had Mark lived, you would have been wed, and only the old gossips would care about the baby's birthdate. If every couple who had a child less than seven months after their wedding were fined for breaking the law, there would be no shortage of funds in the city's coffers and we might need another judge. So the law isn't enforced. You didn't bear a child. If you went to the judge, he would tell you the same. He is much too busy with actual offenses. If you feel you should, donate your forty dollars to the church or an orphanage or use it to care for Amity's child until a home is found for her."

She'd left the reverend with a light heart and with twenty dollars less in her reticule. The rest she would use for Rose.

Sarah took a deep breath and went to join Samuel and Tim.

Samuel had left without her.

The color drained from Sarah's face. "Where is Samuel?"

Tim waited for Sarah to tie her bonnet. "He went on ahead." Tim held out his arm. Sarah's touch was so light he had to look to assure himself she had taken his offered assistance.

He helped her into the buggy. Sarah's hand quivered, and Tim gave it a gentle squeeze.

"You shouldn't be seen with me tonight of all nights."

He had to strain to hear Sarah above the sound of the turning wheels.

"I am where I want to be."

Buggies, carriages, and wagons were parked in every available space around the schoolhouse. Tim maneuvered the buggy near the edge, where he could leave if an emergency arose. He had prayed all day that no one would take ill, shoot themselves while cleaning a gun, or trip over a twig between now and nine o'clock.

Tim helped Sarah down, noting that the quaking had stopped.

"Go on in. I'll be in momentarily. No one need know we came together."

Tim offered his arm. "*I* know we came together, and I am not going in without you."

Sarah gave him a hesitant smile before laying her hand on his arm. "Thank you for helping me be brave."

At least that was what he thought she'd said.

Several fathers of students stood, leaving the open seats for the few women in attendance, other than the teachers, to sit for the proceedings.

Mr. Colburn met Tim at the door. "Dr. Dawes, we received Dr. Morton's note saying you would be taking his place tonight. If you would sit up front. Miss Marden, you can sit over with Miss Page and our new teacher, Miss Brooks."

Miss Page had separated herself from Miss Brooks by sitting on the far side of the male teachers. She had an open seat next to her and gave Sarah a weak smile. Miss Brook's venomous glare caused a shiver to run down Tim's spine.

Sarah didn't move to her seat but instead pulled a paper from her reticule. "Preceptor Colburn, I have a matter for the board."

"You and every other teacher."

"This is my letter of resignation."

Mr. Colburn narrowed his eyes. "Surely *you* are not getting married."

Tim found the rotund man just as odious as he had upon their first meeting in this very room last spring. Did he think all women deserved his disdain? Or just Sarah?

Sarah shook her head. "No. I am not."

"I'll add it to the list of items. But they may vote not to let you go until a replacement can be found. Fall term is close at hand."

Sarah nodded at Miss Page but sat on the bench next to Samuel.

Tim followed the preceptor to the front of the room.

Reverend Palmer led them in a prayer to start the meeting. The reverend's plea echoed in Tim's ears with the amens: "And remind us, O Lord, to love our neighbors as Thou hast loved us."

When Tim raised his eyes and found Sarah's, he had no doubt Sarah had told the reverend everything.

One of the superintendents stood. "Our first order of business pertains to the start of the term…"

Samuel leaned over and whispered in Sarah's ear. "John is willing to let you come with them. And we gave permission for Lettie to go with him as well."

"But she is going to Bradford."

Samuel shook his head. "School has always been difficult for her, and she loves her niece and nephew so. She feels this is what she should do."

Sarah mulled over her niece's choice. Lettie had turned sixteen weeks ago. And no young man she knew of had shown her a bit of interest. Lettie would provide a nice buffer between her and John, who would eventually say something about her disgrace.

"…all those who vote aye?"

Next to her, Samuel joined with the ayes.

Sarah wondered what they had voted on. She looked at Samuel. He had held off telling her about Lettie's decision just to distract her! And it had worked.

"Ayes have it. School will start two weeks later to give time for our farmers to bring in a late harvest. Next, Preceptor Colburn has several matters."

The man stood and shuffled some papers. "There are several letters and items of import, but I am not sure which one to share first. It has been brought to my attention that one of our teachers has not maintained the high morals our school requires. However, this very teacher has also resigned this evening. So I hesitate to read this letter, although I am afraid for the protection of all her students, her deeds must be known."

Several of the women craned their necks to look at the female teachers. Sarah took a deep breath and held her head up. She didn't dare look at Tim. *Be brave.*

Reverend Palmer stood. "Preceptor, may I see the letter?" Sarah held her breath as the reverend looked over the letter she had written to Mark so long ago. "Mr. Colburn, how did you come to have this letter in your possession?"

"I cannot say. It was given to me in confidence."

"This letter is from a young woman to her fiancé, who served in the last war. It contains sentiments never meant for other eyes. Since neither the soldier who has passed or the woman in question would voluntarily give this letter to you or anyone else, I believe the letter may be stolen or possibly forged. I say it is not evidence of any wrongdoing." The reverend folded the paper and put it in his pocket.

Disappointed looks passed among some of the audience. Miss Brooks adjusted her hat. Parmelia shifted in her seat.

Mr. Colburn looked around uncomfortably.

Tim stood. "If the reverend feels the evidence should not be submitted, I suggest we move on to the other business."

"Yes, well … I, um, received three letters of resignation. First, from Mr. Stanworth, who has been offered a position in New Hampshire. The others are from Miss Page and Miss Marden. Both of their reasons for leaving are rather vague."

Again, heads turned. Sarah was glad her face was obscured by the veil. *Poor Parmelia!* People might think the girl was the one, although to the best of her knowledge, Parmelia had no prior fiancé.

"That will leave us without three teachers." Several people repeated the obvious.

Mr. Colburn cleared his throat. "Several applications from *male* teachers I feel should be considered are on my desk. I was going to propose Miss Brooks be offered a permanent position, but I am removing my support of her employment."

The superintendent stood. "Other than your well-known disdain for lady teachers, do you have any reason to not promote Miss Brooks?"

The preceptor tugged at his collar. "Miss Brooks has been unreliable in that I have had occasion to question her integrity."

"I see. Miss Brooks, have you anything to say?"

Reverend Palmer tapped his pocket. Miss Brooks stood and opened her mouth, then closed it, her gaze on the minister. Finally, she shook her head and sat down.

"Thank you for working here this summer. We wish you the best. Mr. Stanworth, Miss Page, Miss Marden, you shall be missed. Mr. Colburn, if you would please give the applications to the board, we will set up interviews for next week. That will give us time to gather a few more applicants, including women."

Mr. Colburn's face reddened, but he handed the papers to the superintendent and sat down.

"I believe that concludes our meeting. We will publish the times of the interviews in case any parent wishes to be in attendance. Good evening."

Samuel patted Sarah's hand. "Just one more gauntlet to go. Keep your head up."

"I need to talk to Miss Page." Sarah motioned for Parmelia to meet her in the next classroom.

As soon as they were alone, Sarah lifted the veil, glad for the fresh air. "When did you decide to resign?"

"Oh, last night. I couldn't be anywhere near Miss Brooks."

"But now that she isn't teaching, you could stay."

Parmelia looked around the classroom she'd taught in. "I never enjoyed teaching like you or Miriam did. I prefer less noise. My aunt has written me several times of a family in Boston who wants a governess for their three daughters. I think I shall apply."

"Do you have any other ideas?"

"Oh, I am not suited to mission work like Harriet Atwood Newell. Plus, I would need a husband. There is always Alphonso in Baltimore, and I think I possess most of the qualities he desires. Perhaps if I am very lucky, I could make him his coffee each day before I ride off in my coach and four." Her smile filled her whole face.

"Please tell me you wouldn't be that desperate!"

Parmelia shook her head. "Oh, never. But I might suggest it to Clara. She deserves such a man."

Sarah laid her hand on Parmelia's arm. "That is terribly unkind."

"Oh, yes, I suppose other than writing a horrible advertisement, he has done nothing to deserve her."

"Gossiping, ladies?" Miss Brooks stopped at the door to the classroom. "Or are you congratulating Miss Marden on saving the shreds of her reputation? At least the reverend knows now."

"Reverend Palmer was aware of my past before he read the letter." Sarah lowered her veil. "Now, if you will excuse me, I hate to keep anyone waiting."

Thirty-seven

A YOUNG BOY RAN UP as Tim led Sarah to his buggy. "Dr. Dawes, Mrs. Morton says you gotta come quick."

Sarah patted his arm. "Samuel is still here. Go."

Unasked, the boy climbed up in the buggy with Tim. "So where are we going?"

"Dr. Morton's."

Tim prayed his hunch was wrong.

"You keep doing that, Rose, and I will need to lay aside black for the rest of my mourning." Sarah wiped at the sour milk Rose had spit on the shoulder of her gray dress. "How do you always manage to miss the cloth?"

Someone knocked on the door. Who could it be this late?

Sarah glanced out the window before opening the door. "Parmelia, what is wrong?"

Parmelia blew her nose loudly. "Oh, we had a terrible row, and Widow Webb told me I need to leave. She gave me until the morning, but I can't stay there with Clara in the house. May I stay here?"

"You are more than welcome providing you don't find Rose an

unsuitable hostess." Sarah eyed the small bag Parmelia carried. "Where are the rest of your things?"

"Oh, I only own one small trunk. I can get it in the morning. It is too late to ask for help. Besides, I didn't know if you would let me stay. I can't pay much as my funds are rather tight."

"You can stay for free if you will cook. You have no idea how tired I am eating of boiled eggs and porridge. I am such a terrible cook."

"Oh, I was too until I got a copy of Amelia Simmons's *American Cookery*. It is ever so much better than *The Universal Cook*. Maybe because it's written by an orphan like me, but I just understand it better."

Sarah led Parmelia upstairs. "I haven't cleaned the room since Mrs. Duncan left. I have been sleeping in the downstairs room since Rose was born. Mrs. Larkin and Mrs. Palmer re-stuffed the tick for me after Amity passed. My room is a disaster, my dresses all over…"

Parmelia held up her hand. "Oh, don't worry about me. I can only imagine how difficult it has been to be alone with a baby."

He shouldn't stop, but he could see two people in the parlor, so Sarah wasn't alone, although it was past ten. Perhaps Louisa had stayed. She wouldn't be the best chaperone but enough for propriety.

Tim tapped lightly at the door.

Sarah opened it, holding Rose to her shoulder. "Dr. Dawes, whatever is wrong?" She opened the door for him.

"Can we talk?" He choked out the words.

"Oh, I'll take Rose."

Not until she spoke did Tim realize who sat in the room. "Miss Page, I am sorry. Am I interrupting?"

Parmelia lifted the baby from Sarah's shoulder. "Oh no, Miss Marden and I were just discussing cooking."

"Miss Page is going to live here for a few days. Come, sit. Do you need tea? What happened?" Sarah bit her lip.

"Perhaps I shouldn't have come. But I need to talk…"

Sarah took his hand and led him to a chair. "Tim, whatever is wrong?"

What had possessed him to come? Looking at the worry on Sarah's face, he was sure he had made a mistake. "I'm sorry. I shouldn't —"

Sarah put her hands on her hips. "Timison George Dawes, you've heard the very darkest secrets of my soul. I don't care what you need to say, you just say it." She pulled over the ottoman and perched herself on it.

"I had to amputate Dr. Morten's leg. There was an infection in the bone."

"Oh no, Tim." Sarah wrapped her arms around him and held him while he wept.

This was exactly why he had come. Sarah was the only one he could tell how much it hurt to be a doctor. Holding her was better medicine than man had ever invented. If he could come home to her each night, he could face the most difficult of days.

Sarah pulled back and wiped his tears. "Will it save his life?"

"Yes, I think so."

"Then you did a good thing."

"It is just so hard. I almost want to join my brother in the shipping trade."

Sarah shook a finger at him. "Don't you dare. I know you. Right now you are counting all the losses, but think about how many lives you've saved just since you have been here."

"But what about—"

Sarah gave him a look that would have had all the eight-year-old miscreants in town shaking in their boots. She reached down and removed her slippers. "Close your eyes for a minute."

Her skirts rustled, tempting him to peek, but he didn't.

"Open them. I've worn my regular shoes since Independence Day. Look at my feet. If you hadn't insisted I take care of them, I might have lost a toe, or worse." Sarah wiggled her toes. "That night you wouldn't let me walk outside when you brought me home with three bricks at my feet." Sarah raised her foot. "Feel them. They are well. And you saved my little nieces."

Tim ran his finger down the small toe he had been sure would need to come off, then set her foot back on the floor.

Sarah covered her foot with her skirt. "You saved them. When you insisted I change my boots in the first place, I thought you were just trying to tell me what to do like a little child, but I knew you wouldn't let me go until I changed. I have my feet because of you." She brought her hand to his cheek. "Don't. You. Ever. Forget."

He mirrored her actions. Sarah's skin was so soft as he rubbed his thumb along her cheek. The familiar desire to kiss her filled him. He leaned down, but she pulled back.

"I think you should go now, Dr. Dawes."

Tim left a more confident doctor but a lonelier man.

The clock ticked in the hallway, counting out the seconds. Sarah ran through the last few moments of Tim's visit. Perhaps she should have been brave one last time. He'd wanted to kiss her…hadn't he?

Sarah had to be wrong. The amputation had upset him. That had to be it. Hadn't Lucy said men got all confused when they had difficult days? And like a little boy with a scraped knee, they just needed a few kisses.

She needed a few kisses.

But then she wouldn't leave with John.

Rose made a mewing sound in her sleep.

Would John let her take Rose?

Thirty-eight

"WE ARE LEAVING MONDAY MORNING, first thing. I need your answer. Tucker, the boy who has been helping me on the farm, is coming with me, so we'll drive two wagons. But you still can't bring too much. Only the necessities." John sat across from Sarah in the parlor.

The day had really come. Here was her chance to leave the North Shore forever. "What about Rose?"

"She isn't your responsibility. If you come, I'll need your help."

Sarah shifted the baby on her lap. "I thought Lettie was going with you. Isn't she help enough?"

John crossed his arms and harrumphed. "Who do you think I need your help with? Tucker has been following her around like she is freshly baked gingerbread."

"Does Samuel know?"

"Of course he does. Why do you think I need you to watch them?"

Sarah tipped her head to look him in the eye. "So if my main purpose would be to watch your children and Lettie, who will be doing the cooking, why can't I bring Rose?"

"She isn't your child. If yours had lived, he'd be the age of my little boy. Is he the reason you wouldn't marry me?"

"John, that topic is forever off-limits. You've always known I don't feel for you the way I did for your brother. Mark wasn't your twin, but he looked enough like you that when I look at you, I see him. If you think I'm going to Indiana to have you or Joe try to take his place, I swear I'll—"

Parmelia's entrance into the house saved Sarah from coming up with a threat. "Oh, I didn't know you had company."

John stood to greet her.

"This is John Wilson, one of Samuel's brothers, and we were just discussing the move to Indiana. This is Miss Parmelia Page. She is staying here for a few days."

"Oh, Indiana. I read a pamphlet about it. The farming is excellent and so many trees. So exciting opening a new frontier where no one has ever lived—well, other than the Indians. You must be so excited."

"I am. However, Sarah doesn't share your enthusiasm." At the door, John put on his hat, then looked at Sarah. "I need to know by morning."

Once John had left, Parmelia fanned herself. "I've seen him at church but never met him. He is more intense than his brother."

"John is really a very nice person, especially when he is around his twin, Joe. But this summer has pushed him to the limits with everything."

Parmelia took off her hat.

"Did you find a position?"

"No, but I did get a letter off to my aunt. I hope to hear back early next week. But to be honest, I would rather trade you places and not go to Boston."

It had been a long night at the Morton house. Tim and Mrs. Morton took turns at the doctor's side. Every time Tim closed his eyes, he saw Sarah rejecting his kiss. How could he carve a piece of wood he couldn't even hold?

Dr. Morton groaned. "I never liked being on the giving end of an amputation. I can't say I like them much better on this end either."

"Would you like some water?" When the man nodded, Tim raised him up enough to sip from a cup.

"Where is my wife?"

"I believe she is sleeping in the room next door. Shall I get her?"

"No. Let her sleep. You should go get some sleep too. Sitting here worrying isn't going to make anything heal faster."

"I was thinking more than worrying."

"About my offer or Miss Marden?"

"Miss Marden. I had already decided to take your offer before last night."

"I am mighty glad of that. You know it will be months before I can do much more than consult. Too bad I read every copy of every medical journal I owned when I broke this leg. I may need to start in on Mrs. Morton's British romances. Maybe then I can give you some advice on the girl, but from what I've witnessed, nothing works quite like just saying the words."

Tim thought of all the words he had bottled up inside.

"Stop thinking so hard. It is only three words, not some Shakespearean play. I've seen it work for married folk, too. They can be all mad at each other because the husband did something stupid and broke some bone, then he says 'I love you,' and his wife starts crying and vowing to care for him. Works every time." Dr. Morton closed his eyes. "The sooner you do it, the better."

Fifteen minutes later, Mrs. Morton came in the room. Tim endured a scolding for not waking her up, then left the house. He ran his hand down his face. He needed a shave before he went and talked to Sarah.

Halfway home, John Wilson hailed him. "Have you found a place for the baby yet?"

"No, we haven't."

"Better do it by Monday. I'm not taking a baby to Indiana, too."

So Sarah had made her choice.

Sorting her life into three piles—Indiana, leave with Lucy, and leave behind—did little to brighten her mood.

Rose was in the last category. "Hey, sweet girl, I wish we could find someone to love you. John says you can't come. But I can't stay. We are in a pickle, aren't we?" The sleeping baby didn't answer.

Voices from downstairs carried up to her room.

"Sarah?"

Lucy and Samuel had come to town? Sarah ran down the stairs and into her sister's arms. "So, you are really going?"

"What else can I do? If I stay here, I'll end up like Dorcas Smith. The rumors aren't as bad as I thought yet, but by the time church ends tomorrow, everyone will be looking at me like I should be tried at a Salem trial."

Rose started to cry. Parmelia beat Sarah to the stairs. "Go talk with your sister. I can take care of her."

Sarah led the way into the parlor. "So, what brings you into town?"

Lucy removed her bonnet. "We needed some more thread and sundries for Lettie, and I wanted to see you. Tomorrow with Thomas Jr.'s and Carrie's families, there will be too many people to talk."

They all took their seats.

The room started to blur. "Saying goodbye is so hard."

"That isn't why we came, pumpkin."

"We think you are making the wrong choice, and, as you know, it is hard to undo some choices. We didn't say anything four years ago, nor did we really listen to what you wanted. I vowed to not make my little sister's choices, but I can't let you go without telling you once that I feel like you are probably making the biggest mistake of your life."

"What mistake? I am not breaking any commandments. I am going to a place where I can hold up my head again."

Lucy took Sarah's hand. "But you are living a lie."

"No, I am not. I've lived a lie for the past four years!"

"This is a different lie. I've watched it grow since the day Emma and Anna were born. Samuel says it was there before I noticed."

Sarah closed her eyes. She was not going to fight with her sister on her last day. "What are you talking about? I haven't lied to anyone."

"You are lying to yourself."

Sarah looked from Lucy to Samuel. What were they talking about? "I don't understand."

"Dr. Timison Dawes—the boy you once claimed smelled like barn cats so you wouldn't kiss him, which, considering that was twenty years ago, you made a wise choice." Lucy smiled. "I've watched you pretend not to pay attention to him for two months."

"But I can't. I am not good enough for him."

Samuel rested a hand on Sarah's shoulder. "I don't think you are the one who gets to decide that."

"But he told me how he feels about the camp followers and women with loose morals. Am I any different?" Sarah looked to Samuel for an answer.

"Wednesday night he asked my permission to court you. Thursday night he drove you to a meeting which, thanks to Reverend Palmer's quick actions, did not end up as any of us feared. Those are not the actions of a man who is putting you in the same group as camp followers."

"Wednesday night? As in the night I came out to confess to the two of you?" The kiss that didn't happen on Thursday night replayed in her mind. What if Tim had been trying to start a courtship?

"But I haven't seen him since late Thursday night."

"When was that? After we talked to Reverend Palmer, I brought you home."

"After Parmelia came, because she got tossed out of the boardinghouse."

Lucy nodded. "So that is why she is here."

"You were saying he came by late?" prompted Samuel.

"After ten. He had to amputate Dr. Morton's leg. He was so upset."

Lucy and Samuel exchanged a knowing look.

"Nothing happened! I mean, I hugged him and told him he'd saved my foot. I did show it to him, but he only saw from my ankle down. I was very careful—didn't let him kiss me or anything." Sarah felt her face warm.

"Some older sister wisdom: You were the person Tim sought out when he was at his very lowest. You were the one he wanted to be with. *You*. If you care for him as much as I think you do, then you should stay. Don't live a second lifetime of regrets."

"But he hasn't been by."

"Most likely he has been with patients or Dr. Morton ever since," said Samuel.

"That isn't it. He tried to kiss me, and I stepped back."

"Samuel, cover your ears. I am going to give my sister some advice."

Samuel walked over to the window, his hands over his ears.

"I can't believe I am telling you this. But sometimes you need to take matters into your own hands—or lips."

Samuel laughed.

Sarah knew she'd turned as red as an apple.

"We would love to stay longer, but we left the babies with Lettie and Louisa, and we must get back."

"That reminds me. John said he needed me to watch Tucker and Lettie. Aren't you worried?"

Samuel shook his head. "Tucker has already asked me for her hand. But he promised to wait until she turns seventeen and they find a minister. He wants his own place before they marry."

"In her case, I advised her not to do any kissing." Lucy laughed, and they all joined in.

Thirty-nine

THE GOSSIPS WERE TALKING MORE about John Wilson leaving for Indiana in the morning than they were the revelations from the school-board meeting. Tim knew he shouldn't be trying to listen to the tittle-tattle before church started, but he wanted to know how bad it went for Sarah.

He tried not to look at her but couldn't resist. She had tied up that ridiculous veil as Seth kept trying to yank it off her head. It looked like every Wilson in the state had turned out for services. No doubt a big family dinner was to be held that afternoon. How was he ever going to get a chance to tell her goodbye—or anything else?

Reverend Palmer stood and gave the announcements, read intentions of some couple Tim didn't know, and reminded everyone to pray for the harvest. Tim stood and sang the hymn and watched the antics in the Wilson pew. They had brought Emma and Anna to church, and Sarah had Rose with her, whom she had already passed off to Miss Page, who sat across the aisle in Mrs. Garrett's nearly empty pew.

Three and a half minutes into the sermon, a child's scream erupted in the Wilson pew. Sarah picked up Stella and hurried out of the church.

"Didn't I yell good, Aunt Sarah?" asked Stella as she wiggled down.

A little too good. "You did very well. Now let's go back to the privy."

"But I don't need to go!"

"Remember, we are going to play a hiding game. I need you to hide in there just long enough to eat this." Sarah produced a candy stick. Stella took it and hurried to play their game.

Please work, please work. Sarah prayed her deception would bring Tim out. A very wicked thing to do on the Sabbath, but he hadn't come around last night, and tomorrow would be too late. Unless she just stayed.

"Sarah? Is Stella ill?"

Sarah turned at the sound of the voice she had been hoping to hear. "No, she is just in the privy."

"You're certain? She sounded like she'd injured herself."

Sarah took three steps closer to Tim. "But I am glad you came out here. I wanted to see you." Sarah's heart raced. She took another step. Almost close enough.

Tim didn't move. "I wanted to see you too."

Uncertainty filled her. *Be brave!*

Sarah took one more step and closed the gap, then rose up on her tiptoes—and hit Tim in the nose with the rim of her bonnet.

She fell back on her heels and covered her mouth. "I'm sorry. That wasn't supposed to happen."

Tim lifted her chin and untied the bonnet, sliding it back a couple of inches. "Perhaps if you tried that again." His hands slid down her arms to support her elbows.

He wants me to kiss him! Sarah stood on the tips of her toes again. *I'm not tall enough.* When she had stretched as far as she could, Tim bent down to meet her. Sarah's hands crept up his arms. She had so much to say and only one chance. Tim wrapped his arms around her, and suddenly she felt like she was floating. When that kiss ended, another one took its place, more desperate than the first. She couldn't lose him.

A little voice called her name. "Aunt Sarah, Aunt Sarah! My candy is all gone, so I came out."

Sarah's feet touched the ground again.

"Did you make me hide so you could kiss him? That is yucky! I'll never kiss a boy behind a church." Stella made a face.

"That is what your aunt said when she was your age."

Stella picked up the fallen bonnet. "Here is your hat. You said ladies should always cover their head in public. Does that mean you aren't being a lady?"

Sarah took her bonnet and tied it back on.

"Why are you are all pink, Aunt Sarah?"

Sarah bent over to pick up her niece. "You ask too many questions. Thank you for your help. I really needed to talk to Dr. Dawes."

Stella made a face. "But you weren't talking. You were being all kissy like Mama and Papa."

Tim wrapped an arm around Sarah's shoulders. "Sometimes a kiss is a very good way to communicate. Church is nearly over. Should the three of us walk around the green instead of disrupting the service?"

Stella wiggled down. "Sure, let's walk."

Sarah took her by one hand. Tim offered his arm for the other.

They walked in silence till Stella broke away to examine a wilting flower.

Sarah looked back at the church. "They can probably see us through the windows."

"Then they won't be too surprised next week when the reverend reads our intentions."

Sarah's feet tangled. "Our what?"

"Before you so eloquently communicated to me behind the Church, I was going to tell you I love you and beg you to stay."

"You were?"

"I still can if you would like, but I am really hoping the kiss said pretty much the same thing."

Sarah knew her cheeks were flaming again. "I was hoping you'd give me a reason to stay."

"Marry me?"

Half the congregation witnessed Sarah's answer through the open window. Those who missed the moment heard it from Stella, who ran inside the church to tell her mama, "Aunt Sarah is kissing the doctor!"

Reverend Porter ended the sermon early, since no one was listening anyway.

Epilogue

Three weeks later

"WHATEVER ARE YOU DOING?" TIM kissed Sarah behind the ear, causing a splotch of ink to mar the paper. "I thought you were just changing your dress so we could leave."

Sarah sat at Emma's old dressing table, the only piece of Emma's that hadn't been replaced by new bedroom furniture. She stared at the letter she had started to write. Once it was done, she would run out of excuses to delay. It was silly to be nervous, but she was more wound up than Miriam had been on her wedding day. "I promised Parmelia I'd write her all the details of the wedding and send it in care of Joe in Indiana. I hope she doesn't regret her decision to join John in his move. She was as exited to go as John was to have someone who could cook well and monitor Lettie on the trip."

Tim placed another kiss at the nape of her neck. "I don't think you need to do that this very moment. We haven't even been husband and wife for three hours yet."

Sarah dipped the pen in the inkwell, her hand shaking. "But I have been so busy these past three weeks. I don't want to leave anything out." Sewing had occupied most of her time. The first order had been a dress that wasn't a mourning color, because black or gray would not be proper for her own wedding, then a new nightgown trimmed with the yards of blue ribbon she never could bring herself to give her nieces.

Tim rested his chin on her shoulder. "You left out the part where Rose spit up on your dress after her christening."

"Well, that wasn't one of my favorite moments, but I did put in her full name—Rose Amity Barns Dawes. Are you sure Mrs. Reynolds will take good care of her while we are gone?"

"Of course. She was Ichabod's nurse and Mother's undercook."

Another kiss distracted her. Sarah had to dip her pen twice to remember the next line.

"I see you also left out Reverend Palmer clearing his throat halfway through our kiss." The words tickled Sarah's ear, and a quick glance in the mirror confirmed her suspicions—she was as pink as her dress. Tim's eyes met hers in the reflection before he added yet another kiss to the nape of her neck.

"That was at the end of our kiss."

"No, I may have ended it then, but I wasn't half done. And I would very much like to finish that kiss." He turned her around on the stool.

A shiver ran down Sarah's spine.

"Only if I finish it now, we may never leave, and we must soon, if we are to arrive before sunset." Tim removed the pen from her hand and replaced it with his own hand. "Come, you need to see your wedding gift. Close your eyes." He led her into the parlor, where Mrs. Reynolds rocked Rose in her new cradle from Samuel and Lucy.

"Open your eyes."

"A bookcase!" Sarah traced the heart shape in the wood of the door. "When did you ask Samuel to build this?"

"The day I asked him for your hand, right after supper while you helped with the dishes."

"He said this wood was for a chest for a bride the night I told— You asked him then? What if things had gone poorly at the meeting. You couldn't have married a woman mired in scandal!"

"I only ever was going to marry the woman I loved. Open the door."

Sarah did as she was bidden. A matching silver handled brush, comb, and hand mirror finer than Swanson's ever carried lay on the shelf. Sarah picked up the brush and ran her thumb over the bristles.

"Samuel also explained a family tradition that I would very much like to keep, starting tonight." Tim took the brush from her but didn't return it to the shelf.

Sarah couldn't keep from blushing. One hundred strokes each night by her husband's hand. Thomas and Emma had no idea what they had started so many years before. She rose up on her toes and thanked him as a not-so-very-proper wife should, not caring that Mrs. Reynolds was still in the room.

"Now, Mrs. Dawes, we've dallied long enough." Tim wrapped an arm about her waist.

"You still won't tell me where we are going?"

"I didn't tell anyone. I want to be your husband for the next three days, not someone's doctor." Tim assisted her back to standing.

Sarah bent and placed a kiss on Rose's brow. "But what if something happens to Rose? Please tell Mrs. Reynolds at least."

"I left a sealed note with Samuel. He is only to open it if there is a true emergency." Tim led her to the front door.

Relieved, Sarah climbed up in the buggy. When Tim sat beside her, she leaned over and kissed his cheek. "Now will you tell me?"

"Not yet."

As the town disappeared behind them, Sarah again tried to learn of their destination by kissing her new husband's cheek. "Now?"

Tim slowed the horse and parked in the shade of a tree. "Not until I finish our interrupted kiss." Tim completed the kiss and whispered, "Seabrook, New Hampshire. A little cottage overlooking the Atlantic," against her lips before starting another.

Suddenly Sarah wanted nothing more than to see the sun rise over the ocean standing in the security of Tim's arms. She broke off the kiss. "What are we waiting for?"

THE END

Historical Notes

THE YEAR 1816, OR "EIGHTEEN hundred and froze to death," also known as the year without a summer, changed the face of the northern hemisphere. The North American drought that started in 1815 continued into the winter, starting off 1816 with mild temperatures and below-normal levels of precipitation. Without Doppler radar, rapid worldwide communication, or scientific knowledge, the inhabitants of the northern hemisphere valiantly fought the enduring frost and famine. Many in Europe looked westward for their salvation, while those in the new world looked farther west still, all in hopes of escaping the largest natural disaster the world had ever known.

It would be almost one hundred years before scientists made the connection between the April 1815 eruption of Mount Tambora and the devastating summer. There is very little exact weather data for the area of Massachusetts where I set my story. A handful of professors, as well as some weather enthusiasts who owned thermometers, took daily temperature measurements. The newspapers reported some weather phenomena after the fact.

Period newspapers show mounting alarm as the summer progressed, and there were some who claimed that things such as the red and yellow snow in Italy and the unusual sunspot activity signified the end of the world. I tried to stay as true to fact as I could with only regional and sometimes anecdotal information available. It did snow in Boston on June 7, and on the eighth, Cabot, Vermont, received eighteen inches of snow. Various parts of New Hampshire and Massachusetts also reported snow. My use of six inches of snow that day may not be accurate for the exact spot where my imaginary Wilson family lived, but it is representative of the weather in the region. Two weeks later, on June 23, someone in Salem, Massachusetts recorded a temperature of 101 degrees Fahrenheit, but by Independence Day, there were several reports of men wearing their greatcoats to the festivities and of wells freezing over.

1816 is the only year to record killing frosts in every month from May to December in New England. In late July and through August, many local newspapers, such as the one in Haverhill, encouraged farmers to try planting again. However, the frosts the first week of September destroyed the late crop as well. One diary mentions starvation among the poor of New England as early as July. Canada's crops had been decimated, and they halted all exports of food and begged for relief.

Facing financial ruin, many farmers gave up, land offices opened throughout New England, and farmers moved to Ohio and Indiana, most leaving between September and December. The migration continued into 1817. Meanwhile, Europe suffered the same fate, with 65,000 Irish dying from typhoid and famine alone. No European country was untouched as they also experienced famine, although in some cases it was from too much rain rather than drought. Perhaps not realizing things in the new hemisphere were just as bad, a wave of European immigrants looked westward for salvation.

There are several excellent books as well as documentaries on the year 1816. I encourage you to read up on that year. Connections to the westward expansion and the industrial revolution are fascinating. Fun fact: some claim that without the eruption of Mount Tambora, there would be no *Frankenstein*. As an author, I think Mary Shelley would have written her story anyway.

Both Dr. Warrens mentioned in the book were real doctors. The *New England Journal of Medicine and Surgery, and the Collateral Branches of Science* was started in 1812. Massachusetts General Hospital was approved by the Massachusetts legislature in 1811 but did not accept its first patient until 1821. Part of Massachusetts General Hospital included the McLean Hospital, also known as the "Asylum for the Insane," which opened in 1818. The property was purchased in December of 1816. The Friends Asylum, established by Philadelphia's Quaker community in 1814, was the first institution specifically built to implement moral treatment for the insane in the United States and was mostly run by laymen. Sarah most likely had heard of both; however, in June of 1816, she was unlikely to know of the location of the proposed McLean Hospital.

The seventeenth century Massachusetts Fornication Law is still on the books today. In 1816, fines for most laws were still written in pounds and schillings, which would be converted into dollars by the court. Still, it was no secret that many marriages started out in haste, but the expectant couple was not usually fined. Fines and jail time were used most often to encourage a reluctant father to take responsibility for his actions.

Bradford Academy, and later Bradford College, did exist. The academy was started in 1803 to provide a coeducational "high-school" type curriculum. Girls were always in the majority of students, with many of the male population choosing to attend Atkinson Academy. In 1836, the Bradford Academy became a women's college, but facing financial difficulties, it eventually opened its doors to men in 1971. In 2000, the college closed its doors forever. The campus still stands in Haverhill, Massachusetts, where the buildings are now a part of Northpoint Bible College. One of the academy's early graduates was Harriet Atwood Newell, an early American missionary who died en route to Burma.

In researching, I stumbled upon many interesting tidbits, some of which I snuck into the pages of this book. The one I enjoyed most was the wife-wanted ad as it appeared in the *Worchester Gazette* on July 24, 1816. I included it in its entirety in the book. However, the editor found the ad as atrocious as I did and prefaced the ad with this paragraph:

> **Who wants a husband?—A fine opportunity now offers to someone who possesses the unfashionable qualifications which are required in the following advertisement.—We are pleased with the prudence of the gentleman in required the lady to be able to make good coffee; though, perhaps, this very requisite will prevent his ever accomplishing his object. For, very few—but here comes the advertisement.**

About the Author

LORIN GRACE WAS BORN IN Colorado and has been moving around the country ever since, living in eight states and several imaginary worlds. She graduated from Brigham Young University with a degree in Graphic Design.

Currently she lives in northern Utah with her husband, four children, and a dog who is insanely jealous of her laptop. When not writing Lorin enjoys creating graphics, visiting historical sites, museums, and reading.

Lorin is an active member of the League of Utah Writers and was awarded Honorable Mention in their 2016 creative writing contest short romance story category. Her debut novel, *Waking Lucy,* was awarded a 2017 Recommend Read award in the LUW Published book contest.

You can learn more about her and sign up for her newsletter at loringrace.com

Waking Lucy

Lucy dreamed of marrying Samuel,
until she woke up as his wife.

Don't miss the first book in the series.

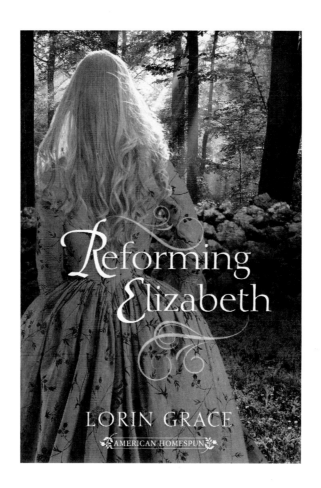

Reforming Elizabeth

Elizabeth Garret is out of control.
Can her great aunt and a disgraced preacher
succeed in reforming her?

Remembering Anna

The key opens a box,
unlocks the past and defines the future.

Made in United States
North Haven, CT
13 February 2023

32553452R00162